Just DIY

by

Diana Johnson

ISBN-13: 9781696878975

For Kate, my inspiration for everything.

I hope you’re lucky enough to always have friends as close as family.

Table of Contents

I am grateful to Beth, Jackie, Jess a.k.a. Turtle,
my sister Susan, and especially Lana.
Your efforts, insights, and support mean the world to me.
And to Kelley for her expertise in headers and footers!

Prologue

In 1856, after a devastating tornado ripped through the tiny town of Chateaugay, New York, destroying much of its municipal structures, Adele St. James opened her Country Day School for the village's young people. She accommodated the classrooms in row houses, spared by the twister's wrath, furnished them with items from her own home, and collected books and supplies from neighboring counties. Prior to the storm, only the town's well-to-do sent their children to school, but Adele opened her doors to every child including those of the migrants who'd contributed to the rising census after the arrival of the railroad opened the town to new commerce.

A single schoolteacher of modest means, Adele worked tirelessly to educate her students despite the criticism and interference from some prominent citizens. One such opponent was Jewel Webster Howerton, the wife of cheddar cheese magnate, Bradshaw Howerton of the New England Howertons. Mrs. Howerton objected to her sons being schooled in such primitive environs alongside the offspring of apple pickers and coal miners. For years she campaigned the Franklin County Commission to take the school over and relieve Miss St. James of her post, but the town was attempting to rebuild and as long as the children had a place to learn, the commission refused to intervene. Eventually she went underground with a small group of investors and covertly created a charity which began contributing donations for improvements and additions to the school. Grateful for the support and without knowledge of the source or motives behind the gifts, Adele accepted them for the good of her students.

The school's development progressed and soon plans for new construction were presented. The new campus would house multiple buildings: one structure for primary grades and another, the senior school. Two more buildings were included for housing teachers, mostly single men and women who commonly lived where they taught in that era.

When Miss St. James was asked to become Head Mistress of The St. James Academy, she was so honored that the new grounds were to bear her name, that she eagerly agreed to the implementation of a board of directors to help oversee the establishment and its operations. After the school opened to students, it would only take two terms for Mrs. Howerton and her cronies to overtake the board, remove Adele as Head Mistress and begin restricting admission based on income and ethnicity. As the trustees became more and more discriminatory, the school's census dropped so dramatically that continuing to operate the sprawling campus while funding it from their own pocketbooks became increasingly harder to do. So, while Adele St. James quietly moved to a nearby county and continued to teach in the public-school system, Howerton and the board decided to convert the facility to a boarding school and to start charging tuition for students wishing to study at the academy.

As with most things in our misguided attempts at capitalism, this country has always gravitated toward assuming the superiority of any version of a thing that costs more. This bet paid off for the officials of St. James Academy and the establishment quickly rose up the ranks of private schools whose admission was sought after by droves of wealthy, spoiled brats whose families attempted to boost their own value by touting their attendance there. As a result, the campus grew yet again to house the boys and girls in separate dormitories and the schools themselves were revamped to accommodate the growing number of students.

Following both World Wars and the stock market crash, the old money behind the academy waxed and waned sometimes barely hanging on to the school's elite status. But as with a score of the behemoths created by money and prejudice during the adolescence of our country, the academy survived right up until the last days of the twentieth century.

Ironically though, in the last decades of operation, the board saw fit to grant scholarships to a choice few young boys and girls who didn't come from wealthy families, but like the kids Adele St. James intended to educate, just needed a place to learn with their friends. The story to follow is about the friendship between two such young women.

Part One

1974-78

Orientation

Parents were not permitted beyond the parking lot on the day of orientation at the prestigious St. James Academy. The young people being deposited were walked as far as the school yard gate, kissed and hugged, advised, and then welcomed beyond the familiar onto the aging campus by a few equally aging faculty members. Each child was issued three uniforms and permitted two suitcases of personals and a satchel for school supplies. Hupp and Eloise O'Hanley walked Aggie as far as the tailgate of the family truck where she promptly stopped them from advancing.

"I can manage from here, Dad."

"We can take you to the gate, doll."

"Let your dad walk you to the gate, Agatha Rose. You go on, Hupp. We'll say our goodbyes here."

Eloise held her daughters face in her hands firmly and smiled.

"I love you, Aggie Rose. You know that?"

The girl nodded despite the grip her mother maintained on her head.

"Well, you *remember* that."

"Yes ma'am. Love you too, Mom."

Aggie turned away and caught up to her father dragging her suitcases behind him.

In the space directly across the parking lot from the O'Hanley's, Patsy and Zeke pulled in with MaryAnne in the back. Zeke drove of course; Patsy's muscle coordination had deteriorated to the point that it wasn't safe for her behind the wheel. He reached into the backseat for her cane and MaryAnne grabbed it.

"This is good, Zeke. I can manage from here."

Patsy shot her husband a convoluted look of acceptance tinged with rejection; a combination she was feeling more and more frequently with the advancement of her symptoms. She touched his arm.

"It's ok, babe. She wants to go in on her own. I get that."

"Yeah, it's like you keep saying, I need to learn how to do stuff myself, right?"

"I guess, whatever you two say. At least let me get your bags out of the back."

MaryAnne waited until his door was shut and leaned up into the space between the front seats.

"I'll call as often as I can, Mom. And I'll send you letters with all the gossip."

She could see that her mother had begun to flush and fiddle with her fingers, a sign MaryAnne knew all too well as Patsy's 'trying-not-to-cry' move. She twisted around to hug her mother's shoulders and kissed her cheek.

"I love you, Mom."

"I love you too, Angel-face."

Patsy stroked her girl's long chestnut hair with her weakening hands and breathed in the smell of her shampoo, then kissed her head and let her go.

MaryAnne was out of the car and around to the trunk in a flash. She took the suitcase handle from her stepdad and popped up onto her toes to kiss his cheek. As she sprinted toward the school, she turned back only for a second.

"Thanks, Zeke!"

Aggie and her dad had stopped short of the bottleneck at the gate to say goodbye and MaryAnne went whizzing past only to come to an abrupt stop just ahead of them. Aggie, barely registering the blur as she blew by, returned her attention to her sweet father.

"I wish I didn't have to do this, Dad."

"I think it'll be good for you, doll. I am going to miss having you around, though; you know you're my favorite."

He reached for his daughter with the worn hands of a woodworker and the weary heart of a loving father pushing his youngest out of the nest.

"I love you, Aggie Rose. I love you just like you are. You remember *that.*"

The fourteen-year-old wrapped her spindly arms around his neck and smashed her cheek into his.

"I love you, Dad."

She left a kiss where her words had been, and they broke apart each one turning away without looking back. Aggie looked down at her feet in an effort to check herself, to keep from losing it, and found her eyes focused on MaryAnne's golden brown calves, exposed only because she had shoved her white knee socks all the way down to the tops of her oxfords. Hers were a stark contrast to Aggie's pink and freckled legs and the momentary study of them was the perfect distraction. The group inched forward a little at a time until they were all moving with some fluidity toward the auditorium.

Edging into the courses of wood and iron seats, MaryAnne and Aggie took their places among the assembly, smiling at the others with curious courtesy. The students wrestled their belongings under their feet in the tight rows, excusing themselves as hair and uniforms got tugged and squished by the occasional overstep. The sounds of friendly chatter filled the hall as returning upperclassmen reunited with their cliques and the newbies summoned the nerve to introduce themselves. MaryAnne was first to stretch out her hand.

"I'm MaryAnne O'Hara!"

"Hi. I'm Aggie Rose O'Hanley."

"AggieRose, one word?"

"No. It's Agatha Rose, really. But two. Aggie and Rose."

"That's pretty. I'm one. M-A-R-Y-capital-A-N-N-E. I don't know why my mom had to be so complicated. And an E on the end. What's that?"

MaryAnne couldn't quit talking. Of course, she was nervous but there was something so sweet and accommodating about Aggie's big green eyes that set her at ease right away.

"I just go by Aggie."

She would have the last word before the auditorium was called to attention.

The presentation of instructors, counsellors, coaches, and administrators was followed by the rules of conduct and class schedules. Dean Springer, whose title and job description had evolved considerably since the academy's namesake Adele St. James' first tenure as Head Mistress, seemed competent and approachable in her welcoming address. She spoke of the history of the institution, the campus' growth and development, and the stellar reputation the school touted.

She then turned her attention to the expectations that went hand-in-hand with a nationally ranked and recognized facility like St. James, Honor, Etiquette, Responsibility, Privilege, Esteem, and Standards. The words were displayed on a huge chalkboard to the right of the podium and Dean Springer tapped the rubber tip of her pointer to the capital letters of each tenet, emphasizing their acronym. A senior boy sneezed, "Herpes!" into the stifling air and the educator engaged in a slow blink that lasted the length of a shallow, tired sigh and continued. The gag ran on pervasively in every copy of these principles listed in the student handbook, posted in each classroom, and displayed on countless banners, posters, and bulletin boards throughout the hallowed halls of every building on campus.

All jokes aside, the tenets that were counted as so integral to the success of St. James students were second nature to Aggie and MaryAnne. They'd been reared by and around some of the best kind of people. But a grand majority of the enrolled came from backgrounds which, despite being infinitely better off economically, were shaky on such virtues. Many of the school's wealthiest benefactors had been sending their offspring to St. James for generations with no clear understanding before, during, or after they graduated of these basic ideals. It seemed that some people thought that paying to be associated with those who expect such moral behavior counted as one actually procuring it. The girls would encounter this painful truth often along their journey at St. James. But for now, they had to settle in.

The students were lined up, instructed to separate into their respective groups, and peeled off to follow the Residential Administrators to their designated dorms. The young gentlemen trekked across the grounds to their halls of residence, and the young ladies were taken to the buildings closer to the school itself.

The tradition that dictated the seniors were permitted the upper floor rooms was initially begun to demonstrate their maturity, and assumed they needed less supervision from the adults residing on the ground floor adjacent to the offices. This also afforded the older students the opportunity to make as much noise as they wanted while the underclassmen were powerless to complain about it. Some traditions fueled the division between the ranks and this one ignited the divide on MaryAnne and Aggie's very first day.

Miss Findley, their RA, was a middle-aged woman of some heft. She stood a towering 5'11" in low heels and her paisley polyester dress stretched over buxom curves and down to ample calves. Upon her gathering their group in the lobby of Wright Hall, their home for the foreseeable future, Aggie couldn't help but fixate on the woman's sturdy legs. Smiling to herself, she also realized that she might be developing a thing for legs as this was the second pair she'd taken note of that day.

Miss Findley called the young women to order.

"Attention, ladies! When I call your name, you will report to the floor and room to which you are assigned."

A few hands raised.

"And before you ask, the answer is 'No'! No one will be permitted to trade assignments or rooms."

More hands.

"No exceptions!"

Now the woman looked down at the defeated students.

"So, if there are no further questions, please listen for your name."

She referred to her list, clutching her clipboard and a giant ring of keys in one hand, checking off names and numbers with the pen in the other. The seniors were called and excused first, then the juniors, and so on. When Miss Findley called and dismissed the final freshman, Aggie and MaryAnne still remained. The woman looked over her cheaters to discover the girls.

"Oh! What have we here? I must have missed someone. Names?"

"O'Hanley, Agatha."

Aggie instantly regretted the military style in which she'd responded, but in a split-second decision to mimic her classmate, MaryAnne doubled down.

"O'Hara, MaryAnne, sir!"

"That's enough of that nonsense. Ladies, this is serious, you're not on my roster."

She instructed them to take a seat and she marched into the office to investigate.

MaryAnne began speculating.

"Probably some stupid mistake. I'll bet it happens every year and Findley always acts like it's the first time this school has ever messed up."

"Yeah, you might be right. But honestly, I wouldn't mind if they left me out of this deal altogether. I'm not exactly thrilled to be here."

MaryAnne urged with an elbow.

"Aww, come on, sister! We've arrived! No more keeping us down on the farm."

Aggie hoped out loud.

"Are you from a farm?"

"No, it's just an expression."

"Well, I *am* from a farm."

"Oh! I didn't mean anything by it."

MaryAnne felt the red warmth of regret rising from her collar and tried to recover.

"Where abouts?"

"Just outside of West Fort Ann. Without the 'e'."

"Touché!"

MaryAnne clapped her hands together and took the opportunity to redirect the conversation. She squared herself around on the wooden bench they shared and locked onto Aggie's face.

"That's in Washington County, just the other side of Lake George from me! Fort Ann was actually named for Queen Anne of Britain, who *did* spell her name with an 'e', but the original fort was built and destroyed so many times, it probably just got lost in the shuffle!"

Even as Aggie found herself leaning back a little from her new friend's enthusiasm, she was being drawn in.

"How do you know so much about Fort Ann?"

"The only history I remember learning was about the territories around the lake because I used to live at the Grand Chancellor Hotel."

"You *lived* there?"

"All summer long for as long as I can remember. I was actually born there -"

"Alright, girls!"

Miss Findley had abruptly returned.

"We have you figured out, now."

Aggie was anxious.

"Is there a problem, Miss Findley?"

"No, we simply didn't count you in the original numbers because you're the only scholarship recipients we've enrolled this term."

A flash of embarrassment overtook both girls and their backs straightened against their shame.

"Not to worry though, ladies. We have made provisions. Follow me."

The girls trailed the paisley covered rump of the administrator up the winding stairs past the first landing for the freshman. The rotund woman's legs swished loudly as her pantyhose heated with friction. The girls couldn't help but notice the nylon humming as they brought up the rear past the half pace to the sophomore floor. They climbed up to the next, housing the junior rooms and paused on that landing to let Miss Findley catch her breath. She ever-so-slightly parted her knees in an effort to quench the fire certain to ignite should she take another step. And when her thighs cooled enough, she licked the sweat beaded on her fuzzy upper lip and continued to the topmost floor of the dorms.

When they arrived on the top floor, the girls looked at one another, wide-eyed. Could they have hit the jackpot, advancing to the senior hall on the very first day of school? What luck! Findley, nearly breathless now, pointed to the right end of the hallway split in two by the stairs they'd just ascended.

"Girls, down at that far end are the showers and lavatories."

She paused, took another salty lick, and waved them to follow to the left.

"But we're going this way."

She labored down the darkened hall, segmented by rectangles of light from multiple dorm rooms open and full of busy girls unpacking and visiting. At the end of the long, paneled corridor, Miss Findley dug in her dress pocket for a single key. She unlocked the door and the three left the rest of the population behind. They had entered a wing of the building originally afforded the cleaning staff and grounds keepers. Two narrow steps down took them into a short hall with two doors on the left, one door on the right, next to a back stairwell, and one door straight ahead. She used the same, single key she'd produced to get beyond the main hall, to unlock *that* door.

The girls followed her into a sprawling room, swimming in light from a wall of windows on either side, where two iron beds were centered. Wardrobes bookended the door, and desks with gooseneck lamps and Windsor chairs with their backs to the beds overlooked the grounds in both directions of the rambling campus. A four-drawer chest where a mix matched pair of shaded lamps sat, separated the beds.

"This will be your home for the next four years, girls."

A chime of the watch locket Miss Findley wore pinned to her dress alerted her to another duty. She handed Aggie the key and left the freshmen on their own.

"Get unpacked and return to the lobby by eleven, sharp!"

The pair, agog, walked around the spacious room, opening doors and drawers, and checking out the yawning view. A giggle escaped Aggie and she clamped her fingers over her lips.

MaryAnne assured her.

"No…you're right. We just got away with murder!"

The teens threw themselves on their beds and squealed with delight!

»«

All the young girls, with the exception of the seniors, poured from the aging building's stairwells, and congealed in the lobby of the dorm. Miss Findley and an assistant handed out name badges to be pinned to every uniform lapel before the newcomers exited for the classrooms. Aggie's and MaryAnne's were blank white rectangles with blue label maker stickers adhered at the last minute. They didn't care. Tagged and accounted for, the group squeezed through the double doors and out onto the grounds.

Concrete paths winding around gardens, fountains, and lampposts guided them to the main school buildings. The sugar maples scattered about the lawn were heavy with bright gold, rust, and red foliage. The canopy intensified the yellow light of the mid-morning sun that owned the clear September sky. The chill of fall was in the air, but the wool uniform coats and knee socks were more than enough to keep it at bay as the girls neared their terminus. The veins of the other paths from the other dorms, converged in front of the central academy steps and Dean Springer appeared at the entrance to announce that upon entering they would find senior classmen to guide them to their homeroom. The day was meant to familiarize the students with the layout of the school.

"Each course session will be only twenty minutes long today, students, including an abbreviated lunch period. And our official first day will conclude with dinner in the cafeteria after which you are free to return to your dorm and prepare yourself to begin in earnest tomorrow morning. So again, welcome and good luck!"

Springer turned to enter, and the masses followed to commence with the day.

O'Hanley and O'Hara were directed to their homeroom, on the ground floor, two doors to the right of the auditorium with which they'd already become familiar. Room 105 marked the start of their journey alphabetically linked. Their classmates were the freshman from the L's through the O's. Their homeroom teacher, Mrs. Amos, handed out a campus map, calendar, cafeteria menu, and class schedules and read a sample of the announcements that they could expect to be briefed on mid-morning, between second and third period.

Near the back of the room, MaryAnne inched her desk closer to Aggie's and, holding her schedule in her outstretched hand to compare to her friend's, scanned the slips for shared classes.

"First period, English."

"Algebra."

"Ok. Second period, History."

"Biology."

"Back here for homeroom, then my third period class is Theatre."

"Me too."

"Yes!"

MaryAnne's enthusiasm was louder than she intended, and the room responded with a collective stare in the direction of the pair. Mrs. Amos stopped briefly to raise an eyebrow from behind her bulletin and then resumed reading. Aggie sunk lower into her seat and MaryAnne shrugged and waved the onlookers back to their own business. She snatched the roster from her roommate's hand and finished the comparative examination of their daily routines as Mrs. Amos concluded her instruction and allowed them free time until the bell.

"I have Home Ec but I don't see that on yours, Aggie."

Snatching the paper back, Aggie examined it herself.

"I'm not taking Home Ec, MaryAnne. I'm taking VoTech."

"VoTech? What is VoTech?"

"Shop Class."

MaryAnne's confusion was evident by the look on her face.

"Home Ec is like the easiest A ever."

"Not for me. I'd catch something on fire if I had to work in a kitchen."

"What do you do in Shop Class?"

"Woodworking, welding, electrical stuff."

"And you won't catch on fire welding wood?"

Aggie laughed at her ignorant friend as the bell sounded.

"I'll be fine."

"Whatever. At least we'll be together in Theatre."

The girls rose and exited homeroom with the rest of their class. Before they separated into the masses in the halls for the rest of their day, Aggie flashed the only key to their room at MaryAnne to remind her.

"Find me in the cafeteria."

"You bet!"

MaryAnne would have met her at lunch even if that weren't the case. She had already awarded Aggie best friend status; her roommate would be slower to commit.

The Howerton Sisters

The cafeteria was a clanging swarm of kids that first day, lacking the order of the normal routine yet to establish itself. Lines going every which way and pointing and redirecting coming from those in-the-know, the girls found each other with little trouble. MaryAnne stood to wave Aggie over to a table she had already claimed by imposition. She edged the girl next to her toward the long end of the bench affording Aggie the end spot and began the introductions.

"This is Aggie, my roommate. Ags, this is Sarah, Morgan, and Katherine, but she goes by Kate."

Aggie nodded, digesting her new nickname and her first bite of fruit cocktail.

"They're all freshman too, Ags. This is the frosh table!"

MaryAnne lifted a plastic fork to declare their territory and nearly stabbed the eye of a passerby in the process. The whole group winced at the near miss. The would-be victim dodged the tines.

Whoa! Watch it!"

MaryAnne shrunk.

"Sorry, I didn't see you there."

Recovering her momentum MaryAnne continued with the personal details she was sure would endear her and Aggie to their new friends.

"Ags and I are in Theatre third period together. I've always wanted to study the theatre. I hope to be discovered one day and act on TV. Maybe on our senior trip. I hear they go to New York City or Chicago every year!"

Kate, already fascinated, probed the girls.

"And you, Aggie? Do you want to act too?"

"No. Well, not exactly. I want to have my own talk show. But I want to know the whole thing…production, direction. I don't just want to be the host. I want it to be *my* show. Like Donahue."

MaryAnne took over the questioning.

"But you took shop! What does that have to do with anything?"

"Set design? Ever heard of it?"

Kate grinned devilishly.

"Isn't Shop Class full of boys?"

MaryAnne took the opportunity to boost her friend in the last word on the subject.

"A: it's 1974 and girls can do anything boys can do. And B: look at her, you guys! What boy is going to object to a beautiful redhead in their VoTech class?"

Just then a clot of older girls gathered at the end of their table, the shadow encroaching on Aggie's space, and their leader spoke up.

"You're the scholars this term, aren't you?"

MaryAnne was confused.

"Scholars?"

"Yeah, that's what we call the poor kids that come here on scholarship…scholars."

Aggie looked up from her plate into the eyes of this new tormentor.

"Yes, we are the scholars."

Cocking her head to one side, the senior looked Aggie up and down.

"I'm Danielle Howerton."

She waited for a reaction. When she got none, she repeated herself.

"Howerton?"

This time Aggie shrugged in response and the girl mocked her.

"Oh my God! They don't even know where they are!"

The gang around her exchanged smirks and stares of amazement and she laid it out.

"The Howerton family built this academy."

MaryAnne tried a shot at some levity to defuse the tension.

"Oh, so your people were carpenters?"

"Hardly!"

All the girls jumped!

"I'm Danielle Howerton, great-great-great-grand daughter of Jewel and Bradshaw Howerton, founders of this institution."

She gawked at the girls' lack of recognition.

"And this is my sister, Thomasina."

She nudged a smaller version of herself out of the fray with an elbow.

Aggie was growing tired of the power play and took the initiative to shut it down.

"Ok. We got it, Dan and Tom Howerton. Hello! We're going to eat now."

"Danielle and Thomasina, scholar!"

Danielle slammed her tray down so hard, her milk carton launched onto the table. MaryAnne reached over, picked it up between her thumb and middle finger, her pinky delicately raised, and placed it on her own tray, then bowed and broke into a royal accent.

"Thank you. I was wondering if we would be treated to seconds."

The Howerton's glowered down at the new girls then met each other's eyes as eerie smiles crept over their faces and Danielle ended the exchange with one word uttered through clenched teeth.

"Cute."

With a flick of her head the menace abandoned the territory, taking her posse with her and the frosh table breathed a collective sigh of relief. Kate spoke her fear of the threat.

"That can't be good."

MaryAnne was pumped.

"Shit! They don't scare me. You scared, Ags?"

She checked her friend who was nearly finished with the contents of her lunch tray already. Aggie tipped her milk up to empty the carton, cutting her eyes toward her brazen roommate.

»«

The quick walk back to the dorms after classes was uneventful for the girls, surrounded by the few new additions to their group. Their way only seemed a little more precarious when they left the other newbies on the second floor and trotted up the stairs.

Thomasina Howerton was a freshman…on the freshman floor, and she and her senior sister, Danielle were poised in her freshman doorway when the girls turned on the landing and kept on up the stairs. The two filed in behind Aggie and MaryAnne and followed past the sophomore and junior tiers to the senior hall. The girls were oblivious to their tail in the noisy stair traffic.

They made it through their private door at the end of the hall and were just about to unlock their dorm room when Thomasina shocked them with a loud bark.

"Hey!"

Both the girls jumped as the sound bounced around the walls of the remote hall and MaryAnne's reaction was just as loud.

"Jesus! You scared the shit out of me!"

"Ha! I distinctly remember hearing that we *didn't* scare you."

The younger Howerton defaulted to her sister.

"Right Danielle? Isn't that what we heard?"

"Yep. You scared too, *Ags*?"

Aggie suddenly decided nicknames were just fine among this foursome.

"What do you want, *Dan*?"

"I want you to give me that key."

"This key?"

She dangled it from her middle finger in salute to the request.

"It's absurd that two freshman scholars should get their own wing in this dorm, when there is a legacy living on the second floor. My sister is not going to be outranked by you two."

MaryAnne moved in front of Aggie, stopping Danielle from advancing over the shoulder of the younger Howerton.

"Sorry girls, but Miss Findley was pretty clear that no one could switch rooms for any reason. And you wouldn't want your sister living in the servant's quarters of this building. Would she, Aggie?"

"Noooo. You wouldn't want to live out here where the *help* had to sleep. Tommy, honey, this is the scholar's wing. No legacies past that threshold. So, off you go."

Thomasina looked back at her big sister for her next move and the elder straightened herself and turned to reenter the main building. With her hand on the knob, she issued a warning to the closed door.

"This isn't over."

MaryAnne grabbed the key from Aggie's finger, closed the door tight behind their new enemies, and locked it.

"That was intense!"

"Yes, intense. Now, can I please get into my room?"

Aggie waved her friend away from the static of the confrontation and MaryAnne jumped to her side to grant them entry.

"Those Howerton's are some fierce bitches. We'll have to watch out for the two of them."

Aggie flopped onto her mattress and puffed out an indifferent breath.

"They're just bullies. My brothers taught me all about bullies."

"But these are rich bullies."

"Money or no, a bully's a bully."

Aggie flipped onto her belly.

"What difference does money make in this situation?"

"I don't know."

MaryAnne pulled her suitcase from under her bed and opened it.

"*They* seemed to think it mattered."

"It might matter to them, but we'd be dumb to let it matter to us."

MaryAnne beamed! *Us* -plural pronouns! They were a unit! She gathered the few things she had packed on top of a smaller case in her luggage which she opened to unveil a portable turntable.

"How about this, roomy?"

Aggie smiled.

"Nice!"

Dean, Bob, and Other Things

MaryAnne ceremoniously placed the record player in the neutral zone, atop the chest between the beds, a gesture of solidarity and good will, and made the pronouncement.

"We will co-DJ. You have fair and equal rights to all records played on this machine, going forward."

Aggie bowed.

"Thank you. What do you like to listen to?"

"Oh, you know, the usual. Top 40, I guess."

"Elton John? ABBA? Chicago?"

MaryAnne responded cautiously.

"Yeah…you too?"

"M-hm."

Aggie was growing uncomfortably warm. A girl's taste in music could bury her. She thought pop was a safe bet. She waited to see if MaryAnne revealed any more before she judged if she could answer truthfully.

MaryAnne broke.

"Uuggghhhh! I can't! If we're going to be roommates, you're going to find out sooner or later. I hate that K-tel shit!"

"Whew, me too!"

The girls dropped onto their respective beds and Aggie started over.

"So, what do you *really* love?"

MaryAnne popped off her mattress and dove for her satchel retrieving three LPs, all still protected by their cellophane wrappers. Holding their covers against her chest she grimaced.

"Don't judge me."

She flipped the albums and hid behind them; Aggie delighted in the revelation.

"Dean Martin?! Oh my God!"

"I know, it's dumb but -"

"No!"

Aggie's tone begged her friend to wait while she dug in her belongings for her own favorites. Now *she* was the one hesitating before the reveal.

"I cannot judge, lest I be judged."

She lowered her head and presented the records with solemn reverence.

"Robert Gerard 'call-me-Bob' Goulet!"

"Aaaahhhhh!"

Their crazy fan screams went out into the room even as the rest of the campus was quieting. Aggie started the evening off with *Summer Sounds* from 1969, while they finished unpacking and MaryAnne began dissecting.

"I don't know what it is about the crooner. They're so much more serious than these boys everyone is all jazzed up about."

“They just look like they smell so good! Not like brothers or dads, but like men. Grown men.”

“Because they *are* grown men! They’re not some teenager trying to sing about love they haven’t had yet. They’ve had it, done it, sucked it, licked it, and slapped it on a bingbong!

A grimace scrunched Aggie’s nose in response to her friend’s well-established over-the-top remarks.

“I don’t know about all that. But I’ve always thought Robert Goulet’s eyes were flat-out gorgeous.”

“And Dean has those yummy, milk chocolate brown eyes and those sexy, full lips!”

Aggie played at her impression of him.

“The better to drink you with my dear!”

“No. Aggie, you know that’s a gag?”

“Huh?”

“The drunk thing Dean does in his Vegas acts, and with the Rat Pack. But never with Jerry, I don’t think.”

“I’m not following.”

MaryAnne educated her friend.

“He didn’t really drink on stage. He was never drunk during his acts. He only acted drunk for the humor of it.”

“I think you’re thinking of Albert Brooks.”

"No. That's *Foster* Brooks. Albert is that Jewish guy with the afro who made that one comedy album. He's on Johnny Carson all the time."

"Oooohhh. So, the drunk thing was an act?"

"Yep. Iced tea. That's the rumor. To look like J&B Scotch. That's what I read anyway."

The girls continued to compare their celebrity crushes, unpack family pictures, refold their tee shirts, and stow their socks and underwear. They hung their spare uniforms and prepared to stroll to the end of senior hall to wash for dinner. Carefully locking their room and hall doors behind them, Aggie tucked the key into her pocket and followed MaryAnne to the lavatory at the far end of the passage.

When they reached their destination MaryAnne leaned into the closed door and met resistance. She rebounded and turned the knob the other way and put her shoulder into it, but still no give.

Aggie shoved her aside to take a turn.

"What is there a trick to it, or something?"

MaryAnne turned away from the door to take in the length of the hallway and saw nearly every doorway manned with a smug, smirking senior posturing with arms folded. Danielle appeared from her room and headed toward the girls.

MaryAnne flicked the pleats of her friend's skirt to signal her to stop.

"There's a trick all right."

Danielle started in.

"Oh, sorry girls, I guess no one told you. That's Luann and Monica in there. They throw shotput on the track team. And they don't take kindly to sharing the facilities with *some people*."

Aggie gave up on the door and turned to face the others.

"Seriously? You're not going to let us use the bathroom up here?"

"You may *reside* above the freshman floor, but you will not *live* above the freshman floor. Your lavatory and shower rooms are three flights down."

Danielle drew her hand in close to her face to wave as if amusing a child.

"Have a nice night, scholars."

Aggie brushed past MaryAnne and headed for the stairs, her friend at her heels. As they descended, the laughter trailing off behind them, MaryAnne began to worry.

"We're going to have to take our shower stuff down three flights every day? I'm not a morning person, Ags. How the hell am I going to get ready in time to make the tardy bell first thing?"

They reached the freshman floor and stopped.

"This sucks!"

Aggie snapped.

"Will you quit it! If they think they're getting to us, they'll keep pulling crap like this and we won't have any peace in this place. Let's just wash our hands and faces and go eat. Why is it so hard to get through a meal around here?"

MaryAnne nodded and followed obediently.

»«

Dinner was surprisingly good, and the girls were convinced that they wouldn't starve to death over the next four years. Even though their bellies were full, they craved the tastes of home. On the walk back to the dorm, the two compared their favorites, each one growing more and more interested in the other's life.

"Fresh eggs make all the difference."

The pride Aggie felt in her family's farm products was evident.

"They look different, they taste different. You don't even have to keep them in the fridge."

"Eggs?"

"Nope. Mom keeps a bowl of fresh eggs on the counter. Dad and the boys eat about three dozen a day between'em."

"Never heard of keeping eggs out."

MaryAnne was always around the kitchen, but she didn't learn much. She was only now suspecting that the staff at the Grand just let her hang out there and nibble as they prepared food to keep her from getting in the way.

"My mom worked in the laundry which was right under the main kitchen. She used to send me upstairs with the aprons, tablecloths, cloth napkins, and tea towels for the chef. Then I'd sit on the counter and sample the goods."

Aggie pressed her friend.

“What was the best thing on the menu?”

“Crab!”

“Mmmm.”

“Any kind of recipe with crabmeat in it - I was all over that shit! Crab cakes, crab balls, crab bisque.”

“Did they show you how to cook it?”

“No. They might have if I ever asked them. It never dawned on me to ask them.”

“I like fish too.”

“Fish? Crab isn’t fish, Ags. Crab is *shellfish*.”

“Yeah. I guess you’re right, there is a difference. But I like plain old fish-fish too.”

“Fish is ok, but shellfish is the best!”

MaryAnne continued her lists.

“Buttery shrimp scampi, lobster with butter, crab legs swimming in butter.”

“Sounds like maybe you like your butter with a hint of shellfish.”

“Shit, I never thought about that either. I love butter!”

They talked all the way to the front porch of their building and stopped when MaryAnne began to whine.

“Man, I hate the thought of going past all that business again just to get to our room.”

“Then let’s not.”

“What?”

“Let’s go the back way.”

MaryAnne thought for a second, then remembered it too.

“That staircase! Come on!”

The girls tore off around the great structure and finding a basement entrance around the far side, Aggie tried their key. It worked! They navigated the dark, labyrinthian cellar until they arrived at the narrow stairwell and began their ascent. Loping upward, incited by their secret freedoms, they reached the short hall outside their room without interference.

MaryAnne celebrated.

“This is sweet! No one can bother us as long as we always come and go through our secret passage!”

Aggie let them in.

“But we can’t, always.”

“What? Sure we can, we just did.”

Aggie cautioned her naive friend.

“If we never come out into the senior hall, they’ll know we’ve found a new way in and out. And I don’t know about you, but I don’t want to run into Luann and Monica in that dark basement!”

“You’re right. And it still doesn’t help us with the shower situation. Unless…”

Aggie waited for the other shoe and MaryAnne held her hand out for the key. Her friend surrendered it and she walked out into the hall, eyeing the three other doors. With Aggie just behind, she played at gameshow host.

"And now, Cheryl will show us what's behind door number one?"

The key fit the lock as it had all the others before, and the pair opened the door to a small but ample private bathroom. A clawfoot tub with shower hose sat under a window that had been painted over, a toilet, fore, and a sink, aft. MaryAnne started to squeak when Aggie grabbed her mouth from behind and whispered into her friend's thick hair.

"Not a sound…not a word…not even a hint…to anyone. You got that?"

The muzzled MaryAnne nodded her head in agreement and when she was released whispered back.

"Let's try the other two."

The room between the bathroom and hall entrance was as big as their dorm, shelf-lined with a window seat, and the one between their room and the stairwell across the hall, appeared to be utilitarian in nature.

They located the valves for the radiators and hot water tank, a fuse box, and a dumbwaiter they presumed went all the way to the basement. MaryAnne marveled at Aggie's knowledge of the plumbing and electrical works. Even though her stepfather was a tradesman, he never taught her how any of it worked. They checked the faucets and turned the valves on to empty the rust from the pipes. They checked the lights and replaced the fuses that had expired. They worked into the night equipping their private little suite.

When the water had time to heat up, Aggie went first in the shower, smiling to herself thinking how proud her dad would be of the job she'd done. MaryAnne waited patiently for her turn, writing a letter to her mom and listening to the velvety voice of Dino, on his 1970 country/folk bestseller, *For the Good Times*.

Going Home

Thanksgiving break was quick, but valuable. Aggie's brother, Jack, had come for her and they made arrangements to deposit MaryAnne at The Grand on their way around the tail of Lake George. Her mother and Zeke were visiting 'the family' at the hotel and wanted her first holiday home to be filled with all the busy, beautiful people who loved her.

The farm was busy too. Jim and his fiancé, Beth, were home from Albany. Bob was on leave from the Navy, which meant he'd miss Christmas with them, but that would have to be ok. Rex was sober, clean, and out of the apartment over Hupp's Hardwoods in downtown West Fort Ann. Their mother couldn't live with the drinking after his accident, so their father fixed up the place above his storefront to keep an eye on him. A full decade since the crash and still no one expected anything else from Rex. Even though icy roads were to blame, he couldn't live - soberly that is - with the fact that his best friend died in the wreck. He'd stay clean for a month or two and get right back on the sauce. It was coming up on the anniversary and the family knew he was trying hard not to mess up the holidays…again. And then there was Jack. Jack tried college for a minute, got 'excused' from the army in basic training, and was now begrudgingly helping Hupp and Eloise on the farm, when he wasn't babysitting his big brother.

Aggie's mother seemed plumper than she remembered at the end of the summer. She stood on the porch in her calico apron and the swirling snow flurries with her arms outstretched for her daughter. Hupp heard the truck pull up and hurried from the garage, stomping off his boots on the backdoor mat. Aggie hugged her mother then wiggled free and made a beeline for her dad. He was thinner, she thought. The momentum behind her hug nearly knocked him over.

"Steady, doll. You're gonna send me ass over tin cup."

She drew in the scent of his flannel, and Camels, and sawdust. *Now* she was home.

The boys teased her and quizzed her about her new school. Beth was sweet and quiet offering to show her something new with her hair if she wanted a change from her signature ponytail. Eloise was pink from her labors in the kitchen and the joy of all her children gathered under one roof again.

After dinner when the men had retired to the living room and Beth and Aggie had run the matriarch out of the kitchen they started the dishes and gossiped about West Fort Ann.

"I know you've been away too Beth, but have you heard anything about Bill?"

"No, honey. Bill's gone. And never coming back is my guess."

The older girl stopped drying the dish in her hand and touched Aggie's hair.

"Honey, a pretty girl like you, you don't need someone like Bill."

Aggie stopped washing.

"I know how it is with your first crush. But you need to forget all about that now. That's not what you want."

Aggie smiled at how little her future sister-in-law knew about what she wanted.

"There it is. There's that winning smile. That's what's gonna get you your very own TV show some day, Aggie Rose and I can't wait!"

Aggie plunged her hands back into the suds and her heart back into being home and being loved. Even if she never felt understood, she knew she was loved. Beth listened intently to the teen and her life plans. Though she and Beth were cut from very different cloths, Aggie loved her brother's girl and longed for the day when they would become real sisters.

»«

"MARYANNE!!!" the party shouted as the teen entered the service entrance to the main kitchen. She was hailed like a soldier back from the war: hugged and kissed and held at arm's length to get a good look at. The service staff of The Grand Chancellor on Lake George, who made up the closest thing to a family MaryAnne ever knew and spoiled her shamelessly, was a motley crew. And they'd all stayed over to celebrate Thanksgiving with their favorite kid.

Everyone was there. Joseph Moynihan and his deaf brother Jonathan were the groundskeepers. Jonathan ran the big mowers and snowplow because the sound didn't bother him. When she was little, MaryAnne asked every summer, "Is he deaf because he runs the loud machines, or does he run the loud machines because he's deaf?" Every year she was given an answer that escaped her on her first day back to school in the fall.

Hank and Peg Halpenny managed the boat rentals and all the lifeguards. Peg taught MaryAnne how to swim when she was a tot and Hank let her steer the motorboat at the end of the season when they needed to bring in the safety rope dotted with blue and white floats that cordoned off the swimming area. The Halpenny's stayed on in the winter tending the shallows of the lake as an ice rink through the spring.

Frank Belcastro ran the restaurant and the formal dining room that was used for big conventions and important weddings, and his daughters Lisa and Celeste ran the pool and lakeside snack bars, respectively. Celeste always let MaryAnne scoop her own ice cream. Lisa was older and not nearly as warm, but she was never unkind and would occasionally put two straws in the Coke floats she made knowing it got a grin out of MaryAnne every time.

Dr. Haynes was the manager in charge of the whole staff. He ran a tight ship, but he too was hospitable and not just to the guests but to those who worked in their service, and lucky for MaryAnne, also their families. He wasn't a real doctor, but everyone called him Dr. Haynes; another bit MaryAnne quizzed her mother about at the beginning of every summer and forgot again by the first week in September.

Summers at the The Grand Chancellor Hotel were MaryAnne O'Hara's favorite thing in the world. Ever since she could remember, her mother had worked the season in service at the majestic resort.

Patsy was barely seventeen when she had her daughter, on the fifth of June 1960. When the rabbit died, her friends at Butler High School, called it a 'virgin birth' because she was that one girl who got pregnant the first time she *did it*. The carnie that called her to go out on the last night of the fair, never called her back. Her parents called it a sin and kicked her out. Patsy packed some clothes and her books in the 1950 Henry J her Grand-dad Bill left her when he died and drove north. The shore of Lake George was as far out of southwestern Pennsylvania as she could get on her babysitting money. When she arrived at The Grand, she negotiated a room in exchange for a job and started the next day in the laundry, folding linens and filling the housekeeping carts. Once the baby came, Patsy was allowed to keep her close, carrying the little thing around in wire laundry baskets lined with warm white towels.

Of all the employees at The Grand though, Mrs. Norman was MaryAnne and Patsy's favorite. Dottie Norman ran the hotel laundry. She had taken pity on Patsy from the start; they all had a strange sense Mrs. Norman had a sad baby story of her own; and fell in love with her newborn baby girl. They were closer than blood relatives and MaryAnne loved her.

It was Dottie who allowed Patsy to stay on through to the end of her pregnancy, something that was frowned upon in prestigious places like the hotel even as the Age of Aquarius was dawning. When The Grand hosted guests like the bishop of the Albany diocese, the image of an unwed mother in the hotel's service was not one management wanted openly conveyed.

Dottie saw that the teenager remained out of sight once she began to show and Patsy was grateful for her efforts. Mrs. Norman even kept Patsy on the payroll without Dr. Haynes becoming the wiser while she was still in the hospital and then when she returned to the hotel but was unable to do more than care for the baby. The whole laundry staff covered Patsy's duties until she was back on her feet. The young mother got back to work as soon as she could, determined to return all the good will she'd been granted.

Once she was regularly working her full shifts, it was Dottie Norman who encouraged Patsy to attend classes in nearby Warrensburg, just a few ticks west of Lake George.

When MaryAnne was just three months old, Dottie watched the baby while Patsy took a course to get her G.E.D. and then enrolled in night school in a small teaching college from which she graduated early with her education degree.

MaryAnne was five when her mother secured a position on the faculty of Warrensburg Elementary, where she had done her student teaching. Dottie gave them some old furniture and a few dishes, and they made a home out of a third story, two-bedroom in the Libby apartments, within walking distance of the school. Patsy and her kindergartener started the term together that fall, away from their friends at the lake but every summer that followed, the pair spent the whole season from Memorial Day to Labor Day working and playing among the resort crowd at The Grand. And every summer, MaryAnne loved it!

The girl made her way around the room chatting with everyone as they prepared dinner and when she finally got to Dottie, she blew her bangs and widened her eyes to take her in.

"Dooootttiiiieeee! It's so good to be home!"

"We've missed you so much, MaryAnne!"

Dottie's eyes were welling as she grabbed MaryAnne's face, kissing her long-lost girl over and over.

"Look at you. You're grown already!"

MaryAnne closed her eyes and twirled for Dottie to size her up thoroughly; and when she felt properly assessed by the woman, she opened them and confronted her.

"Dottie, where's my mother?"

Dottie lost her shine in an instant and her brows caved in above her worried eyes.

"They'll be here real soon, honey."

"Is everything ok?"

"Everything is –."

Suddenly, there was a mechanical bang and the back door swung open.

It was Patsy…in a wheelchair!

Zeke had muscled the contraption past the screen door but was unable to get to the next knob, so he rammed it with the footrests of the chair, even as Patsy's feet occupied them, and cursed it.

"Damn this thing!"

Patsy grinned and waved to the shocked crowd.

"And a Happy Thanksgiving to us all!"

A beat, and then another rousing cheer came from the group.

MaryAnne did not cheer.

Instead, she stood motionless, her eyes filling with hot shock. Dottie gently squeezed her hands to get her to move.

"She's still your momma, honey. She's had a rough time of it lately."

The girl blinked and tears were loosed down her cheeks.

"It's ok, MaryAnne. Go to her."

Dottie pushed her charge toward the gathering and MaryAnne wiped her face before she got through. Zeke saw her coming.

"There she is! There's our MaryAnne!"

She stranded him with his arms outstretched behind her mother and dove into Patsy's arms. Her coat was so loose it crowded her neck when her daughter embraced her. Patsy held on to her girl with everything she had. They both began a silent cry. A hush fell over the crowd and many of those assembled teared up or turned away.

After a few awkward seconds, Zeke sensed they might need spurred to recover so, taking his Giants cap from his head and flapping it against his jeans, he began to lament.

"So nuthin' for the old stepdad, huh?"

He dropped his head.

"I see how it is. I'm just chopped liver!"

MaryAnne laughed out loud in her mother's ear, raised up and leaned over to grab the strapping man.

"You know I love liver!"

And another hardy cheer rang out from the galley of The Grand.

When the kitchen had been cleaned and closed and everyone retreated to their bungalows, MaryAnne trailed behind watching Zeke push her mother across the gravel to the few wooden steps leading to the porch of theirs. He locked the chair and bent to lift his wife from it.

"Is that really necessary?"

MaryAnne asked the question too quickly and with a judgement that surprised her. She felt embarrassed for her mom and wasn't sure Zeke knew how it looked.

"She's lighter without the chair. Plus, these old steps can't take the bangin'."

Patsy shot her a glance that the girl was not truly sure how to read. MaryAnne thought it was shame but couldn't discern if she was ashamed of being carried or of her daughter for being uncomfortable about it. They both blushed in response, but Zeke carried on unaffected.

He took her inside and placed her gently on the couch, helping her off with her coat and boots, and settling her under a crocheted afghan. When her pillows had been adjusted perfectly, he held her face and kissed her lips tenderly.

"I'm going outside for a smoke before I get the fire going, ok?"

She smiled without parting her lips as if to keep hold of the kiss for longer. MaryAnne had shed her own coat and boots and stood self-consciously before her mother with her hands on her hips.

"Well…he might have lit the fire first. It's cold in here."

She didn't know how to begin to talk to Patsy about her condition. She'd been walking on her own with only the occasional need for her cane in the summer and here it was just three months later, and she was in a wheelchair. She could feel her heart beating faster and she didn't want to cry again, so she flew into action.

"I'll light the damn fire!"

"MaryAnne, leave it. Zeke will be back in two minutes."

"Mother! In the next two minutes, this hearth will be ablaze! Just you wait."

"Angel-face leave it. Come sit with me. You know you don't know the first thing about starting a fire."

MaryAnne abandoned her post at the fireplace and knelt in the space between the couch and the coffee table.

"I know. I just wanted to do something for you."

"You're here, that's enough."

Patsy twisted slightly at the trunk to raise her hand and comb her fingers through MaryAnne's hair. She used to do this very thing when MaryAnne was a tot and woke in the night to a bad dream. She remembered how it soothed them both, but she wasn't sure if she still had the touch with her weakening hands.

She did…and MaryAnne felt a little less like crying already.

"When did this happen, Mom? When did you get the chair?"

"You make it sound like I'm on death row! It's only been a few weeks, I guess."

"Why didn't you call me or write about it?"

"That would have been a great letter; Dear MaryAnne, I can't trust my legs anymore so I'm going to live in a wheelchair now."

Patsy's tone registered as mocking in MaryAnne's ears and she erupted from the floor.

"Jesus Mom! It's not funny!"

"MaryAnne I'm sorry! I didn't mean to make light. I'm sorry, come on and sit back down here."

The girl returned to her knees and held her mother's hands.

"It's ok. I'm ok. This is just what happens. I had a good summer, hardly any progression at all. And then when it got colder, I just started slowing down."

"But you were in remission last year when it got cold. Remember we sledded on Butt-Breaker Hill."

"Wow, was that only last year?"

"Yes. That's what I'm saying. This is happening so fast."

The teen was trying to disguise her panic as a right to know. She was feeling both, strongly.

"It's just because you've been away that it seems like it's happened fast. It's mostly been a steady, gradual thing. MaryAnne, you knew this was coming. You've known since the beginning. I've been honest with you since they diagnosed me."

"I guess it just looks totally different now."

Patsy's brow furrowed incredulously.

"Are you worried about how it looks?"

"Not how it looks to other people, Mom. How it makes you feel like *you* look."

She wasn't at all sure she phrased her thought the way she meant to.

"Does that make sense?"

Patsy's voice began to harden.

"I have accepted this, MaryAnne. This is my reality."

They heard the car door slam and Zeke folding and heaving the wheelchair and luggage onto the porch. Patsy retrieved her hands from her daughter's grip and shot her a final look that closed the discussion.

»«

The girls lapped up the attention their respective families lavished on them over the long weekend. They filled their homes with talk of their first semester away. Both made sure there was a full description of the campus, their private wing, and their newfound friends, Sarah, Morgan, and Kate. They afforded each subject its due according to importance. So, it made sense that neither could shut up about the other.

Aggie kissed her mom goodnight the night after Thanksgiving and kept on at the arm of her dad's recliner well past his yawns and flickering lids. She confessed that MaryAnne 'cussed a little too much', but she 'loved the same music', and 'she grew up in a hotel!'. When she got around to reporting that they'd incurred the wrath of the founders' heirs, she was honest about worrying just a little over what they were capable of.

Hupp cautioned his daughter.

"We gotta be fireproof, doll. Otherwise, we'll be afraid of every damn fool who lights a match!"

As always, her dad fortified her resolve with the truth of one sentence and she worried no more.

MaryAnne wore Patsy out curled up on the opposite end of the couch by the fire for two straight nights recounting every detail of what she saw as Aggie's unshakeable courage and crazy trade skills. Patsy hung on every word as she struggled to stay awake.

"Plumbing, Mom! And electric, and she's gorgeous! It's like if Trooper John Thornton and Mary-Katherine Danaher had a baby. A beautiful redhead with Kelly green eyes but tough enough to fight and smart enough to fix anything! Quiet Man II, the sequel…Quiet Woman!"

On the last night, Zeke, who'd fallen asleep draped over the loveseat, roused to hear her still going on, checked his watch, and stretched.

"Sounds like a great kid, MaryAnne. Maybe you could bring her to The Grand this summer for company."

He tossed the quilt from his middle and moved toward his wife.

"You 'bout ready, babe?"

"You go on to bed, Mom."

"But I don't want to miss a word, Angel-face."

"We'll still have time for a little more tomorrow morning…although I can't think of anything I have left to tell you. G'night."

She was sure Zeke knew best what her mother needed, and his efforts conveyed that he'd let them carry on long enough. She kissed them both and watched as he lifted her, afghan and all, to disappear behind the bedroom door. She started to retire to the room assigned to her in the bungalow but chose the comfort of the already warmed couch, close to the fire. She listened to the sounds of her mother being helped on and off the pot and Zeke getting her out of her clothes. There was muffled giggling and low, sweet talking. She wondered how they could do it, either of them. She had a lot to digest.

The clans were so enrapt in their daughters' tales of one another that both extended invitations for the other girl to share in the next trip home. Calls were made and arrangements followed and, by the time Jack loaded Aggie and then MaryAnne back into the truck for the ride back to school, both the girls were already counting down to the next break. So, the branches of their family trees began to grow in reach for one another. Over the seasons to come, they would knit and knot in a way that seemed almost impossible to break.

The Suite

It surprised Aggie how happy she was to be back at school. MaryAnne was both less surprised and happier. They caught one another up on family business and the anticipation mounted for them to visit each other's people. But school life would have to be tolerated in the meantime, so they set about it, each growing closer to and more empowered by the other.

Even though MaryAnne swore it wasn't her, news of their clandestine apartment was leaked. It was only their three closest friends who knew, and they weren't telling a soul. They were only permitted in the large shelf-lined chamber that the girls dubbed The Library. Neither Aggie nor MaryAnne wanted anyone in their private bath, and their dorm room, while bigger by half than those of the other girls, was no big deal. Sarah, Morgan, and Kate were stealth in their comings and goings since they'd been threatened within an inch of their lives if they got discovered.

Aggie could be terrifying when she locked her teeth and pointed her finger in your face. MaryAnne loved to see her in action but never felt a smattering of fear for herself. She secretly wondered if Aggie had the stuff to back it up. Living with four brothers can make you appear tough, but she wasn't at all sure when push came to shove if Aggie would push *or* shove to make good on her threats. Lucky enough, throughout the end of their first year and into the next at St. James, the challenge remained unproven.

The quintet filled The Library with books, magazines, and posters, branding the sacred space. They spent their downtime away from the other cliques and clubs playing cards, braiding hair, taking magazine quizzes, comparing crushes, and even studying upon occasion when the need pressed them.

Aggie easily ranked the highest grade-point-average among the group and MaryAnne would have had the lowest if not for her partner in crime helping her at every turn. Aggie wrote her assignments, finished her projects, and warned her friend every time it would be the last time she'd help her. But MaryAnne always came up short and Aggie always scooped her up and saved her. MaryAnne did not lack the brainpower, but she was pitifully thin on motivation. Her spoiled childhood was starting to show its detriment and Aggie was chafed by it more and more each time. The couple was developing a co-dependence the likes of which neither girl was emotionally mature enough to name, and it was deepening, along with Aggie's resentment. But in the moment, that too went unidentified.

One night, exasperated with her roommate's devil-may-care response to an upcoming exam for which they were preparing, Aggie confronted her.

"Don't you care at all about your grades, MaryAnne? I mean do you want to settle for just passing by the skin of your teeth every time?"

"Aggie, I'm doing the best I can!"

"I find that impossible to believe. You are brighter than this!"

"Am I?"

Aggie sat stunned at her friend's response.

“Do you really think you aren’t smart?

“I have no clue how smart I am, Aggie. I was never encouraged to find out. My whole life, people took for granted that I’d do okay because I was pretty, but no one ever really taught me anything. They’d say things like ‘you’ll get it’ and ‘it’ll come’ and I still don’t know what they were talking about!”

“Wow. I had no idea.”

“At the lake I only learned about The Grand Chancellor. And at school, there was always someone telling me how pretty I was, but never how smart. Do you think that’s why I’m so vain?”

“A little vanity is good. It makes you get up and take a shower and brush your teeth every day. Look you’ve made it this far, MaryAnne; besides, you know you can’t get by on your looks forever, you are going to have to rely on your brains at some point in the game. You have to believe you are intelligent.”

“I believe I am witty and clever.”

“There! You see, you’re clever. That’s the way to think about it.”

“Aggie, criminals are clever. That doesn’t help you pass tests, that makes it easy to cheat on them or to weasel out of taking them. Clever is not the same as smart.”

Aggie wasn’t sure how to help her friend with this dilemma, but she knew they wouldn’t get anywhere parsing words.

“You want me to shoot you straight?”

"Always."

"Clever is better than nothing. Clever means you can think on your feet, problem solve, and use what you got. So be clever about this classwork and find ways to agree with it so you can keep it in your mind with everything else you know to be true. Don't look at it as new stuff you've never heard of; everything you've ever learned is like that at first. Imagine you just haven't learned it *yet*."

Nodding, MaryAnne felt understood in a way that was totally new to her. She felt seen and grateful. She was beginning to love Aggie more like a sister every day.

"Thanks, Ags."

Aggie realized that she'd let her friend share a painful truth about herself and feel better for it. In the seconds that followed MaryAnne's heart-felt gratitude, Aggie wondered if she too could share her private pain and get some acceptance and relief as well.

A moment more, and her courage was gone.

Not now. Not yet.

Their study sessions continued to devolve into talk about school itself as kids of that age are prone. No one was allowed to bring petty bickering into the suite though. You couldn't gossip or judge anyone outside the group, except the Howerton's; they were always fair game for criticism. With the end of the freshman year, their threat was lessened by half when Danielle graduated and left only Thomasina to devil them. She, it would turn out, seemed either less of a menace *than* her sister or *without* her sister. And although Aggie and MaryAnne never even entertained the thought of befriending her, they didn't spend their energy worrying over her like they had when Danielle was around. By the end of their sophomore year together, they were almost civil to her. That currency would open a portal to fine and dangerous things to come.

The Caper

Following their quiet stint at the farm sophomore summer, Lake George teamed with activity. The Moynihan boys taught the girls new card games, Aggie finally learned how to water ski, and a new lifeguard had MaryAnne swooning at the pool.

The girls returned to the campus of St. James by Greyhound that year. Rex had gotten bad again on the fourth of July, so Jack couldn't take them. Bob was deployed, Jim and Beth were in Albany, and Hupp and Eloise couldn't leave the farm for any longer than the short trip to deposit the girls at Lake George. And the staff of The Grand was always too swamped at the end of the season to take leave for anything but emergencies. It was Zeke's idea to send them by bus, knowing that Patsy would have a terrible time on a drive like that. He let her surprise them with the tickets when he took her to visit the hotel for the weekend before their return. He was right in assuming they'd love the idea of a road trip together and unchaperoned!

They called the school from the bus station and asked to speak to Kate. They wanted to brag to someone about their excursion and remembered that Kate had stayed on campus for summer school. Their friend delighted in catching them up on all the latest gossip.

"This skunk was living under our dorm porch, but the grounds keeper, Mr. Simms was off having hernia surgery or something and his lawn guys couldn't bring themselves to kill it, so they caught it in a trap, and they've been feeding it all summer. It's huge! It can barely move in that cage. Mr. Simms comes back next week, and they said he was going to bash it over the head with a shovel!"

The two holding the bus station phone between them winced and uttered a whispered, "Jeez!" in unison. Then MaryAnne asked if anyone else was up to anything nefarious and the stories kept coming.

"Turk and Buck Brinley's big brother Hawk is parking a car down the dirt road past the lake behind campus. Buck and Thomasina are sneaking out every other night or so and going joy riding around town, then sneaking back in before dawn."

The mention of Thomasina's name brought Aggie and MaryAnne both to attention. But it was Aggie who asked for more.

"And they haven't gotten caught?"

"No one's ratted on them yet."

The call came over the loudspeaker for their bus and they said their goodbyes to Kate and boarded. They started their ride home plotting their part in the rescue of the school skunk. MaryAnne thought aloud.

"We just can't let Mr. Simms bash that poor thing to death. We'll take it off campus and set it free!"

"Let's sneak out ahead of Tom and Buck one night and take Brinley's car and drive it out into the woods."

"But how will we get the keys?"

"We don't need keys, MaryAnne. I'll hot-wire the thing."

Pumping her fist and proclaiming to the ceiling above her seat on the bus, MaryAnne squealed.

"I have the coolest roommate in the free world!"

The two spent the remaining length of their jaunt planning the entirety of their junior year; what colleges they'd apply to, what changes they'd make in their class schedules, what charities they'd volunteer for, and what events they'd plan for the suite.

They arrived to little fanfare and settled into their apartment as easily as they had in the previous two years, minus the aggravation of the senior's antagonisms. Once they'd unpacked and reunited with Sarah, Morgan, and Kate, the old gang was right back in the swing of things.

»«

Kate gave them the heads up the night before Mr. Simms' return that Hawk Brinley had indeed left his car for his brother in 'the spot' and Morgan and Sarah pledged to help the girls with the rescue. Kate ran interference with Buck and Thomasina while the foursome went for the cage in the sandy lot behind the maintenance building. The animal spared them his usual defensive spray as he had become quite accustomed to being cared for and fed by the staff and students for the summer. Each girl took a corner and heaved the dense thing waist-high and hurried in lock step across the grounds to the dirt road past the lake. Morgan and Sarah leaned against the car catching their breath while Aggie hung under the steering wheel connecting the ignition wires to start it. The engine came alive and MaryAnne jumped and cheered.

"Help us get him in!"

The four teens crammed the cage into the back seat and shut the fugitive rodent inside. MaryAnne hugged her friends in thanks and they took off back to the dorm. Aggie hurried her roommate into the front seat and spun the car around to head away from town to the edge of the forest.

They reached the turn to the old logging road and veered off the main route. The dirt road behind the lake was like a paved interstate compared to this cow path. Deep divots dredged by tractor tires ran parallel on either side of a weed-covered rise in the middle that rubbed along the under carriage of Hawk's car making the girls grimace with every bump and dip. When they agreed they were out far enough they went a few feet further to a wider spot in the road and turned the car around. Engine still running and headlights on, they each opened the back-seat doors and Aggie pulled while MaryAnne pushed on the count of three. It would take multiple counts of three to tip the cage out into the high grass.

Aggie huffed and puffed in the cool night air.

"Ok…now what?"

MaryAnne shimmied through the backseat and stood over the fat skunk staring blankly at his abductors.

"Now we open the cage, and he goes home. Right Stinky?"

MaryAnne opened the metal latch and the animal remained motionless. She coaxed.

"Go on. Go on home and find your family."

Still nothing. She waved her arms and kicked gently at the cage.

"Shoo! Get out!"

Aggie began to see the humor in the situation and started giggling.

"What's so funny? You try!"

"He doesn't want to go. He's no dummy. He isn't going to get table scraps from the cafeteria way out here in no man's land. He's not going to go!"

MaryAnne reddened at the idea of the skunk having the upper hand and grabbed the cage and gave it a hearty shake.

"He'll go God damn it or I'll…"

Aggie's giggling turned to hard laughing at the sight of her precious friend shaking a skunk out of a cage in the middle of nowhere. And the harder she laughed, the angrier MaryAnne got.

"Stop that shit and help me, Aggie! He's too heavy for me to do this myself!"

"I can't! I can't! You look so ridiculous right now! You should see yourself!"

Exhausted, MaryAnne dropped the cage and sat down hard on the ground next to it. Hair eschew, sweat pouring down her face, she looked up at Aggie and joined her in laughing at the absurdity of it all.

"We come all this way and the damn thing won't go! You're right, Ags, this *is* ridiculous!"

After a minute, the two settled down and watched as the skunk poked his nose out the opening to the cage. They sat still, holding their breath as he inched further and further out, until finally he was more out than in. The girls jumped to their feet and tipped the back end of the cage up, emptying the remainder of his rump and freeing the thing once and for all. They erupted into cheers!

"Yea! Yes! Finally!"

They watched as the obese animal lumbered slowly away from the car into the wet grass and Aggie called the project.

"Ok, that's done! We have got to get this car back before someone reports it stolen. Come on, MaryAnne let's go."

"Gotcha!"

MaryAnne pitched the cage as far away from the road as she could and scrambled around to the front seat. Aggie got behind the wheel, put the car in drive, and stepped on the gas. They didn't move.

"What's wrong, Aggie? Why aren't we moving?"

"I don't know. We must be stuck in these deep ruts. I'll rock it."

Aggie shifted and gassed the engine, drive, reverse, drive, reverse, drive. Still nothing.

"You'll have to get out and push us, MaryAnne."

"Me?"

"Yes you!"

"What good would that do? Aggie you're tons stronger than me. *I* should drive and *you* should push. You know I'm right."

She was. Aggie tried a cuss.

"Damn it!"

She popped out and MaryAnne slid into her place behind the wheel. Aggie went to the back bumper and got low in the center of the car.

"Ok, now put it in drive and slowly give it some gas!"

MaryAnne followed the order and Agatha Rose pushed from behind. Nothing.

"Stop! Stop! Stop!"

MaryAnne hung out the window.

"What now?"

"We'll try it in reverse. We just have to get out of this rut then we can steer our way clear. Make sure you go in reverse. I don't want to die out here tonight!"

Aggie took her position just below the hood latch in the front of the car and gave the signal to MaryAnne. The engine revved and Aggie pushed and bounced the bumper until it broke free and she stumbled forward as the car lurched back out of the rut. MaryAnne's face was beaming until she felt the back wheels roll over another obstacle. She braked.

Aggie ran to her window.

"What was that?"

"I don't know, Ags. I felt the tires come up out of the rut and then they rolled over something again. Don't tell me I drove into another hole!"

Aggie stepped lightly along the side of the vehicle until she came to the rear tire.

“Oh my God.”

“What? What is it Aggie? Did I break something?”

MaryAnne left the engine running and followed her friend. She looked down and discovered the black and white tail of their liberated captive protruding from under the whitewall just as the scent from the animal’s anal glands leaked from its hind end.

“Oh my God! Noooo! Stinky! Noooo!”

MaryAnne fell against the trunk and began to wail. Aggie grabbed her and gave her a gentle shake.

“Stop it, MaryAnne. Get a hold of yourself.”

Sobbing and choking, MaryAnne quizzed her friend over and over.

“Is he dead? Did I kill him? Is he dead, Aggie?”

“You get back in the car. I’m going to pull up off him and we’ll see.”

MaryAnne slunk into the passenger’s side and Aggie took the wheel and eased the car up a few feet. She made MaryAnne stay put and she went back to assess the damage. She could see by the eerie red glow of the taillights that the poor thing’s entire hind flanks were flattened; but his upper half was still intact. She’d seen too many accidents on the farm to hope he could survive. She knew what they had to do. She got back in the car and confronted her accomplice.

“You didn’t kill it.”

“Oh good. So, he’s ok? Did he run away?”

“No. MaryAnne, you didn’t kill it, but it can’t survive. It’s ass end is completely squished.”

“No.”

“It *will* die, there’s no doubt about that.”

“Oh God! Aggie we can’t just leave it to suffer. Oh my God! What are we gonna do?”

“MaryAnne! You have to stop. Listen to me. We can’t leave it like this. We’re going to have to run over it again to finish it off.”

“Oh God! Oh my God! Aggie this is awful!”

“Shhhh. Shut up! I don’t like this any more than you do but it’s the most humane thing we can do. So, we’re just gonna have to do it and get it over with. Alright?”

MaryAnne was past speaking now. She just nodded in agreement, tears streaming down her face.

“Ok. Brace yourself.”

Aggie put the car in gear and as she gave it the gas, she and MaryAnne instinctively let out a joint scream to keep from hearing the thump as they drove back over the struggling skunk.

“AAAAAAAHHHHHHHHH!”

The car settled back beyond the body and the two inhaled to reset. MaryAnne still clutching the dash, raised her head.

“Is that it? Did we do it?”

“God, I hope so. Wait here.”

MaryAnne sat back against the seat and wiped her face as she heard her roommate's tense voice utter more expletives from behind the car. Her eyes widened in disbelief and she whispered to herself.

"Surely not. Oh no. Poor Stinky."

Aggie climbed back in the car and grabbed the wheel.

"Once more ought to get it."

She looked at MaryAnne's face greening in the light of the dash.

"Are you ready?"

MaryAnne nodded faintly and resumed her hold on the car. The two screamed again as Aggie cranked the gear shift down and stood on the gas.

"AAAAAAAAAAAHHHHHHHHHHHHHH!"

The sickening bump of the rear tire cut off their scream and they sat still for a moment to catch their breath. Aggie put the car in park and left to review the situation once more. MaryAnne was feeling weak. She thought she might pass out. She rolled the window down to let in the cool night air. She was fanning herself with her hand when Aggie fell back into the driver's side and slammed the door.

"I cannot believe how stubborn that little thing is."

"Aggie you don't mean…"

"I think I know the right angle now to finally get it where it counts."

"Jesus, Mary, and Joe. Will this night ever end?"

"Stop being so dramatic, MaryAnne. That's not helping!"

MaryAnne looked out her window and held onto the armrest just below it to brace herself.

"Go! God damn it, go!"

Aggie yanked the wheel to the right a few degrees, put it in gear, and stomped the gas pedal to the floor as the two girls screamed from their guts.

"AAAAAAAAAAAHHHHHHHHHHHHHH!!!"

She barely waited for the vehicle to stop when Aggie slammed it in park and jumped out again. She couldn't believe her eyes. Was the car too light? Were the tires too thin? Was the skunk too fat? She couldn't figure out why in hell the damn thing wouldn't die. She slowly returned to her door and opened it standing with her elbows suspending her above it for a moment. She wiped the sweat from her face and lowered her head to check on her passenger. MaryAnne looked sick. She asked after her.

"You alright, MaryAnne?"

Her friend's head loosely pivoted from the window toward her voice and she answered.

"Do I look alright to you? Aggie, for the love of God, tell me the thing has gone on to meet Jesus."

Aggie dropped her head and shook it. MaryAnne's head flipped back to look out the window again. The mixture of adrenaline, the scent of the skunk, and the thought of the poor thing in anguish was almost more than they could bear.

They would scream and drive over the campus pet three more times until Aggie was convinced the thing was dead. They were too exhausted to move once they achieved their objective. The two sat in silence for nearly half an hour contemplating the night's gory turn. As the shock wore off, Aggie played every attempt over and over in her mind's eye and a smile crept onto her face. And then a trickle of laughter eked out. MaryAnne turned to look at her partner in crime.

"What in the Wide World of Sports is so fucking funny?"

Aggie's face grimaced and she laughed all her air out, tears escaping her tired eyes. She spat out her observation in fits and starts.

"Can you imagine…how hilarious we looked…repeatedly running over that poor animal…while we screamed bloody murder every time!"

MaryAnne smiled at the comedy of errors and mimicked the gestures.

"Drive, AAAAAAAAAHHHH! Reverse, AAAAAAAAAAHHHHH! Drive, AAAAHHHHH!"

The girls gave into the outrageousness of the whole affair and laughed until they cried.

"We were going to save the campus pet! We were going to be heroes!"

"We couldn't let Mr. Simms bash it's head in with a shovel, Aggie!

"No. Not us! We were going to take it out into the wilderness and run it over in a stolen car twenty-two times until it finally gave up the ghost! MaryAnne, this was a crime spree!"

They laughed even harder and louder than ever, holding their ribs and crying their eyes out. Even after they quieted a little, they kept erupting over and over until they were worn out. This night would be one neither of them would forget or be able to tell anyone else about. They swore one another to secrecy and tried to compose themselves enough to get home.

"Oh, O'Hanley and O'Hara do it again, huh Agatha Rose?"

"You bet. Stolen cars, murder; there ain't nothing this gang won't do."

"Seriously, Ags. I wish we could do something to Hawk's car just to make up for the hell we've put ourselves through tonight. Just a calling card of our caper."

"The skunk fur burnt onto the muffler won't do it for you?"

"The fur itself doesn't stink though."

"Well, I'm not about to perform an autopsy to extract the things glands, if that's what you're after."

"What about the whole carcass? To be discovered in the trunk."

"MaryAnne O'Hara! You couldn't even think about killing the thing and now you want to pick it up and put it in the trunk of this car and drive it all the way back to school?"

MaryAnne shrugged then nodded.

"Come on, Aggie! The bastard's have it coming, getting to sneak out and go joy riding every other night! Thomasina will be furious!"

"And they couldn't tell administration because they'd be ratting themselves out for stashing the car in the first place. This could be beautiful!"

MaryAnne clapped and squealed.

The girls turned off the car, picked the lock on the trunk, and retrieved a wool blanket from inside. They wrapped the dead skunk as best they could and awkwardly lifted it into the trunk. They gagged, laughed, shuddered, gagged and laughed some more, then wiped their hands in the wet grass.

It was well after 1:00 am when they got back to the dorm. They crept up the back stairwell and into their private rooms and collapsed into bed.

By breakfast, the rumors were already starting about the missing skunk. It would take longer for the details involving the car to emerge but even when Morgan, Sarah, and Kate interrogated them about that night, they stood steadfast in their lie that they released sweet Stinky into the wild and returned the car in mint condition. The rest was left to fester into urban legend along with countless other storied pranks of the institution.

MaryAnne turned her attention to tutoring their friends in the art of tong, the wagering, rummy-like game they'd learned at the lake. She dove into the distraction with such vigor, the other girls became obsessed and the commotion was all but extinguished.

"Joseph Moynihan said that he knew of a game between Dan Clelland and Marty Johnson that lasted all night! At the end they'd played a hundred hands and eaten a dozen-and-a-half hard boiled eggs!"

Morgan grimaced.

"Are the eggs a part of it? I can't eat eggs."

Aggie assured her.

"No, Morgan. The eggs are just part of MaryAnne's story."

Playing cards in The Library again seemed to signify the end of the gossip surrounding that night in the Brinley brothers' car, and while Thomasina Howerton remained suspicious of her two rivals, she didn't breathe a word.

The Truce

Aggie went at it hard in her drama and speech classes, junior year. She was amassing a portfolio of playbills and competitive debate prizes to bolster her application to Northwestern. She knew that Phil Donahue was from and filmed his original show in Ohio, and she loved the thought of attending college in a place outside of the usual New York and L.A. channels. Chicago offered tons of arts culture and spurred many TV personalities to fame. She followed all the Chi-town alumni; Bob Kurtis, Siskel and Ebert, John Chancellor, Ann Landers, and who could forget Studs Turkel for God's sake? She had her sights set on newscasting and then hosting an audience participation talk show like Donahue. The way of Mike Douglas and Merv Griffin was over, it was infinitely more entertaining to have the crowd ask questions of the guests than just the host following a scripted format. She wanted to pioneer a female take on the whole concept and so remained focused and driven.

MaryAnne continued to be nonchalant about her student career as she had about her plans for the future beyond school. She wanted to be a *star* and was all but certain she'd just get discovered in a shop on Fifth Avenue or working the ticket counter at a theatre, or maybe even sunbathing on the shores of Lake George if the right guests were registered at the hotel any given summer.

She still tried out for every major role in every dramatic production the school put on. She really was a natural and by far the most beautiful girl at St. James with her olive coloring contrasted against her sea green eyes, and her thick head of chestnut hair. As confident as she was though, MaryAnne truly didn't know how beautiful she was. A fact that probably kept her from becoming a huge slut. Aggie, on the other hand, was accidentally gorgeous and commanded every performance with a solid, confident stage presence. Their tracts, though similar, diverged just enough that they didn't compete but instead held each other up in true support and sisterhood.

In auditioning for the part of Katherina in the school's production of *The Taming of the Shrew*, MaryAnne found herself up against none other than Thomasina Howerton. Though their feud had cooled considerably over the last two years, Aggie still didn't trust the girl but MaryAnne had made every effort to build a more amicable relationship. The competition for the leading role in a Shakespearean play in their pivotal junior year would change the course of that relationship.

"MaryAnne, don't be dumb. She'll play the heiress card and get the director to pick her, like always."

"There's no 'like always', Ags. We've never been up for the same part before."

"You know what I mean. She's going to get it."

"I really don't think she's like that, Aggie. Her sister? Hell yes! She'd have pulled everything in the book to keep me from getting it, but Thomasina probably doesn't even know how much I want this. Don't you think I'm good enough?"

Aggie rolled her eyes.

"You know that isn't what I'm saying. I just don't want to see you get your hopes up, that's all."

"No. I get it. You only tried for stage manager because that's all you could get so you think I'm no better than that either."

Aggie bristled against her tone.

"Wait. What? I told you I wanted to manage because I thought I needed the backstage experience to learn more about production."

"I got news for you Agatha Rose, I *am* good enough. I could act circles around you and Thomasina Howerton!"

MaryAnne headed for the door and Aggie tried to stop her.

"Will you please not do this?"

"Do what? Get something on my own? Without your help or even any confidence in me? *Do it yourself next time, MaryAnne. This is the last time I'm gonna help you, MaryAnne.*"

She stormed out and left Aggie pleading with the slamming door.

"MaryAnne wait!"

Alone with her regret, she quietly cursed herself.

"Damn it, Agatha Rose! You chump!"

MaryAnne ran down the back stairs and across the campus to the auditorium. She found a script backstage and began rehearsing a scene from the play. Hearing it in her head, gesturing, and miming the dialogue, she got lost in the stillness of the hollow room. Deep in her presentation, she startled at the clang of a backstage door slamming behind the curtain.

She was sure it was her penitent friend.

"Not interested in your apology, I have work to do if I'm going to beat the heiress for this part."

The heavy blue velvet curtain parted and out stepped Thomasina Howerton.

"You mean me?"

MaryAnne's hands fell flat against her sides.

"Shit. I thought you were Aggie, Thomasina. I'm sorry."

"Ok. What exactly for?"

MaryAnne took in a deep breath and decided to trust her own version of the teen in front of her.

"Aggie said you would try to use your clout as the founders' grand-daughter to get the lead and that I shouldn't get my hopes up."

The Howerton girl poked her tongue into her cheek and folded her arms.

"So that's what the almighty Agatha Rose thinks of me after all this time? And you, MaryAnne? Do you think I'd do a thing like that?"

She struggled with her answer.

"No. Not really. I don't know."

"Seriously? I know Danielle terrorized you two freshman term, but the last couple of years I think we've come pretty far as friends, don't you?"

"That was my argument, Tommy."

"See? I don't even mind the whole Tom and Dan thing anymore. We've gotten past that childish stuff, MaryAnne."

"I know. I think so too but…"

"But Aggie calls the shots!"

It sounded like an accusation coming from her. Her tone put MaryAnne on the defense.

"She's not calling any shots, Tommy. She just doesn't want to see me get hurt."

"Would it *hurt* you if I got this part, MaryAnne?"

"Well, yes, I guess. I really want to play Katherina, Tom. I was sure you didn't know how badly I wanted it when you signed up for auditions."

She swallowed the rest of the risk.

"I said that if you knew, you wouldn't try anything unfair to sabotage my chances."

"I wouldn't! And frankly, *I'm* hurt that you'd even think that about me!"

"Not me, Thomasina."

MaryAnne's voiced trailed off as she threw her best friend under the bus.

"Aggie."

Thomasina shook her head and began plotting.

"Listen. We don't have to let Aggie ruin this for us."

"She doesn't mean to ruin anything."

"Hear me out, MaryAnne. I will withdraw my name from the auditions."

An audible gasp escaped MaryAnne's face and her eyes widened.

"I don't have time to practice a lead role right now. I'll throw my name in for Bianca and you can have Katherina, ok?"

"Thomasina! You do not have to do this. I don't mind competing with you for the role. I just wanted you to play fair is all."

"Fair, MaryAnne is that you should get the part. You're tons more talented and you're gorgeous!"

The girls giggled at the end of her compliment and Thomasina extended her hand.

"Fair?"

MaryAnne took the outstretched hand in hers and squeezed.

"Hell yes!"

The main doors of the auditorium opened and the stage crew, including their manager, Agatha Rose, poured in to work on sets and lighting. The actresses' private exchange quietly transformed into an offer to help MaryAnne practice if she knew of a place where they could be away from the noise of the theatre. And despite the club rules, MaryAnne escorted Thomasina Howerton across the campus, back to her suites at the end of senior hall…and granted her entry to The Library.

»«

After finishing with the crew, Aggie climbed the back stairway to her room and opened the door just as her roommate was showing Thomasina out into senior hall. She stood frozen in disbelief. MaryAnne shrugged and pushed past her into their room.

"I know what you're going to say, and I don't want to hear it, Aggie."

Aggie moved like she was sinking in quicksand and one wrong move would cost her life. She turned into the room and stood at the foot of her bed, staring at her friend.

"Thomasina Howerton? In The Library? And escorted out the door to senior hall?"

"I was pretty clear that I didn't want to hear it!"

"Thomasina. Howerton. In The Library. And – "

"Yes! Thomasina-fucking-Howerton, in The Library, and escorted out the door to senior hall!"

MaryAnne seethed and drove her hands through her hair pulling her hot, red face tight.

"YES!"

Aggie blinked and rattled her head in disbelief.

"I…I mean. What? Who else was in there with you? Did Kate and Sarah and Morgan say they didn't care if THOMASINA-FUCKING-HOWERTON was allowed to come into The LIBRARY?"

"Jesus, Aggie! What? *What* is the big deal? I mean how childish to keep people out of 'the club'!"

Her air quotes were close to clawing at her friend.

“I didn’t ‘check’ with anyone else. This is my space too. I invited my ‘friend’ to help me rehearse for the play.”

“She’s helping you rehearse?”

“She’s dropping out. She doesn’t have time for practicing all the lines for the lead. She’s letting me have it.”

MaryAnne’s tone was returning to normal.

“I told you she was ok.”

Fully shaking her head now, Aggie’s eyes narrowed and for the first time in their relationship, she was genuinely mad at her friend.

“You cannot possibly think that opening up our private space – a space we have protected and kept secret and pure for three years – to the girl who has been after us, torturing us, hounding us, and judging us all that time, is a good idea.”

MaryAnne sat unsure on the edge of her bed now. It did seem like an impulsive and reactionary move. And no, she hadn’t *thought* about any of it. She wanted to be right this time. She wanted Aggie to have misunderstood Thomasina, but she lacked any real conviction that she had. She went ahead without it.

“You’re right about The Library. I should have asked. It wasn’t fair of me to let just anyone in. But you’re wrong about Thomasina. There’s more to her than you think.”

She looked for some yield in Aggie’s face.

“It seems like *you* are the one judging *her*, Ags.”

"Huh. We'll see, I guess."

That night the two readied for bed with little more to say. Something had changed between them. The trust that had been forged by all the collective battles against the Howerton girls and the others that followed their lead was eroding. Aggie fell asleep feeling unsettled and unsafe about the snake in the grass. MaryAnne felt the same but because she was beginning to question Aggie's motives. Neither of them slept well but the morning came anyway, and they had to do their best to get past it.

Tong and Other Rummies

After a brief period of awkwardness and the introduction of a bottle of Malibu Rum, the group welcomed Thomasina into the fold almost without reservation. Aggie of course, still maintained that she was not to be trusted and, even though she enjoyed the cocktails, remained leery of the new addition to the crew. And the crew was growing more and more every semester. When Thomasina found out they played cards for money, she began inviting all kinds of kids. For the first time ever, boys were snuck in after curfew and The Library grew into a little speakeasy. No one was willing to risk expulsion, so all the kids kept it to a low roar, but there was something happening in the suite every weekend night.

Aggie usually remained completely sober when the card games involved booze but one night she sipped a little Boone's Farm and was herself feeling slightly Tickled Pink. MaryAnne, who had taken to the rum and the rummy like a pool hall champion, fell into bed that night after winning the pot. Significantly impaired, she began to think out loud to her roommate.

"Maybe it's 'cause I got the carnie blood, huh?"

"What is?"

"That I can drink and smoke and play cards like that."

"You don't smoke."

"Oh yeah."

MaryAnne was feeling buzzed and brazen.

"You wanna smoke? I can teach you."

Aggie giggled at her friend.

"But you don't smoke! How can you teach me to smoke if you don't smoke?"

MaryAnne rolled over and propped her heavy head in her elbow.

"Can you smoke, Ags?"

"Hell yeah, I can smoke! My brothers taught me how to smoke, and chew and spit and scratch my dick!"

"Ahhhh-haha! I knew you had balls, but a dick? That's fantastic! What else did you learn down on the farm, Aggie of Green Gables?"

"I learned how to kiss. Bill taught me how to kiss, NOT my brothers!"

"Ohmagod!"

MaryAnne sat straight up in the bed and slid promptly to the floor in one fail swoop.

"You have to teach me how to kiss!"

Snorting at her stunt, Aggie looked down at MaryAnne's crumpled body and the tousled hair covering her face.

"Where did you go?"

Clearing her mug of the mop, MaryAnne rose to her knees in front of her friend.

"Seriously, Aggie. I have to kiss…fuckin'…Petruchio in the play and…"

"Yeah. Jason wants to kiss you so bad he can't stand himself."

"I can't stand himself either. I mean it's gonna be bad, Ags. I've never kissed anyone before. I need help!"

Her eyes were just slits looking up at her friend's face, but Aggie registered her desperation and took pity.

"Ok. Get up here."

She hoisted the limp girl up by her armpits next to her on the bed.

"So, in the play he'll be like here."

She positioned herself toward her student.

"And you'll be here."

She adjusted MaryAnne's shoulders.

"And he'll probably do something like this."

She slapped her hands on either side of her girlfriend's face and held her wobbling head still. Looking into her bloody, blue-green eyes behind their heavy lids she turned her head slightly to the right.

"Close your eyes!"

Then she moved in toward her mouth. Their lips, barely open, touched and pressed against each other. They puckered and separated, then did it again. The next time, they opened up and their tongues gently passed one another, trading Malibu Rum for Boone's Farm, innocently learning.

Aggie opened her eyes to see a light in the doorway from the hall. A figure stood silhouetted in the entrance.

Thomasina.

Aggie saw the glint of her narrow eyes and watched paralyzed, as the dark figure silently disappeared behind the closing door. She told her friend she was a natural and had nothing to worry about, then deposited her back on her bed and returned to her own.

MaryAnne passed out seconds later, but Aggie, her mind racing through 'what ifs', laid awake for hours.

The next morning brought out the best in MaryAnne despite the low-grade hangover she sported. She remembered every bit of her lesson and she was grateful to her friend for treating it with such dispassionate expertise.

"I can't thank you enough for last night, Aggie. I won't feel like such a virgin when I have to do the kissing scene with Jason now. I'm so relieved."

Aggie nodded and walking out of their room a few steps ahead found a note taped to the door that read 'Chateau GAY'. She ripped it away and stuffed it in her pocket before MaryAnne could see.

Aggie wanted so much to tell her that Thomasina had seen them kissing but she was unsure if she could rely on MaryAnne not to make things worse. She still didn't trust the Howerton girl further than she could throw her and if MaryAnne tried to 'explain' things, she was liable to think more of it.

She wasn't sure either whose opinion she was more worried about, MaryAnne's or Thomasina's. Aggie was not attracted to MaryAnne but MaryAnne wouldn't have guessed that was even a possibility. She was oblivious to alternative sexuality except for the occasional dots connected by the showbiz rags about cross-dressers, drag queens, and Liberace. She led an inexplicably sheltered life among the hotel staff but would have had a completely different take if she had befriended some of the more interesting guests. But Thomasina was more worldly and was sure to have picked Aggie up on her gaydar by now. Maybe that's what she didn't trust about Thomasina. Aggie was uncertain of what would happen if she were found out and that made Thomasina even more of a threat. Agatha still felt no safety in confessing to her roommate yet. Maybe after the play.

The week to follow was busy. The play took on momentum and all the kids were preoccupied with their parts in the production. No one gathered in The Library after class or before lights out, so Aggie had no chance to confront Thomasina about the incident. She kept her distance and found herself running interference so MaryAnne wouldn't have much time alone with the interloper either.

The play ended to a standing ovation and MaryAnne's Katherina was the crowning jewel. Aggie gained a new appreciation for the stage crew and production of a presentation, and Thomasina even seemed pleased with her supporting role. The cast and crew took over the auditorium after the audience cleared out and celebrated until Dean Springer returned herself to shut it down.

They took the party to The Library.

Drinks and games ensued, and the evening wound around and around the fun they'd had in their rehearsals and the final performance. With the on-stage kiss between Katherina and Petruchio, couples who hadn't before, began making out in every corner of the party. Jason and MaryAnne went at it hard on the window seat. Kate and Parker Holyoke paired up, Sarah reluctantly gave in to Bobby Williamson, and Morgan was all over Emory Choate.

Tong hands were dealt and played by the single kids in the bunch and the drinks kept flowing freely into the night. Aggie and Thomasina found themselves reaching for the rum at the same time and stopped to recognize the stilted air between them for a moment.

Thomasina yielded the bottle and in polite response, Aggie poured the other girl's portion first.

Thomasina watched the sweet booze fill the red cup.

"So?"

Aggie kept her eyes trained on her task.

"So what?"

"Are we going to talk about it?"

"Again…what, Thomasina?"

"Ok. Come with me."

She took Aggie by the hand and led her out of the room, across the hall and into the utility closet. They surprised a freshmen couple, elbows deep in each other and Thomasina ran them out.

"Juniors and seniors only in utility, you know that!"

Aggie giggled at their clumsy exit and opened the sliding door to the dumbwaiter where they hid the bottles. She pretended to inventory the bar with her back to Thomasina.

"This should be enough. Everybody's probably within an hour of passing out or going to bed."

"I didn't drag you in here to stock the bar."

Turning toward the confrontation now, Aggie readied herself.

"What *did* you drag me in here for then, Tommy?"

"I know *you* know I saw you and MaryAnne that night."

"What you saw was not what you think."

"What I saw, was what I was pretty sure I knew about you but had no proof of."

"All you know about us could fit in a thimble. MaryAnne is as straight as they come! She wanted to know how to kiss Jason in the play and I showed her, that's it!"

She was heating up.

"I swear to God, Thomasina, if you start that around the school, I'll kill you!"

Thomasina's eyes widened.

"Easy…easy, Aggie. I have no ulterior motives here. I am a friend."

The hair was standing up on Aggie's arms and her heart was beating faster with every word from Thomasina's mouth. The snake was no longer hidden in the grass and, unable to look away, Aggie was fascinated by her colors.

"I believe you, Aggie."

"You do?"

"Yes. I thought MaryAnne was probably straight so that only leaves you."

"And?"

There was no mechanical motion in the way Thomasina covered the three feet between them, she just blended into the space that Aggie's breath occupied and connected their mouths in a deep and passionate kiss. Aggie's brain wet with rum and thumping with fear and lust crackled with static. She clutched Thomasina's waist and held her own body pressed against her. There was no bitter taste, no salt. Tommy was soft and sweet, and Aggie was immediately lost in her. They moved each other around the tiny room, pushing up against the ladder and the door, knocking over their red cups and slipping around in the spilled spirits.

A break for air and Aggie turned away and grabbed her swimming head.

"Shit! Shit! Shit! What is this?"

"Ags, don't you see? This is why I wanted this part of the dorm from the start."

"What?"

"I knew my chances of getting caught with another girl wouldn't be so high if I could have a hideout like this."

"But you never said anything."

"What was I supposed say, Aggie? Hi, I'm Tommy Howerton and don't tell anyone because I'll get kicked out of school, and my family, and the goddamn world, but I like girls."

The venom hit her nervous system and Agatha Rose O'Hanley fell for her enemy like a barrel over Niagara. She dove into her mouth again and held her head, feeding her hands through Tommy's hair. They only kissed but all the way up until their energy waned, and then they thought it best to say goodnight.

Both the girls went to bed that night with electricity in their veins. Thomasina felt triumphant and Aggie Rose the familiar fear and exhilaration of another forbidden romance.

MaryAnne finally came to bed after pushing Jason toward the back steps just before dawn and heavily hit the pillow, already close to sleep.

"You good, Ags?"

Aggie was filled with the spell of doubt and anticipation Thomasina had cast but admitted nothing.

"I'm good."

Educating MaryAnne

The summer before senior year, like always, started on the farm and ended on the lake. Jim and Beth got married and Aggie and MaryAnne were the maid of honor and bride's maid. Once the newlyweds left for the honeymoon, the girls helped to break down the festivities and spent the remaining days cooling in the pond and predicting their life arcs from the inner tubes in which they bobbed. The senior trip would be announced upon their return to St. James and they were speculating what they'd do in the various venues they hoped for. Aggie was rooting for Chicago and MaryAnne, New York. Each had her own plan that overlapped the other's just a bit so either would suit them. They laughed at the possibility of some random place neither of them wanted like Baton Rouge or Atlanta. But St. James never did the deep south for their senior class trip, how gauche!

Hupp and Eloise kissed the girls goodbye at the bus station and MaryAnne held on a little longer than usual. A haunting foreboding filled her heart, and she was reminded that as she and Aggie approached the inevitable separation of graduation, she was liable to lose track of these fine people who had been so good to her the last four years.

Aggie felt a similar twinge when they approached the shore of Lake George; it might be the last time she spent with some of these folks and she was genuinely going to miss them. As usual, the girls were accommodated in one of the staff cottages and enjoyed the run of the place until Zeke and Patsy arrived.

The couple landed at the cottage while the two were out on the boat with the Halpennys. MaryAnne and Aggie squealed with surprise when they returned from the lake to find them settled in and chatting with Dottie, who'd delivered a spread of sandwich stuff and fresh fruit salad. Zeke was out front smoking when they came up the path and he muscled them in with his heavy arms around their towel wrapped shoulders.

"Look what washed up on the beach, babe!"

Patsy's face opened wide with glee at the sight of her girls, but her arms didn't.

The young ladies lunged for the frail woman enveloping her in their embrace. Aggie too excited to register her flat response started in on how good it was to see them and to be back on the lake. But MaryAnne was quick to notice the flaccid limbs of her shrinking mother and the fact that she had made no effort to sit in the upholstered furniture. She quizzed them.

"How long have you been here?"

Patsy whispered.

"We got in a couple of hours ago. Dottie says right after you two got on the boat."

"What are you whispering about, Mom?"

The girl scanned her mother and the chair she occupied, searching for clues. She spied a yellow tube coming from the pantleg of Patsy's seersucker capris and followed it to a bag hanging just under a sweater that was draped over the handlebars of the chair.

"What is that?"

Zeke chimed in to save Patsy's voice.

"The MS is affecting your mom's vocal cords and bladder, honey."

Patsy nodded in support.

"She can still talk…"

She smiled to comfort her stunned daughter.

"I can still talk, just not very loudly."

Now MaryAnne nodded as the picture got clearer and she tried to hide the fear and dread that was materializing in her head. Her voice? Her bladder? She could feel her eyes heating up and as she had so many times before, she looked to Aggie to rescue her.

Suddenly aware of her friend's panic, Aggie flinched and took hold of the moment. She grabbed at MaryAnne's towel.

"We should get changed. Come on."

Dottie prodded them on.

"Yes, get yourselves out of those wet suits and come out for lunch."

The girls disappeared behind their bedroom door and MaryAnne grabbed her mouth, tears pouring down her flushing cheeks. Aggie wrapped her arms around her friend and held her close until she had silently relieved her broken heart. Then she pulled her wet mane off her shoulders and lifted her head to look her in the eye.

"She's still here."

MaryAnne took in a deep breath and bobbed her head in agreement.

"And we're here *together*. You have to toughen up, MaryAnne. She needs to know you're going to be alright."

The rest of the visit was spent with MaryAnne earning her mettle as the actress she was to become. She smiled and carried on like nothing her mother was enduring was out of the ordinary. They spent the last days of the summer playing games and listening to records and absorbing every ray of the sun and the season they had left between them.

Aggie thought her friend was dealing with enough and decided again, as she had dozens of times before, not to come out on this trip home. She'd find a better time in the course of the next year when MaryAnne was back in her groove at school.

But things were changing rapidly for them both; a trend that would continue in the fall.

The Senior Class Trip

Aggie and Thomasina had opted to stay in The Library when Kate had burst in to announce that they were posting the details for the senior class trip outside the offices in the administration building. A mad exodus emptied the room, and the whole upper floor beyond the suite, leaving the two alone. As they had on many occasions when they had been afforded such accidental privacy since they discovered one another last spring, they kissed and touched with a vigorous passion.

The young women pushed and pulled at the clothes that bound them and connected hands to flesh beneath. Warm, wet kisses heated unbuttoned breasts and probing pairs of fingers pumped in and out of the wet places under their skirts. Thomasina pulled at Aggie's hips and got her to her back in the window seat, where she climbed on, both teens bending their long legs to fit the space as they struggled to stay on their perch.

"Why are we doing this here? Your bedroom is less than twenty feet away."

Thomasina tried to stay connected to her mouth but was unable.

Aggie stopped the effort altogether and slid back up to sitting.

"Wait. Wait! Just stop a minute."

"What, Aggie? What's the matter?"

Aggie seemed agitated.

"I don't know…just wait!"

"What'd I say?"

"I can't. Not in the bedroom. Not in *that* bedroom."

Thomasina's skin and disposition were cooling rapidly.

"Why not? What's the big deal?"

"Not in my and MaryAnne's room. Ok?"

Now Thomasina was the one who seemed agitated. She straightened herself and began tugging at her disheveled blouse and blazer, retying her tie, and tucking in as she stood to challenge her lover.

"I don't know why you don't just tell her, Aggie. I don't get it."

Aggie looked up at the girl and shook her head, then lowered it again.

"Who have you told, Tommy?"

"No one. Not a soul. Not even my sister!"

Her raised voice surprised them both; she flinched and lowered it.

"But I don't have a best friend like MaryAnne."

Aggie stood and started putting her own uniform right.

"That's precisely why, Tom. She is my very best friend, and I don't want anything to change that."

A low rumble could be heard nearing the building outside and the girls darted their heads around to peek out the window. Far below, through the boughs of the giant sugar maple they saw the topic of their conversation leaping from the path singing.

"These vagabond shoes..."

They laughed and retreated from view for one last embrace and kiss before they surrendered their secrecy to the group once more, cheering in tandem.

"New York!"

»«

All through that last first semester, the students of St. James Academy buzzed with their plans for the New York trip. They colonized into groups to schedule their time for attending different shows and exhibits; tickets were purchased, and chaperones selected.

Even though Aggie and MaryAnne did odd jobs on the farm and at Lake George every summer to afford the trip, Hupp and Zeke had each snuck them enough to buy a set of tickets to a show. They wrangled Kate and Parker, Sarah and Bobby, and Morgan and Emory into seeing Henry Fonda and Jane Alexander in *First Monday in October* at the Majestic.

MaryAnne wasn't worried about Jason agreeing to the plans. Since the play he was following her around like a pup waiting for the sex she kept promising him. Jason was cute enough, but he was no prize. MaryAnne could have had one of the Bradford boys or Russell Warren or even Henry Appleton; all more handsome and intelligent, not to mention richer than Jason. But MaryAnne had a theory that if she chose a boy who was lacking a little, he'd stay truer. Plus, she'd never kissed anyone before Jason and had made up her mind that her virginity should be awarded to the gentleman brave enough to have been her first kiss. Kind of a two-for-one deal.

Aggie and Thomasina secured their usual beards, Turk and Buck Brinley. Buck had confided in Thomasina long before she and Agatha had become a thing that he and his twin brother were also gay, and the four teenagers trusted each other to keep up the collective façade. Aggie felt a low current of guilt every time they did anything together since she'd never owned up to the skunk incident. She counted on a measure of safety from them with her biggest secret, but somehow fessing up to that night with the skunk felt like she'd be endangering MaryAnne too, and Aggie was more loyal than that.

The holidays sped by none of the seniors caring much about the long break leading up to January 15th, 1978 when they would leave for The Big Apple. Most of the students came from families with businesses and property in the city but Aggie and MaryAnne did not count among them. And they were both filled with the hope of the coming possibilities, not just for the trip, but of a life beyond the tiny towns from which they came as well as the sheltered grounds of St. James.

At a party, the night before the trip, MaryAnne signaled the group with her red cup raised above the huddled mass in The Library.

"I would like to propose a toast. To the trip!"

Her peers raised their own drinks.

"Not just to N-Y-C, but to the big trip to come. The one we're all due to take about a hundred thirty days after our return from the city."

She sounded wistful now and Aggie feared she might break down, so she moved through the elbows to her friend's flank.

MaryAnne closed her eyes and put a hand on her heart.

"To all the places we'll run to and from. And to all our safe returns to those we simply cannot leave behind. Salute!"

A cheer rang out from the group!

MaryAnne leaned into her friend and hugged her neck declaring her love for her through her long red curls, then whispered a secret.

"I need you to cover for me tonight. I'm sneaking over to Jason's dorm for 'it'!"

Aggie's eyes widened. MaryAnne released her and winked, then booped her nose, and left with her beau.

Thomasina watched the couple exit the room then shot a look back to Aggie. They smiled at each other and waded through the room to connect.

"What's that all about?"

"They're going back to Jason's room for 'it'!"

"It?"

They giggled and looked down at the floor with a blush of embarrassment then Thomasina recovered.

"I've got an idea! Meet me in your room in five minutes!"

Aggie Rose watched as the young woman darted out of the Library and out of sight. She filled her cup and another with Boone's Farm and navigated her way out of the throngs. She kicked the door shut behind her and was at once cooler and on fire with anticipation. She juggled the drinks in one hand as she unlocked her bedroom door and entered the dark space. She placed the cocktails atop the nightstand and sat on her bed, waiting, her heart pounding, for what she had resisted all these months.

When Thomasina returned, Aggie sat up straighter and the hair rose on her arms like it had that first night. The sweet smell of Love's Baby Soft wafted in ahead of the girl as she closed the gap between them. The couple linked as they had a thousand times before but this time, there would be no hesitation.

Thomasina kissed hungrier that she ever had, and the sweat beaded on her forehead as she dove deeper and deeper. Aggie held her at the waist as Thomasina unbuttoned her blouse with one hand, dipping into her bra to cup her breast. First one strap, then the other, then except for the St. Christopher medal dangling just past her collarbone, Aggie's torso was bare. She kicked off her oxfords and stamped her knee socks to her ankles, slipping out of them altogether on the hard wood floor. Thomasina grabbed the hem of her girlfriend's skirt and yanked the waistband over her slender hips, pulling her cotton panties loose. Sliding her knee between Aggie's trembling legs, Thomasina gently drove the rest of the girl's clothes to the floor. The young lovers stood hand-in-hand, gazing at each other. Aggie was wide open and invited Thomasina to do the same.

"Now you."

But before she could take another breath there was a loud, slamming sound in the hall outside her room. Thomasina screamed and swept her leg against Aggie's and the two were on the floor in an instant.

"HELP!! HELP ME!"

The door burst open and Miss Findley stood, flushed and rigid with the blinding beam of a flashlight trained on the spectacle of Aggie's pale pink, naked body smothering Thomasina's, fully clothed.

"What is going on here?"

Thomasina summoned tears and backed out from under the exposed Aggie.

"Miss Findley! Thank God you came in when you did! I don't know what I would have done if you hadn't stopped her."

The snake lunged for the matron's shoulders and buried her face in her bosom to complete the performance.

"Get your clothes on this minute, young lady and get downstairs to my office!"

The administrator directed the hysterical girl in her arms to the hall and slammed the door.

Aggie sat dumbfounded on her empty clothes, looking around the room for an answer, flashing back through all the moments from the past year and a half with this girl.

This bitch.

This cunt!

She moved only as much as she needed to gather her things and dress herself. Alone in the dark of her and MaryAnne's room, nothing but the light of the campus lanterns illuminating the stillness around her. What would happen now? How could she let this happen? She knew! She knew that Thomasina was no good and she let her in anyway. What would MaryAnne say? What in hell's half acre would she do now?

The party had ceased, being raided by Miss Findley on her way downstairs with Thomasina in tow. The few kids left straggling out watched as Aggie left the safety of her room, then senior hall, then descended the stairs. She sat on the wooden bench she had shared with MaryAnne on Orientation Day and pondered her fate while she listened to the muted phone call she overheard between Miss Findley and Dean Springer.

After what seemed an eternity, Findley opened the door for Thomasina to return to her room and ushered Aggie into her office.

"Dean Springer is on her way, Miss O'Hanley, come in and take a seat."

Re-Educating MaryAnne

It would be less than an hour before the sun came up as Jason kissed MaryAnne good night and tiptoed down the backstairs to hightail it back across campus. She lilted in to drop on her bed and whisper to her confidant.

"Well, Ags, it's done."

She waited for an answer or a grunt or some sign that her best friend had heard her pronouncement, but nothing came. Without ceasing to stare at the soft blue of dawn taking over the ceiling, she excused her friend.

"You're tired. I'll tell you all about it on the bus."

The alarm clock sounded only a couple of hours after her head hit the pillow but MaryAnne popped to her feet like she'd slept for a week.

"It's time! Wake up Aggie Rose, we're going to New York Ci-tay!"

She jumped from her bed to Aggie's and landed on nothing but the bedding. Confused, she flipped on the lamp and surveyed the room. She spied the open wardrobe across from Aggie's bed, climbed off the bed and crossed to the light switch to take in the whole scene. She walked cautiously to look for her friend's things but found nothing. Standing stunned in the middle of the half-empty room she didn't hear the door open behind her.

Thomasina stood dressed in street clothes for the bus, one arm draped in an expensive overcoat the other outstretched toward MaryAnne.

"Oh, MaryAnne. I'm so sorry, you must be in shock."

"What?"

"I feel so badly. But it wasn't my fault, you know. I didn't even imagine she was like that."

"Who?"

Still confused MaryAnne felt a panic set into her chest.

"Where's Aggie?"

"Oh my God, you didn't hear?"

"Hear what, Tommy?"

MaryAnne grabbed the girl, coat and all.

"Where is Agatha Rose?"

"Expelled! They put her on a bus late last night after…"

"After what? What the hell happened last night?"

"I'm so sorry, MaryAnne."

Miss Howerton loosed herself from the grips of the bewildered girl and began to spin the tale.

"After you and Jason left the party, Aggie asked me to meet her in your room. I thought she wanted to talk about the trip or something."

"Yeah?"

"But when I came in here she was all alone and drunk and NAKED!"

"What?"

Shock washed over MaryAnne in a wave, but she resisted.

"She wasn't naked, Tommy. Not Agatha Rose."

"I swear to God, MaryAnne. Not a stitch of clothes on. Not even her socks!"

"And she was drunk?"

"Very! She started talking about how she was looking for someone. That she wanted to be close to someone. She told me how you two had kissed and that she felt a real chemistry between you two and that she wanted to make you jealous, so you'd drop Jason and…"

"What in hell are you trying to tell me, Thomasina?"

"She's gay!"

The bitch managed to conjure up the tears she hadn't used in her last show and began to cry.

"I told them you didn't know a thing about it. I told them that it was all her and that we didn't give her any reason to come after us like that."

"You told who?"

"Miss Findley. And she told Dean Springer. And they called her mom and dad in the middle of the night and put her on a Greyhound back to whatever barn she was raised in!"

MaryAnne dropped to her bed.

"I wasn't here…I was with Jason…I was going to tell her all about it on the bus."

"Oh, honey, let's get you on that bus. Come on, MaryAnne, you've got to get dressed. Are you packed?"

She dropped her coat on Aggie's bed and scurried for MaryAnne's clothes and luggage. MaryAnne sat paralyzed on her bed staring across at the expensive coat that singly occupied the place left behind by her very best friend in the world.

Part Two

Six Years Later…

Aggie Rose

The apartment Aggie rented was a ten-minute walk from the admin building, housing her advisor's office on the campus of North Western University, and she was two stoops away from the walk-up when she stopped at the corner store for her second cup of morning coffee. Her final semester in the master's program was to begin the following week and the twenty-four-year-old communications major managed to secure a spot in every course she needed to graduate in the spring. She could hardly believe she was so close to realizing her dream. Her internship the last two summers at WLS-TV had earned her a spot on the production crew of the evening and late news editions and once she graduated, she'd go to work full time at the station and try for a spot on their morning show, AM Chicago. She blew on the hot coffee through the tiny slot in the lid and slipped past incoming patrons and the two doors down to her address. She was up the stairs and unlocking the door when she heard the phone ringing inside. Hurrying and trying not to spill, she made it through to reach the phone in time.

"Hello!"

"Agatha Rose."

The stern and somber sound of her brother Jack's voice landed heavy in her head.

"Jack? What's wrong?"

His voice cracked.

"I have bad news, girl."

She immediately thought of Rex. He'd done it, she bet. He'd finally drank himself to death. She resolved in a split second never to forgive him. And poor Jack!

"What is it, Jack? Is it Rex?"

"No, honey."

Confused and growing afraid, she pressed him.

"Jackson Paul, what the hell is it?"

"It's Dad, Aggie."

She went numb. Before he could finish, tears welled and fell down her shocked face.

"He's gone, honey. He died."

Her brother went on to explain that Rex heard a noise in the shop downstairs that woke him out of a dead sleep about 6:00 am, their time. She looked at her watch; how long?

"Rex ran down and called an ambulance, but the paramedics said he was most likely dead before he hit the floor. A massive coronary. You need to get home, Aggie Rose. Mom needs us all home."

The next hours were a blur as she attempted to wrap her mind around the loss of her father and fill in all the blanks of the trip home and the beginning of her last semester. She called her boss at the station and her advisor for emergency leave and booked her flight. She went to her downstairs neighbor to ask her to take in her mail and surrender her spare key when *Hart's Desire* came on the television in the living room. The familiar sultry music, too heavy on the saxophone, played while the main characters vogued for the camera, their credits displayed at the bottom of the frame. And there she was, 'Faline Farah as Delia Blackwell'. Even after these past six years, with all the makeup and stylists, and changing her name (and quite possibly her nose), her sea green eyes and chestnut hair were the same.

Aggie felt a pang for her as fresh as the ones in the last half of their senior year. Dean Springer had allowed her to graduate early because she had the credits, but she would have her signed diploma mailed to her on the farm. She wouldn't be permitted to walk at graduation. She had written MaryAnne on the bus ride home and every day after that for the first year but never got a response. How weird to be thinking about all this now. She wished for her friend of all those years ago. She needed her for this. Her dad, her hero, was gone. How could she make it through burying her father without her best friend?

The quick flight home hypnotized her, and she felt hungover when she landed. Jack and Rex were there to meet her, and she clung to them like she'd been rescued from the scene of a crash. It felt good to have her arms around them. They had both kept their distance from their complicated sister after she twice shamed the family, and she wasn't sure what to expect from them now. Whatever they'd thought about her lifestyle wasn't important to them in the moment though; they were just family, happy to have one another.

Jack looked the same as he always did but Rex looked better than she'd seen him in years. He was clean-shaven, dressed halfway decent, and had an air of responsibility she couldn't remember ever associating with him. On the ride to the farm the boys informed Aggie of their initiating contact with Jim and Beth, who were separated, and did she know that? And of course, they were in touch with Bob's ship to get him family leave, but he was on maneuvers in the Pacific and they'd need to wait for him before the service. Mom was insisting that they wait for Bob.

"And how is Mom?"

Jack attempted to answer but couldn't quite get to it.

"Uh…Mom is…"

Rex took up the slack.

"Mom is being mom, Aggie. She is pouring it on when people come to the house and cussing Dad like a sailor when no one's around!"

Jack couldn't hold it together anymore.

"She's making me sick! He never told that woman 'no', not once in his whole life and it was never enough for her!"

Aggie reached for his shoulder and tried to calm him.

"He treated her that way because he loved her, Jack. And she loved him too."

Rex would have the wisest words to share on the subject right before the truck turned up the farm road.

"He was just better at showing it."

They squared themselves and braced for the show.

The week to follow was filled with the usual arrangements of funeral details and insurance claims. The family attorney was at the house on a couple of occasions making sure Eloise's interests were protected. Their insurance agent called twice and visited once before the day the funeral started. And of course, all of Washington County came to Mason's Funeral Home for the three days of viewing. Hupp wanted to be cremated, but Eloise wasn't having any of that! Every day more family and friends washed by the casket and handled the siblings and their mother like buckets at a fire brigade, grabbing hold for a moment and handing them off to the next person in line.

The boys helped Hupp's Army buddies and Lion's Club members away from their father's body when they welled up, walking them outside for a cigarette or getting them a cup of coffee in the pantry beyond the parlor. Eloise stood steadfast at Hupp's head with her handkerchief tucked in one hand and her other gently fiddling with his beautiful silver hair. Aggie focused hard on that hand and what it meant for her mom to hold on to that last little bit of the man she loved. When she went theatrical again, her daughter would conjure that image over and over to excuse her mother's behavior and remain supportive.

Once the droves had left the farm, following the burial, the house got rigidly quiet. Beth and Jim who had carried on like they needed to for the funeral now sat Eloise down to give her the cold facts about their perishing marriage. Beth cried and promised to stay in touch, that they were still family, and she could always count on her as a daughter. Jim apologized and reassured his mother that they still loved each other but that they wanted different things and were better on their own.

Eloise said she was glad Hupp wasn't around to see this. She told the couple she hadn't even told him the truth about their separation for fear it would kill him on the spot. So, it was better they waited until after he was safe in the ground to tell about the divorce. The old woman was moving into survival mode and stacking ugliness where she thought guilt would render support.

With the burden of their news delivered, Jim drove Beth home to Albany the next afternoon. The following morning they'd bid goodbye to Bob. He'd be rejoining his ship to finish his mission.

Eloise cried from the snowy porch after Bob's car disappeared from view.

"Everyone is leaving me! First your dad and then Beth and Jim, and now Bobby's gone. Why is everybody leaving me?"

Aggie gently ambushed her mother with a quilt from the bedroom and directed her back into the house where she helped her into bed, calling on the image of her mom's hands in her dad's hair to trigger some compassion. She kissed her head and went to the kitchen to brew her a hot tea. She was steeping the bag when she heard a knock at the door. Expecting the brother who just left, she chided as she opened it.

"What d'ya forget, Einstein?"

A man stood, head bowed, holding a basket of fruit wrapped in cellophane and tied at the top with a gold and red ribbon. He lifted his head, and she could see his familiar eyes smiling out from under the bill of his Giants cap.

"Zeke!"

Aggie cried and lunged for the man's neck.

"Hiya, honey!"

She welcomed him like family, taking his coat off and leading him to the comfort of the kitchen. They sat around the table over coffee, cutting pieces of apples and pears to share, and talking about their summers at the lake.

"I'm so sorry we couldn't make it to the funeral, Aggie. Patsy isn't doing very well and it's really hard to get her transported these days. As a matter of fact, I've had to put her in a nursing facility."

"Oh, Zeke, you can't beat yourself up for that. You did everything for her for so long. Surely she doesn't blame you for having to make that decision."

"No, no. You know Patsy. She knew when it was getting to be too much for me, and she insisted."

He was trying not to cry and jumped subjects to keep from it.

"MaryAnne is paying for the whole thing! Well, Faline, I guess? It's a really nice place. It's close to the lake so if MaryAnne – um – I mean, Faline ever wants to visit, she'll be right there, close by."

"She's not been home much, I take it?"

He shook his head.

"She sure isn't the same kid she was way back when, you know?"

"None of us are Zeke."

"True, true. But you haven't changed much, Aggie Rose. You're still as sweet and pretty as ever."

She smiled and leaned in for a hug. The afternoon grew older and closer to dusk and he excused himself stating the ride home would be easier before it got too dark. They hugged and kissed and promised each other they'd keep in touch. Aggie thanked him for the fruit and the visit and passed on her love to Patsy and MaryAnne or Faline or whichever one he spoke to next. She ended her day with a flicker of the warmth she had in her young heart in the cottages on Lake George. These were good people. She'd make the time to see Patsy before she went back to Chicago.

»«

The morning Aggie planned to head home, Rex and Jack woke their mother talking of their proposal to close their father's shop and she was livid.

"What do you two think you're up to?"

Rex explained.

"Mom, neither of us can run the shop. I mean, we can sell out the pieces he finished and his tools, but then we'll have to close it."

Eloise began to redden.

Jack tried next.

"Maybe we can get that little appliance store to move in. They could use the same space. Stock for sale in the front and the workshop for repairs."

"We're not selling that shop!"

"Mom be reasonable! You sure as hell aren't doing any wood working and Rex and I don't want it!"

"Don't want it? You and Rex don't want it?"

Aggie had just turned off the shower when she heard the raised voices coming from the kitchen. She dressed in a hurry and went to see what had everybody up in arms.

"What's up doc?"

"Your brothers are talking about selling your father's heart and soul, that's all."

Jack attempted to enlist his sister.

"Christ Aggie, will you explain this to her, please?"

"Sure. You explain it to me, and I'll explain it to her?"

"Mom, we were waiting to tell you until after everything settled down, but Jack and I have been offered jobs in Saratoga Springs at the track. Jim knew a guy that was looking for stable managers, we went down to see him, and he hired us on the spot. We told Dad right before he -…"

Rex stopped short when he realized he was setting his mother up for the grand finale.

Eloise leapt at her sons, jabbing her finger in their faces, her chair launching out from under her.

"YOU KILLED HIM!"

Aggie reached for her just as she fell to the floor.

"OH GOD! MOM!"

She was kneeling at her side on the kitchen floor, both her brothers stunned, standing over the two women. Eloise was wild-eyed, face drawn, drooling.

Aggie screamed at the men.

"Don't just stand there, call for help!"

»«

Dr. Green pulled the door shut to the intensive care unit and took a seat next to Jack in the corner of the waiting room where the three had gathered.

"Ok. The bad news is, it's bad. This was a major stroke. We have her heavily sedated in an effort to let her brain rest and recover. We aren't going to know the full effects or prognosis for recovery until she takes that time."

His audience looked hopeless.

"The good news is timing is everything with these things and you kids were spot on getting her here in time. The meds administered in route no doubt saved her life and kept things from escalating out of control. If she makes any kind of recovery, it'll all be because of your quick response."

The family listened and heard about their mother's health, but Dr. Green couldn't offer any information about what the hell they were supposed to do next. They stared blankly at his face waiting for the things he wouldn't be explaining.

"What is the time frame we're talking about here, doctor? Weeks, months?"

"It's impossible to gage that right now, Aggie Rose. It is truly up to your mom. She is a strong ole farm girl, but she's been through a lot losing Hupp and everything."

Rex's shoulders slumped with guilt.

"So, we'll just have to see how she does. The nurses are changing shifts right now, but you can go in at the top of the hour."

He patted Jack's wringing hands and excused himself.

Aggie watched as his white coat blended into the walls down the hall then she looked at her brothers.

"I need a Coke."

She tapped them both on the knee and they followed her to the elevators.

»«

Aggie finished up on the pay phone in the empty hall outside the day room in the rehab wing of the Nursing Center at Glen Falls; the facility where her mother was receiving therapy. She was a fixture at the place, getting to know all the therapists and their assistants, the nursing staff, housekeeping, and even some of the other residents. It was the same institution Patsy was in, located almost exactly halfway between Warrensburg and West Fort Ann, and Aggie regularly sat and visited with her friend's mother even though she was nonresponsive most days now. Zeke happened to enter the main hall to begin his day with his wife when he spied Aggie sitting alone.

"Morning' sister! What'cha doin' all by your lonesome, honey?"

"Hey Zeke. I was just trying to figure school out…my advisor."

She gestured with the receiver she hadn't yet hung up.

"What's the scoop? They gonna let you withdraw?"

"Yep."

The defeat in her tone signaled the man that she'd given up.

"Now, Aggie. This isn't the end of it, girl."

"I know. It's just not where I wanted to be right now, you know?"

"I know."

And he did, all too well. Zeke looked down at his feet, fumbling his Giants cap in his meat hook hands.

"I'm sorry, Zeke. What is it you always say? I'll be drunk by noon if I don't stop with all my 'wining'!"

"Yeah, honey. There's no use in complaining. Nobody wants to hear you bull."

He brightened.

"Let's go see our girls."

"You go ahead. I have one more call to make then I'll get Mom and we'll meet you in Patsy's room."

He waved her to her task and lumbered down the hall.

She dialed the station and asked for the production manager.

“Sherman, it’s me.”

“Oh, hey, Aggie.”

She caught him in the booth, and she waited while he asked the crew to excuse themselves so he could take the call.

“I’m just checking in again.”

“Yeah, how’s your mom?”

“Still no progress with her affected side or speech, but she’s eating better…swallowing now, at least.”

She heard a heavy sigh coming from her boss and hurried to change the subject.

“I was thinking about something we might try for the lead-in to the early edition…”

“Aggie, we have to let you go.”

“What?”

He sounded genuinely sorry.

“You ran out of leave last week. The donations of sick days from the crew only gets you through tomorrow. We just can’t keep the position open indefinitely.”

“I know I’m out of leave. I don’t want paid, just please don’t replace me. Sherman, I’m coming back. Please don’t do this.”

"It's out of my hands, Aggie. Network is nervous about the last place ratings for the morning programming so they're hiring some black girl out of Baltimore, Ophelia, or something like that? I forget. She'll replace the anchor on AM Chicago and they're filling the day crew with her people, so ours are shifting around to nights. They're hoping maybe she can compete with Donahue."

He waited a beat, then tried an excuse.

"Nobody's happy about it."

She sat staring at her distorted reflection in the metallic panel around the cubes of numbers on the face of the phone.

She looked scary, grotesque, unrecognizable.

"Sherman, I'm sorry, man."

The line was quiet.

"I'm just trying to do what's right here."

"I know, Aggie. If you get back to Chicago, come see me. You never know, there might be another spot open once you're done with school and everything."

The call ended without her will or engagement. He promised her a letter of recommendation and she thought about how little that meant if a female anchor was being brought in to star on AM Chicago.

That was *her* gig!

That was what she was trying for since her teens. *She* was supposed to be the new girl on the set. Not black Ophelia from Baltimore, but ginger Aggie Rose from West Fort Ann! She could get another job at another TV studio. But she couldn't be the first woman to compete against Donahue on a daytime talk show.

For a moment she hoped the new anchor would fail. Maybe she wouldn't even last one season and the network would be ready to try with someone new, and she'd be done with the farm and back in the city, and ready for anything! Maybe…maybe not.

Doubt seized her and she hurried to the nurse's station, reporting that she wouldn't be sitting with her mom for the day, and headed back to West Fort Ann. The whole way home she tallied her resentments.

"Damn you Mother! Blow a God-damned gasket over my brothers, and who gets stuck taking care of you? Me! Not Jim! Precious Jim has to go back to Albany to divorce his wife. And Bobby, hiding out in the Navy halfway around the frickin' globe! And Rex? What about good old, drunken, Irish, junkie Rex?"

She let out a rage-filled chuckle while she wrung the steering wheel with her sweaty hands.

"Why, Rex has finally decided to clean his ass up and be a productive member of society; haven't you heard?"

Her breath was hot, and she could feel her pulse in her temples, a familiar sign of tears she refused to let go.

"And poor Jack, just can't let his big, grown-ass brother go to work all the way down in Saratoga without someone alongside him to make sure he doesn't start drinking again and get his stupid, big, square head kicked in by a racehorse!"

The nineteen-minute commute back to West Fort Ann was quicker than usual; her gas foot weighing more when her soul was heavy. She wiped tears that snuck out and cussed the curves of the road and the miles of woods. She took the final turn onto Route 149 and followed it to where she found herself stopped in front of Hupp's Hardwoods.

She sat idling with her head on the steering wheel for a moment. She raised up and looked the street over to take in the blight that had steadily crept into her hometown. Storefronts boarded up, vacant lots sprouting wild sumacs through the crumbling, ghost foundations of buildings long gone. And the sidewalks connecting the remaining businesses strewn with litter, blown out of neglected dumpsters, and dropped by tourists passing through to better places. She declared the town's demise to her father's ghost and the fogging windshield.

"It's dead, Dad. It's dead. You're dead. We're all dead. Dead in West Fort Ann…without the 'e'."

The door opened easily enough, though she still had to pull up on the knob when she turned the key to get it just right on the first try. She could do it since the first time Hupp showed her, but her brothers never could. There were a lot of things she could do her brothers couldn't. She could stain without streaks, she could cut a perfect dove tail, and she could pound a wooden dowel so perfectly flush and with such finesse her dad had a hard time discerning it from the grain around the pilot hole. She could do everything better at the shop and things on the farm just as well. And now, she was the champion-of-the-world at dropping everything and staying with their mother in bum-fuck-New York while everyone else's life went merrily along.

She walked around the darkened shop picking up odd objects and running her hand over the glow of the pop machine like a genie's lamp. The counter was gritty with sawdust. The windows cloudy with years of unworried dirt. She found the cash drawer still sticky from her dad's hands, coated with tongue oil, reaching in for change to drop in the boots of the firemen when they tapped on the door to collect for Jerry's Kids.

She looked on the floor behind the counter where Rex found him that morning. She spied a drop not colored like the dark walnut, cherry, and maple drips spread all around the floor by Hupp's work boots. This was black.

Blood.

She bent to touch it and sticking out from under the file cabinet against the wall, she saw his carpenter's pencil. She abandoned the stain and reached for the pencil. She raised up, holding it flat across the palms of both hands, and the pain poured from her eyes that she hadn't yet taken time to feel. It was as if this pencil, perpetually behind her father's ear at this dirty wood shop, was absolute proof that he was really gone. Perched on a metal stool, she folded her arms under her head on the counter and cried herself to sleep.

An hour later, the phone woke her from her exhaustion, and she took the call from a customer who was so sorry to hear about her dad, but had he had a chance to finish her table legs? Aggie checked the recipe box Hupp kept his work slips in and then the wooden crates stacked on the shelves in the back of the shop for the finished products. She returned to the phone with good news; he had finished them, and she would be there for the next several hours if someone wanted to come pick them up. She ended the call and smiled triumphantly.

This would be a whole lot better than all day at the nursing home.

She snatched all the work slips out of the recipe box and read each one, written in her dad's cryptic shorthand, deciphering every project to which he last laid his gentle hands.

This would be her therapy.

The days blended one into another and before she knew it spring had turned to summer. The boys had visited Glenn Falls on Mother's Day and left crying because Eloise still looked so frail and hadn't yet regained her speech.

Every interaction with her brothers left Aggie feeling more and more like her father wasn't exaggerating when he called *her* his favorite. Who were these grown men who couldn't keep it together enough for more than one Sunday in May?

Weak…cowards…pussies!

She kept her daily dates at the rehab center but was content to shorten her visits to get back to tending the farm and working in the shop. In a matter of weeks, she had the sheep rotated to the alternate pasture, the garden plowed, and the barn cleaned. At the shop, she had finished everything Hupp had started and none of the customers could tell her work from his. She took enormous pride in the talent she'd inherited and the techniques she'd learned from him. This left only the full pieces he had repaired or restored for resale in the shop. A different curious townie quizzed her with each new day, what would she do with the shop when all the dwindling inventory was gone?

She hadn't committed to an answer as she was unsure herself.

»«

Half her day on the farm done by ten o'clock one late summer morning, Agatha Rose freshened up and headed to see her mom. She caught the speech pathologist coming out of her room and the two women walked into the courtyard for an update.

"She's approaching a milestone that we need to be aware of going forward, Aggie. Stroke patients usually progress in the first six months to a year after their event. After that marker, we rarely see improvement. It's been eight and your mom still isn't speaking."

"So, if we don't get any more progress with the speech, she might never get it back?"

The therapist nodded.

"She tries for about half the time then she just quits. We've tried games and phone calls and just about everything in our whole bag of tricks."

"I know, you've done a great job."

"She just can't or *won't* do anything more for us."

"She is a stubborn old bat, my mother."

Aggie exhibited, guilt-free, the trace disrespect she still felt for the myriad things for which she held her mother responsible but then asked, sincerely.

"What can I do to step it up?"

"I know you talk to her every time you visit, and that's what she needs. But don't go easy. Get her excited. Piss her off. *Make* her respond to you."

Aggie crooked a curious brow and a smile crept over her face as she accepted the challenge.

"That should not be too difficult. I'll give it a whirl."

Upon entry to her mother's room, Aggie spun a wooden chair on its hind leg to straddle it backwards and sit face-to-face with the slumping woman. Eloise was dressed in a magenta, velour track suit, not exactly her style, and covered at the waist with an heirloom quilt from her own cedar chest back home. Her right arm was wedged flaccid in the wheelchair, her left holding on to the arm rest.

Aggie stared into her lopsided face and began.

"Hey Mom, remember Bill?"

The old woman's good eye widened.

"I was just thinking the other day that we never really discussed Bill and me after that whole 'last piano lesson' thing, did we?"

Her mother began to squirm.

"I had a lot to say on the subject, but every time I would try to bring it up, you'd shut me down. Well, today, I think we're going to talk aaaaall about Bill!"

A devilish grin overtook Aggie's face as her mother sat agonizingly helpless across from her.

"Bill and I were in love. I knew it the moment I met her, way before she started teaching me piano. I was turning thirteen and she was just sixteen. I saw her stopped at the light down from Daddy's shop in the Driver's Ed car when she was taking her test. She looked at me and winked and I fell, just like that!"

She snapped.

"I followed her around all year and when she posted those flyers, 'Piano Lessons with Willena', I brought one home to show you and begged you to let me go. It's funny now that I think about it; you didn't suspect a thing. I had vetoed clarinet, violin, dance, and girl scouts but when I suddenly wanted to take piano lessons, you sent Dad out that night looking for an old upright for the living room. Didn't you realize that I couldn't play a damn lick on the thing. Didn't you hear how utterly awful I was at it?"

She laughed and kept on telling while ignoring her mother's obvious discomfort. How cathartic to be able to lay this all out and not have any negative feedback to interrupt her emptying heart.

"Well for the whole time she *taught* me, I fantasized about kissing her. Just kissing. I didn't know people did anything other than kissing at that point. I hinted and teased and gave her every opportunity to do it, but she kept me at arm's length."

Aggie adjusted in her seat now because she was coming to the heart-breaking part.

"Then on our last night together, she told me that her parents were sending her away to school and she wouldn't be able to teach me anymore. Well, I was devastated! Why? Who would do that to their daughter? Just send her away for no reason like that! Then she told me it wasn't for no reason."

She leaned in toward her mother's contorted face and began speaking *at* her.

"She told me she was *gay*. I didn't even know the name of it, isn't that funny? *Gay*. She was gay and she told her parents that she was in love with one of her students."

She pressed her palm to her chest and closed her eyes to recall the sensation of the moment.

"Me!"

She breathed in long and slow.

"*Me*, Mom. Bill was in love with *me*."

She leaned back, circling, holding on tight to the chair.

"I was numb! I blurted out, 'I love you too!' and I went for her. We wrapped our arms around each other and held close and still for this beautiful, brief moment. Then…it happened…my first kiss! It was the most amazing thing that had ever happened to me. There I was, barely fifteen and kissing the woman I had obsessed over for nearly two years. I knew she had just told me she was leaving but in that instant, I didn't care if we lived or died."

Totally unaware of herself, Aggie was streaming tears down her blushing cheeks.

"I was loved! I was gay, and I was seen, and I was understood, and I was loved! I was reborn that night, Mom! Do you get what I'm telling you? Me, Agatha Rose O'Hanley, the *real* me, was reborn that night in the arms of my piano teacher."

She sniffed, her nose running now too, and wiped a palm across her wet eyes. She noticed tears on Eloise's cheeks as well. She reached for the tissues on the nightstand and blotted the old woman's face.

"And then she was gone. And all those hushed conversations with her mother, and the women in the church. Never once did anyone ask *me*, talk to *me*, tell *me* anything! Dad couldn't even tell me what was going on. You had him in the dark right along with me!"

Now she was connecting to the anger and fear she had felt in those nights after Bill left town.

"Man, I wish I would have told my dad about it!"

She stood, abruptly enough to startle her mother, and kept mindlessly crying as she shook her head.

"I wish I'd have said, 'Daddy, I'm in love…with a beautiful girl…who loves me too."

She crossed to the window to shut her mother out of her memory. She didn't deserve to see her cry over it. Not then and certainly not now. It was none of her business who she loved!

"I wish I'd have told my father what I'm telling you so he could see me as I truly am."

She hung her head.

"Dad would have been cool with it. He would have been fine!"

Her tears had dried, but she kept her focus outside. Out there somewhere, she *had* told her dad and he *was* cool. And then a scratchy sound squeaked from behind her in the room.

"He…knew."

Aggie's breath froze in her lungs. She turned back into the room and gazed at her mother's struggling face.

"Mom?"

Eloise labored with every syllable.

"He…knew…Ag-gie. Your…dad…knew…a-bout…you."

"He did?"

Contrite, the girl dropped to the floor at her mother's side pleading for more.

"He knew about me and Bill? About me being in love? And was he fine with it? Was he cool with it?"

The woman answered her daughter with a wink and a thumbs up from her unaffected side and Aggie fell into Eloise's lap and wept with abandon.

It seemed ironic that the subject that finally loosed Eloise's tongue was one that the family was content never to speak of before her stroke; but Speech Therapy was pleased with her breakthrough and encouraged the patient and her daughter to discuss more and more.

On a rainy day at the beginning of autumn, Eloise sat with a photo album across her legs at a table in the empty day room and Aggie quizzed her on dead relatives and abandoned places repeated in the pictures.

"This one, Mom. Who is this with Dad?"

Her eyes softened and a nearly symmetrical smile overtook her face.

"That's his first wife. That's who you're named after."

"Whaaaat? What are you telling me right now?"

Her mother nodded.

"Daddy was married before you? Am I the only one who didn't know this? And I'm named after this person?"

Eloise took in a long breath before attempting the tale.

"Before we met, he was the youngest foreman in the sawmill, and he was in love with Agatha Rose Shahady."

She plucked the handkerchief from her right fist with her left hand and tried to wipe the moisture from the corner of her mouth. Still struggling to recognize her paralyzed side, she missed, and Aggie held up a small, make-up mirror to guide her.

"Agatha Rose was younger by a couple of years, but this was back in the late nineteen twenties, so girls as young as fifteen and sixteen were often married to men older than them for security."

Aggie hung on every word.

"Well…Hupp asked her father for her hand and he shot him down."

"Oh no! Why? Who would turn Daddy down?"

"Her father told him she was sick. I can't remember now what she had. Something with her blood…or her lungs. TB maybe?"

She waved her hand to erase her feeble attempts at the details.

"But her father said, he couldn't do that to Hupp. He couldn't saddle him with a dying wife."

"Oh my God, Mom! How tragic!"

"No! Not tragic. Because do you know what your dad did?"

Aggie shook her head.

"Your dad eloped with that girl."

Her daughter's mouth dropped open.

"What a rebel! Who knew Hupp O'Hanley was such a stud!"

"No, no, no."

Eloise tempered her telling it.

"It wasn't like that. They ran away and got married and he kept her by his side every minute of every day after that. He made her breakfast and dressed her and bundled her in quilts and flannel and drove into the mill every day with her by his side. He placed her by the stove in the room where he worked and checked on her with every in and out. Then they'd ride home together, and he'd make dinner and hold her by the fire."

"This is something else, Mom."

A tear appeared in Eloise's eye as she touched her wrinkled hand to the image of the couple.

"She lasted exactly one year to the day longer than the doctor gave her. He was holding her in their bed when she took her last breath."

Aggie's wet eyes were trained on her mother's face.

"I knew the story when I married him; everybody in town knew. But we never spoke about it until you were born. After all those boys named after my folks and his, when it came time to name his little girl, he said, 'El, would it be alright if we named her Aggie Rose?'"

Aggie fell back in her chair, wrung out from the emotional ride.

"Holy shit, Mom, that's just the most beautiful thing I think I've ever heard."

"Yep. My husband was a beautiful man."

Without any awareness, Eloise raised her bad hand to catch a tear that had held on her lash long enough.

"I meant you, Momma. It was beautiful of you."

»«

Eloise continued to improve through the shortening days of fall and the dark winter that followed. The boys came up on holidays and then retreated over and over to their respective lives away from home. Her treatment team speculated that discharge may be possible within the coming year and that gave Eloise and her daughter something to look forward to.

Aggie survived the shearing season, the lambs' arrivals, and plowing and planting the garden again with little to complain about, but her salvation was the shop. What time wasn't used repairing things on the farm, she toiled happily with the projects she took on at her father's shop.

She restored half a dozen pews for the church renovation, helped the guys at Ace Hardware make the new bleachers they donated to the little league field, and she was creating some amazing pieces of her own design. Word quickly spread about her talent and abilities and she was becoming a bit of a tourist attraction in her own rite. The mayor even included a picture of her at the lathe in the 1985 West Fort Ann Community Calendar after some random travel reviewer wrote about "Aggie O'Hanley's Wonderful Wood Workings in West Fort Ann".

Acceptance, if not relief for her change of course bathed her in gratitude on a daily basis when she was working with her father's tools. She couldn't have foreseen the turn in her trajectory when she pulled up in front of the shop on that gray day in April.

A woman stood with her back to the street, peering into the shop at the display window, the dangling leg of a toddler hooked at her waist. Shutting the truck engine off, Aggie jumped down and the woman spun around, startled.

"Oh! I didn't even hear you pull up."

Aggie stood for a moment in shock, then blinking in disbelief.

"Bill? Is that you?"

The woman removed the yellow rain slicker hood from her blonde bob and smiled.

"Hey, Aggie. It's good to see you."

Snapping to, Agatha opened her arms to guide Bill and the child out of the mist and into the shop. The familiar tinkle of the bell above the door caught the baby by surprise and his head swam in his own hood, looking for the source of the sound, until his mother freed him from it.

"I'm sorry to just show up like this, but when Mom and Dad told me you were back in town, I just had to try and connect. You know?"

"No, no. I mean, yes, sure."

Aggie was blind-sided and struggling to articulate what she wasn't even sure of herself.

"How are…who is this little guy?"

"This is Thatcher. Say, hi, Thatcher. This is my good friend, Miss Aggie."

Aggie squatted to meet the boy's eyes.

"Hi Thatcher."

He spoke just above a whisper and tucked his head behind his mother's calf.

"Hi."

"You're such a beautiful boy."

He was. Golden hair and a smile he couldn't contain despite his shyness, and deep blue eyes like marbles, like his mother's.

She knelt now too, to meet Aggie's eyes.

"Miss Aggie and I have known each other for a long time, Thatch. But it's been so very long since we've seen each other."

"So very long."

She stared back at Bill's own deep blue gaze for a moment then checked herself.

"This is no place for us to visit. I'm not exactly kid-friendly with all Dad's tools and blades."

The two women surveyed their environs, then Aggie engaged the little boy.

"You know what? I can take us to where we can see some sheep!"

They agreed on Bill's car for the ride to the farm for Thatcher's safety in the car seat and headed for the city limits. Bill pointed out icons from their childhood to her son who seemed perfectly content just to study the pretty redhead in the front seat watching his momma. She showed him the Washington County Movie Palace, the high school, even the vacant building where the Tasti-Freeze used to be.

"That was Mommy's first job, baby. I served ice cream there."

His eye's brightened.

"Ice cream!"

"Not now, honey. Maybe after we see the farm."

Bill kept narrating the tour until she passed the United Methodist Church. The building where two years of piano lessons had changed their lives forever, rendered her dumb.

The farm wasn't far past the church and the sun had nudged its way from behind the grayness to cast a storybook light on the muddy fields. Thatcher hit the ground running, although his arms moved faster than his legs, and he was quick to the barn before the women. Aggie took him by his chubby hand and walked him through and out the back into the field where the sheep, alerted to the sounds of their shepherd, began the long walk from the back pasture, the bells on their necks clanging.

Aggie's dog, Culpepper, loped from among the wooly bodies to greet his mistress and welcome her guests. He licked the boy's nose and made him giggle and guard at the same time. They took in the sensations of the sheep, feeling their cropped fleece bellies and their velvety noses. They sprinkled feed into troughs; Thatcher delighting in the sensation of the coarse meal pouring over his hands. And they tossed the dog's tug for a tiringly long session of fetch.

Thatcher started to lose his sense of humor after he and Culpepper collided in competition for the tug and Bill scooped up the toddler and asked if he was getting hungry? Aggie reacted instantly.

"Oh my gosh, Billie! I totally lost track of time. Let's go in and get some lunch."

A belly full of grilled cheese and tomato soup, and a giant glass of chocolate milk, and the little boy was out like a light, sprawling as if he'd fallen from the ceiling on one half of the loveseat. Bill sat in the remaining space and laid her hand on his pudgy feet.

Aggie whispered to the young mother.

"Can we talk?"

"Yeah. He's fine. He sleeps hard, just like his dad."

"So…"

"So, his dad?"

"Yeah. That seems like a good place to start."

"When I left town, or excuse me, was *sent* out of town, I went to live with my Great Aunt Nellie in Brooklyn. She was a telephone operator for thirty years, never married. My mother thought it would 'help' me 'get over' my 'issues'."

Aggie nodded, eyes rolling at the words Bill attacked with her air quotes.

"Needless to say, Mom knew nothing about her grandmother's sister. She may have been the original lesbian!"

"Ha!"

The loud laugh escaped Aggie's face and she grabbed her mouth afraid she'd woken the baby.

Bill grinned.

"It's ok, Aggie. I'm serious. This kid can sleep through anything.

"Go on, I'm sorry."

"Well, after a whole summer of running errands and driving her and her girlfriends around, I started my first semester at NYU; double majoring in psychology and music."

"Wow, impressive."

"I needed both in undergrad to get into graduate studies for Music Therapy, and that's where I met Thatcher's dad."

She continued to tell how they both played the cello, she tutored him in biology, they commiserated about the gay dating scene on campus, and after their freshman year, they moved in together. They were one another's beards at family functions, each one content to help the other fake a straight relationship for a little less heat at home. They dated different people off and on but by the end of their third year, they had been in enough relationships that didn't work out for one reason or another, to start to think about their own a little differently. They both wanted a traditional family, spouse, kids, house. So, they began to contemplate an open marriage arrangement that would afford them the opportunity to have kids together while still maintaining their private love lives.

"So, a couple weeks after graduation, we eloped and got pregnant right away."

Aggie's eyes were wide with interest.

"Wow. You're married?"

Bill looked at her naked left hand.

"No. Not anymore."

She inhaled deeply and continued.

"He was thrilled about the baby and things were going well until he met this guy, Christian. He said that he was still on board for raising our child together but his interest in the pregnancy started to taper off and they started to fight about him spending time with me. It just wasn't working out the way we planned it. You know?"

Aggie nodded even though she was sure she didn't know.

"And then right after Thatcher was born, he came to me in tears and said he couldn't do it. He couldn't take care of another whole person. He wasn't done living his life."

Bill shook her head and frowned.

"Whatever that means. I mean, what the hell am I doing if not living my life? Right?"

Aggie agreed.

"Right!"

The questions in Aggie's head were getting checked off one by one and she was growing more hopeful with every word.

"So, annulment? Divorce?"

"Divorce. He asked for nothing. Gave me custody of Thatch and puts four hundred dollars in my bank account every month. I mean, it's not perfect, but even if we had stayed 'married', how perfect would it have been?"

Aggie's empathy came sincerely.

"I can't imagine how much that sucked for you, Bill. But you have this tiny human who is obviously the best ever, and you don't have to share him with anyone!"

Bill smiled and took in her son as he slept beside her, then a tear formed in her eye and she looked back at her friend.

"But I want to."

Aggie waited, listening, and Bill continued fumbling.

"He's amazing…and hard…and amazing! But babies are meant to be shared. The love and joy and the responsibility. I need someone to check me on my shit. How do I know if I'm doing this right if it's just me?"

"Is that why you came home…for help from the family?"

"I wanted to be closer to my parents for sure, Mom and Dad are in their eighties. For them *and* for Thatcher. But I didn't make the move back to West Fort Ann right away."

She only had a couple more cards she hadn't yet played, and she was trying to summon the nerve to go for broke.

"When I heard that your sweet dad died…"

Aggie's head dropped and Bill reached for her across the ottoman.

"I'm so very sorry, Aggie."

Aggie looked up and registered the sympathy in Bill's eyes.

"Thank you, Billie. Truly, that means the world."

"I'm sorry I didn't make it in for the funeral, but Thatcher caught a bug from daycare, and I was struggling about what to do with him, and these are all excuses, but I want you to know that I was holding you in my heart when I heard."

Her hand, resting on top of Aggie's now gripped it and held on for dear life.

"The real truth is, that I guess I've been holding you in my heart all along. I didn't make the choice to move back until I heard that you were back on the farm again, taking care of your mom."

Aggie closed her fingers around Bill's.

"I didn't come home for my parents. It's a bonus that they get to see their grandson, but… I came looking for you."

Aggie was reeling from the reverie. Was any of this real? Was she actually sitting hand-in-hand with her first love hearing how she'd come home to reconnect with her?

"Bill, I…I don't know what to say."

"I'm sorry, Aggie."

Every time she said her name, Aggie's heart beat a little faster.

"Don't apologize."

"No…it's too much maybe."

"Who's to say what's too much? I was on track to work in television until my world took a ninety-degree left turn and landed me back here working on the farm and in my dad's wood shop. And you were pretending to be married to a gay guy so you could have a family and that didn't work out so you're here…in my living room…telling me that you came home for me."

Hearing her own voice made it sound even more bizarre than she originally thought.

"Too much? Life is crazy! How can we say what's too much?"

Bill left her reservations behind her with her divorce, and her Aunt Nellie, and all that had preceded this very moment, and planted a kiss on Aggie's lips. A kiss that might have come after that first one, at their last piano lesson, when they were too young to choose the path for their own lives together. A kiss that connected them to the girls they were and the women they had become.

A kiss that settled it.

This was the purpose the universe had in store for Aggie with every winding curve she stumbled through. This moment that she'd only dreamed of had suddenly clarified every other before it.

They both knew with that one kiss, that their hearts were home.

The couple, quietly determined, informed their families of their intentions, and moved Thatcher and Bill to the farm. Aggie confronted her mother and sent the boys heart-felt letters letting them know their acceptance would be appreciated but their blessing was not something she found necessary to follow her bliss. They responded with love and support; who were they to judge their baby sister for anything? They didn't have all the answers either. If Aggie was happy and Bill was good to her, that's all they cared about. Even Bill's parents were an easy sell.

It was no mystery why the whole thing met with such resounding approval; they all fell in love with Thatcher.

The girls were joined in a private commitment ceremony in the Unitarian Church in Glenn Falls and second parent adoption papers were drawn up so that Aggie could assume her official place in their son's life. His father relinquished all claims to the child and their little family was born.

In the spring Eloise was discharged home and was even able to help a little on the farm, moving around with just the help of a quad-cane for support. She and Thatcher worked in the garden and walked in the pastures on cool days and played Go-Candy Land (a hybrid of Go Fish and Candy Land they created) in the barn on hot ones. He grew and thrived in the love and attention of his Gram.

Time rushed by like water over a damn, and Thatcher went from a curious toddler of three in those early days to a ten-year-old in the blink of an eye. Eloise slowed a little but remained sharp enough to challenge the rest of them from time to time. The devotion between Aggie and Bill deepened with every season. Aggie felt so safe in the love of her family that she couldn't remember wanting anything else.

Agatha Rose divided her time equally between the farm and the shop and was gaining more confidence in her work with every piece she crafted.

Bill got a grant from the state and traveled throughout the tri-county area working with her mental health clients. She even volunteered one Saturday a month to play at the Nursing Center at Glenn Falls. It was after one of those visits in the autumn of '92 that she came home with a heavy heart.

Aggie and Thatcher returned from a matinee of *School Ties* and found Bill and Eloise at the dining room table. Thatcher kissed them both and darted up to his room.

"Hi Mom! Hi Gram!"

Aggie waited until she heard his door slam and reported.

"Well, if you had any doubts, our son is a liberal. He said he was going to write a letter to the ACLU on how to start a culture club in his school."

She sat down and continued, grinning.

"Full disclosure, as despicable as Charlie's character was, I found myself wanting to see more of the shower fight. Thatch has a come-to-Jesus moment over the mistreatment of the Jewish people and I have a hetero flash watching teenage boys wrestle naked in the locker room!"

She laughed at herself then registered the solemn expressions on the women's faces.

"Uh-oh. You two look super serious. What's the matter?"

Bill broke it to her…Patsy passed away.

»«

Zeke stood at the front of the chapel on the grounds of The Grand Chancellor Hotel on Lake George next to an easel holding a bank of photos of Patsy and MaryAnne, and all their friends on the staff, their wedding pictures, Patsy on water skis, Christmas in the hotel galley. Visitors were stopping to pay their respects and share their stories of his lovely wife. The urn was placed in a lighted curio to the right, surrounded by flowers.

Aggie slipped in and scanned the register for her old friends from the lake. She was really looking for MaryAnne's name or Faline's but thought she probably wouldn't sign in at her own mother's funeral. She added her name to the book and then scoped out the crowd in hopes of spying her friend. Instead, she found Dottie, the Moynihan boys, Hank and Peg, and the Belcastro sisters; their father had gone on last year. Dr. Haynes had retired to Florida, but he sent those gorgeous dahlias someone pointed out. She made her way through the line to Zeke and held him with all the love in her heart, then settled in for the service with the crew from the lake. She kept an eye on the door, but no one else came.

When the service was over, Aggie, the last one to leave the chapel, hugged and kissed Zeke just outside the doors, apologized for not being able to stay for the wake, got in her car, and headed back to the farm. The day had darkened with a gray rain and she stopped to gas up before she got on the highway.

A limo pulled into the gas station just as she got out to pump. She smiled in the direction of the tinted windows thinking that maybe it was the funeral directors returning from the interment. The driver got out and went into the store; he wore a chauffer's cap.

That was not the funeral director.

She watched the man go to the counter inside and felt her guts start to warm. Her eyes followed him as he returned to the car and the window in the back slid down. A hand reached out to receive the cigarettes he purchased, and Aggie could hear the passenger talking on the limo phone.

"Tell him I just couldn't do it. Tell him I'm sorry."

The driver was back in the car. She looked at the woman in the back seat.

She *had* come. It was MaryAnne.

The woman looked out the car window into the eyes of her first best friend and confessed.

"I just can't."

Aggie judged without thinking.

"That's not good enough."

The window went up, and she was gone.

Faline Farah

Sam Burgess had been her agent since he discovered her on the senior class trip. It had been just as she imagined it; she was trying on sunglasses at Bergdorf's and he spotted her. The trauma of losing Aggie just days before, left her in a kind of haze, and the charismatic way Sam talked to her left her spellbound. He gave her his card and the classmates around her crowded in and congratulated her.

She felt empty.

It was supposed to be the best thing that ever happened to her, her big break. But all she could think of was how she wished Aggie was there to see it.

She wouldn't remain at St. James to finish her last semester either. Sam came through with an offer to set her up and she called home and told Zeke and Patsy she was moving to New York City.

No longer MaryAnne O'Hara, Faline Farah debuted as Delia Blackwell, the illegitimate daughter of Nathanial Hart, the dynastic tycoon whose family constantly tried to beat each other out of the will on daytime TV's second most watched soap opera *Hart's Desire*.

Delia was twenty-eight but Faline was just shy of her eighteenth birthday when Sam convinced her to emancipate herself and sign the contracts; just a formality she had reassured her parents but a necessity because of her age. They were naturally worried for her safety, but Burgess had taken excellent care of her. He wasn't into starlets as a kink, too much drama. He was good at spotting talent though and even better at representing it.

She was thirty-two now, and in the middle of her fourteenth season on the soap and it's rising ratings were largely due to her; a detail that wasn't lost on her agent and one that would make his job exponentially harder with every performance.

This day he stood, gently knocking on her dressing room door and pleading as usual for entry.

"Faline? Honey, let me in please."

"Why, so you can tell me how awful I am? So you can tell me how I'm never going to win an Emmy?"

"Honey come on. You know that's not true. Just let me in so we can talk it out."

The door to Faline's dressing room swung open and she flung herself to the chaise in the corner crying.

"Faline its ok. Those Emmy's are political, you know that. We have that discussion every year."

She had worked her way into more and more scenes over the past fourteen years by pseudo-seducing the writers and producers (she promised much and delivered little on her guarantees for sex), until she was playing a major role. She had tried for other projects and landed a couple of commercial spots but none of the movie studios would look at her since she had the 'soap stink' on her already. Once an actress passed a certain threshold of episodes, they were deemed unmarketable on the big screen; the fourteenth season was thirteen past her limit.

She cried now, sincerely. Despite being acutely aware of all the shortcomings of her career, she remained content with her stardom being limited as long as she continued to achieve all this genre had to offer her, and that meant awards!

"No one was better than you during sweeps, Faline."

"Then why didn't I get past the damn nomination, Sam?"

The aging man sat down on the chaise next to his client and ran his plump, coarse hands through her hair. For a moment she flashed to her mom and what that soothing deed meant to her as a child. Her heart broke a little at how far away that all seemed, and she cried harder than the current failure warranted.

"Faline, maybe you need a break. Let's get you out of town. Where do you want to go, honey? Anywhere you want, I'll take you."

A knock interrupted the two and a production assistant squeaked from behind the door.

"Miss Farah?"

Faline didn't even look up to bark back.

"What? Come in!"

The petite girl skulked into the dressing room and handed off a slip of paper to Burgess. He read it and closed his eyes to brace against her reaction. The P.A. made a quick exit and he squared up to break it to her.

"Faline honey. I'm afraid I've got bad news."

Her stepfather had written almost as often as Aggie at first, receiving dictated responses typed by this assistant or that intern. He called her directly while Patsy's voice was still detectable over the phone but gave up on that too once she lost it completely and entered the facility in Glenn Falls. It *was* good of Faline to pay for everything. But he thought she owed her mother that much. She could have come to see her more. She showed up once when Patsy was first admitted and again the Christmas after that, and he heard that she had returned to The Grand the following summer with a flock of sycophants from the show, but that they treated the staff like shit, and it broke everyone's hearts.

Clear up until Patsy took her last breath, though, Zeke kept his tongue about her daughter. It was never a situation between them that he felt like he couldn't criticize her, he just knew there was little to come of such interference but hard feelings. Instead, he filled his wife's final couple of years with caring for her daily needs, romancing her, and reliving the memories that made her heart keep beating while her body shut down.

When her manager broke the news to her though, Zeke fully and rightfully so, expected a phone call…from MaryAnne!

He would be disappointed.

"I'm sorry, honey, but this note says that your dad called and -…"

Faline sniffed and frowned with irritation.

"What? What do they need now?"

"Honey, your mom has passed."

Faline's body ejected itself from the chaise without her conscious control. She felt as if she had fallen into ice water. Her breath caught in her chest and she felt a white-hot pain shoot through her whole body. She collapsed under the charge and felt her mind closing down while the room filled with shouting scrambling people…

She came to as the paramedic was removing the cuff from her arm and his partner was waving an ammonia capsule under her counterfeit nose. She thrashed her head around and accidentally came in contact with the capsule, its caustic serum painting the tip of her rhinoplasty.

"Ugh! Get that shit away from me, God damn it!"

Sam breathed a sigh of relief.

"There she is! She's back. She's ok."

She searched the crowd for his face.

"Sam?"

The E.M.T.s continued their examination, lifting her eyelids and manipulating her pupils with penlights and directives.

"Miss Farah, do you know where you are?"

"Can you follow my light? Can you tell me what day it is?"

"Get the hell away from me you dickheads!"

Faline was small but strong and she pushed at both the men with a growing intensity. They persisted.

"Ma'am, can you please tell me what day it is?"

"It's the day my mother died, you asshole!"

She broke down and cried and Sam took the lead.

"That's enough fellas."

He waved the onlookers to disperse and handled the shoulders of the ambulance crew.

"Let's let her up, guys. I think she'll be ok if we give her some air."

They followed the directive and rose gathering their equipment to retreat with their gurney to just outside the dressing room. Sam helped Faline to her feet and walked her to the chaise once more. She nodded to him and he walked out and closed the door behind him.

She bent in the middle, elbows resting on her knees, her head in her hands, looking at the floor between her feet. She spied the note. Sam must have dropped it in all the commotion. She picked it up and held it in both hands to read.

Message from: Zeke

Re: Patsy

Passed away this morning 10:20 am at Glenn Falls. Waiting 2 days for cremation so you can have a private viewing. Funeral Saturday. Come home.

She felt the surface of the thin paper between her thumbs and fingers. What was she trying for? If the ink wore off, was it real? If the paper wore through, did it happen? If she didn't call him back…if she didn't go…would her mother really be gone?

Sam returned and sat down next to her. He put his arm was around her, gently pulling her under his wing.

"We'll get you whatever you need, sweetie. I'll get you on the next first-class seat from JFK."

She leaned into his armpit.

"I don't want to fly, Sam."

"Ok. Whatever you want, Faline, honey. We'll get you a limo."

The producers weren't the least put out by the unexpected absence. Faline was growing to be more trouble than she was worth and the whole cast and crew bid her farewell when she left the set and headed north for Lake George; the day *after* receiving the news. The trip was under three hundred miles so she should be at The Grand by the evening of the last day to view Patsy's body before the cremation. The Chapel on the hotel grounds was where the service would be conducted, and she was sure she could convince the funeral directors to hold the procedure at the crematorium until she'd had a drink and a nap.

She wouldn't wait for her arrival at the hotel to have the first of either.

The bourbon flowed freely in the spacious back of the black limousine. She started out mixing with diet ginger ale but four or five in, just settled for the rocks. Winnie, the assistant du jour Sam sent with her, sat across from the star buttoned up to the neck in her wool coat and pinned securely to the seat, nervously checking the attachment of her seat belt with every cocktail she watched disappearing down Faline's hatch.

A minor accident well ahead of them on the highway forced a detour of traffic into a poorly marked neck of the woods that temporarily confused the driver, and he stopped the car at a lodge along the route to ask for directions. Faline interrogated her stiff companion when she realized they'd quit moving.

"Where is he going?"

Winnie barely spoke above a whisper for fear of incurring her drunken wrath when repeating what the driver had just said to them.

"The detour wasn't very well marked, Miss Farah. He's gone into the motel to ask directions."

"Hotel?"

Faline's senses attempted a rally.

"I used to live in a hotel."

"Motel."

"Huh?"

"I believe it's a motel, ma'am."

"Puh-tay-tuh, puh-tah-tuh, let's go!"

Faline's rag doll posture launched her around in her seat and out the door of the limo before her assistant could unbuckle her belt. The surprisingly agile Faline landed outside in the gravel lot surefooted and still in possession of her full glass.

The girl shut the door behind them and hurried alongside her, hooking Faline's free arm in hers and stepping carefully between the divots in the lot, filling with rain. When they reached the lobby, Winnie handed her charge off to the driver and checked the three of them into separate but adjoining rooms "...until Miss Farah could properly rest for the remainder of the journey." The assistant was assured that their anonymity would be protected in exchange for a hefty tip of folded twenties.

Her traveling staff escorted Faline to her room and upon them relegating her to the bed, she promptly blacked out until morning.

The physical frame of Patsy O'Hara-Goodwin would go to the fire without a final touch from her only child; an act of self-sabotage by that child that would make closure nearly impossible.

Faline's binge would render her useless until the morning of the funeral. It was well after noon before they arrived at Lake George and the service had all but concluded. She made the chauffer hide the limo in the drive behind one of the staff cottages and she skulked around to the porch to stand out of the light rain as she looked down at the little church. She could barely hear the piano and the singing of Amazing Grace for the drops on the tin roof above her.

The singing ceased and in a moment familiar forms began emerging from the wreathed doors. She shrunk back behind the porch post and peered over her dark glasses; the circles under her eyes rivaling their purple lenses. She squinted at the distant figures identifying them all by their posture, their gait, and the way they handled one another. These people used to be hers, her family. Now, without Patsy, she didn't feel connected to any of them; or anyone else for that matter.

She recognized Zeke and without realizing it she searched for Aggie Rose in the group. She should have come. She would have come if things were the same between them. She looked away and tiptoed down from the porch and into the limo just missing her friend as she made her way out of the service.

Faline poured another bourbon rocks and reached for the pack of Eve 120's she'd exhausted on the road the day before, crumpling it and pressing the button to lower the window to the chauffer.

"It appears as if they carried on without me, Jenny."

"It's Winnie, Miss Farah."

Faline ignored the correction and turned her attention to the driver.

"Hey, brother, before we get back on the highway, I need you to stop for some cigarettes."

"Won't we be driving into the resort for the wake first, Miss Farah?"

"Nope. I don't think I would be very welcome down there right about now."

She slurped at the surface of her full drink to keep it from spilling from its glass.

"Let's just head for home, shall we?"

The car pulled out of the main entrance to the hotel grounds just ahead of the funeral procession. Faline stared out the tinted windows and threw back the remainder of her drink.

"Get Sam on the phone, honey. I need him to do something for me."

The girl made the call and handed the phone off to Faline.

"Sam?"

She tucked the receiver into the crook of her neck and freed her hands to refill her tumbler.

"I missed it!"

She poured the caramel-colored liquor over the melting ice and watched it settle into the bottom. She pictured it doing the same thing in her blood, swirling around and numbing bits of her head, heart, and nerves. She listened to his consoling attempts to excuse her irresponsible behavior as grief while downing the fresh drink, then ordered her agent into action.

"I need you to send another flower arrangement to the house…no! To the hotel…no! To the house, to Mr. Zeke Goodwin."

She filled her glass again and this time sat back against the leather upholstery and held it up to the gray light flooding the back seat from the open window. She took the cigarettes from the driver.

"Write a note and tell him I just couldn't do it. Tell him I'm sorry."

The driver was back in the car. Faline looked out the window in the direction of the gas pumps and spied a woman silhouetted against the dim glare of the rainy day and felt the urge to confess.

"I just can't."

The woman dispensed her judgement.

"That's not good enough."

She *had* come. It was Agatha Rose.

»«

Once back in the city, the drinking continued despite Sam's best efforts to get his client to sober up. She became more and more unreliable in the scenes opposite her costars and at the behest of the producers, the writers were paring her part down gradually with every episode.

Sam tried everything short of inpatient rehab to dry her out, which she flatly refused, but she was losing ground every day. She drank until she blacked out every night then needed her prescription of phenedrine the next day on the set to stay awake long enough to get through her scenes. Sam begged the producers to give him more time to get her help, explaining how her behavior was just her way of working through her grief, but he was lectured again and again on how they couldn't keep making exceptions for her.

He called in another favor when she fell in her dressing room and broke her nose, and the writers were instructed to create a car wreck scenario to work with the real-life bruises on her face. What Sam couldn't bring himself to tell her until they came back to the studio was that they had put her character in a coma indefinitely to keep from putting up with her bad behavior for the rest of the season.

Every soap star knew that once the coma card was played, your odds of returning to the story were reduced by half, if you were lucky. From a coma, it was all too easy to just pull the plug. It was nearly always the last step before a character was killed off.

As was another unprofessional habit since the drinking began, she only read the scripts just before she was called to the set. She chuckled when she ran across the bit in the story about the accident.

"A car wreck? Kind of cheap don't you think?"

"No Faline, not at all."

Sam was tiptoeing to keep her calm.

"This way you won't have to endure all that time in makeup."

"Do I look that bad?"

She spun around in her chair and leaned into the mirror.

"Ooof!"

"Now before you get all worked up, Faline, you are going to heal just fine. The doctors said no permanent damage was done and that you were lucky because your original nose would never have been able to survive the impact."

"My original-…"

"Sorry, honey. You know what I mean. You look great!"

“Mmmm-hm.”

Her eyes narrowed and she glared at the man through her heavy lashes. Then she softened her face and looked him in the eyes.

“I am sorry I’ve been such a pain in the ass, Sammy.”

He reached for her hand.

“We’ve all been so worried about you, Faline, honey. In all this time since you lost your mom, you’ve never taken the time to recover. They just want to give you some time to rest and take it easy.”

“It’s just a car wreck, right?”

She nervously flipped through the script scanning for more details.

“I mean it’s not like they’re putting me in a coma or anything…right?”

The tail end of her rhetoric coincided with her finding the dialogue of another character announcing the bad news that ‘*Delia has fallen into a coma!*’.

Wild, breath heaving, Faline sprung to her feet, rolled the script in her hands and screaming, ran for the sound stage.

“A COMA!!!”

Sam lunged for her and missed and scrambled to his feet to follow her. She was swift to her target and upon reaching the director’s chair, hurled the script into his lap freeing all the pages into a snowy blast.

“A coma, Michael? A fucking coma!”

"What the hell, Sam? You were supposed to have told her before she got on set today, man!"

Red-faced and panting, the agent reached for Faline's arms and tried to intervene without sounding like he was making excuses.

"Now, Faline, honey…"

"Don't you *honey* me, you jackass!"

Lunging toward the man in charge of the set, her arms pinned by her agent, she kept up her rant!

"A coma! Delia can make it through a God damned car wreck without falling into a coma, for Christ's sake! Last season she got shot in the head by her nanny and came out smelling like a rose! And she has a blow out on the way to Drake's wedding and she's in a God damned COMA!"

"Get your client out of my face, Mr. Burgess!"

The man took control of his set and directed an assistant to get the producers on the phone to report Faline's behavior.

"Yes! Get the producers on the phone and remind them how much money I've made them over the past decade, genius!"

Sam muscled her away from the growing crowd, holding her close to him while he forced their tandem steps back to her dressing room.

"Tell them Delia Blackwell is a much better driver than that! Coma my ass!"

Sam's thinning hair was glistening with sweat when he slammed the door separating her outburst from the rest of the crew. He took a handkerchief from the breast pocket of his suite coat and dabbed his forehead and upper lip.

"Jesus, Faline! You're gonna give me a heart attack one of these days! I can't keep doing this!"

"You?"

"Yes, me!"

He sat down at her makeup table and looked at his own aging face in her mirror, then beyond to her in the reflection. He took in a long, calming breath.

"And neither can you. Faline…honey…please be reasonable."

She froze to meet his eyes in the mirror.

"Reasonable? They put me in a coma, Sam. Do you know what that means?"

"Yes. It means they didn't write you off the show. It means you have a chance to make this right. It means Delia can lay still in every scene until Faline can get her shit together and sober up."

Her frayed edges abated some and she suddenly *heard* what this kind soul had been saying. She had just been confessing that she was sorry for everything. She was not wholly unaware of how hard she'd been to work with. But a coma? She didn't realize she was that bad…until now.

"I had no idea, Sam."

"Look, all is certainly not lost yet, honey."

She looked down at his hands tenderly holding hers and then back to his gentle, sweaty face.

"Oh God, Sam. I don't want to blow it."

Sincere tears streaked from her blackened eyes down her rage-red cheeks.

"And you won't, Faline. You will lay still on set and we will get you the help you need in your down time and you won't blow this. I promise."

She sat down hard on the chaise, defeated. He reassured more and she cried more and when he left to smooth things over with the cast, the crew, the director, the producer, and the writers…she poured herself a drink.

»«

The scene began with a zoom out from the interior of the intensive care unit in which Delia lay comatose, to the hall outside the observation window. Her face still bruised, she sported an oxygen canula under her nose and an I.V. prop taped to one arm in the private room cluttered with monitors and equipment, beeping out her vital signs. She only had to lay still long enough for the characters outside the window to meet and discuss her case.

ACTION!

"It's still too early to tell what function she'll regain if any, Mr. Hart."

"If any?"

"I don't want to give you false hope."

"Doctor, are you saying she could remain a vegetable for the rest of her life?"

"If she doesn't start to show some improvement soon, you should consider gathering the family to decide what course you want to take."

"She has no other family. And neither do I. She's all I've got, doc..."

"CUT!"

The director charged onto the set blasting past the two men into the hospital room.

"What the hell are you doing, Faline?"

"Was I still in the frame?"

"You have one job, Jesus! Get makeup back in here!"

He was sweating under the lights.

"Chalk her lips up some more."

"I thought I'd open my eyes for just a second and give them a tiny bit of hope! So, you could see it? How did it look from out there?"

"God damn it, Faline! She's in a coma. No eyes! No movement! Nothing! Just lay there! Where's Burgess?"

"No, no, no! Don't bother Sam! I got it. No eyes. Ok. I'll just lay here."

"Can you do this please? You're costing me thousands of dollars not to mention years off my life!"

"No eyes. Got it. I'm ready on your mark."

Faline's hangover was dissipating. If they'd only been ready to shoot a couple of hours ago, she would still have been groggy enough she might have fallen asleep on set. But she had already taken her speed and her nerves were energizing. She reset and waited for the cue.

ACTION!

"It's still too early to tell what function she'll regain if any, Mr. Hart."

"If any?"

"I don't want to give you false hope."

"Doctor, are you saying she could remain a vegetable for the rest of her life?"

"If she doesn't start to show some improvement soon, you should consider gathering the family to decide what course you want to take."

"She has no other fam-..."

"CUT! I swear to God, get Burgess down here!"

The director barreled back through the door throwing down his script on the foot of Delia's bed.

"What the hell was *that*?"

"I didn't open my eyes, Michael. I just smiled ever so softly at Nathaniel's heart-felt admission of love for his long, lost daughter. Delia is in there somewhere, just *waiting* to come back to her daddy. Michael that was perfect timing."

"No, Faline. It wasn't. Perfect timing for a smile or to open your eyes is when we've written that *'Delia smiled'* or '*Delia opened her eyes'* but that hasn't been written into the script yet and at the rate you're going, you'll be lucky if it gets in there at all!"

The whole set was frozen until he finished berating the jittering star.

"Take FIVE!"

Production assistants cleared the set leading the actors to their dressing rooms and the Kraft services table for hydration, sustenance, and rest.

Michael stormed past Sam on his way onto the set.

"FIX IT!"

Sam smiled pulling up a prop chair to the bedside of his client.

"Honey, how's it going today?"

"They're not open to any feedback for my character, Sam. That's not what my contract says."

He held her bare knees, to keep her legs from swinging over the edge of the bed.

"That was your old contract, Faline."

She squinted at his face.

"Are you positive?"

"Yes, honey. That was seasons two, three, and four that you had creative license with the character but then several years ago, the studio offered you more money per episode if they could take that clause out, remember?"

She cocked her head and tapped her fingers on the bandage covering her I.V. prop.

"Oh yeah. Now I'm remembering."

She wasn't.

"You bought the condo with the raise; it was a good trade."

"It *was* a pretty good trade, Sammy."

"Yeah. So, you can't improvise, honey. You have to play the part as written."

He softened the blow as much as he could, but her eyes darted around wildly as the amphetamine took hold of her brain. The tempo of her voice accelerated, and she began to chitter like a rabid squirrel.

"Ok. I can do this. I'll just lay here. I just thought, how cool would it be to see through the glass behind Hart and the doctor, the beginnings of Delia coming around just as Hart is getting the news that she might not wake up…and maybe she only wakes up when no one else sees it…you know, just the audience, in the background of every scene and not any of the other players so it's just between the viewers and Delia…you know, a secret thing between my people out there rooting for me to wake up and me the comatose beauty waiting to be kissed awake or something like a fairytale…or…"

"Ok. O-ok, honey. I think we should pack it in for now. They probably aren't going to finish filming this scene today."

He helped her down from the bed and an assistant appeared to wrap a robe around her shoulders as they started for her dressing room. She prattled on and he glanced up at the booth to see the director, arms folded, following with his eyes as they turned the corner out of sight.

The next morning Sam arrived on set before his client and replaced the little white pills in the bottle she kept hidden in her dressing table with valium. She arrived moments later reeking of booze and barely awake.

"Good morning, Faline!"

"Shhhh!"

"Sorry."

She negotiated through swollen eyes.

"I need a minute, Sammy. Tell makeup and wardrobe to wait a second, ok?"

"Sure, honey."

He left her to her routine, and she sat in front of her reflection and examined her puffy face and blotchy skin. She leaned in for a closer look and pulled at her cheeks to tighten her flesh up and out into her hair. That ironed out the crepey bits but made the dark circles under her eyes much more prominent.

"What a hot mess you are MaryAnne O'Hara."

She opened the drawer and retrieved the tainted bottle her agent had just tampered with and shook one of the pills into her hand without even looking at it, then popped it into the back of her throat and swallowed it effortlessly with what little spit remained in her dry mouth. She signaled the waiting crew.

"Ok! Let's go!"

When the set was ready, Sam and an assistant walked her to the hospital bed and tucked her in.

Stagehands replaced the I.V. and turned on the prop meters and gages, then props came on set with an intubation tube.

"Miss Farah, Michael wants to add this piece to the takes today and see how it feels."

He checked her face for resistance and found none.

"Just hold this piece between your teeth and we'll tape the rest to your cheeks."

She glanced off stage at Sam and the director standing shoulder to shoulder next to the camera and flashed them a drowsy smile and a thumbs up, then complied with the instruction she'd been given and allowed them to plug her mouth and tape it shut. The crew positioned her, covered in the bed, and moved on to set up the rest of the actors for the scene.

By the time they were set to their marks, Faline was sound asleep and motionless.

ACTION!

"Since we've had to intubate her, there's been no change. And it's still too early to tell what function she'll regain if any, Mr. Hart."

"If any?"

"I don't want to give you false hope."

"Doctor, are you saying she could remain a vegetable for the rest of her life?"

"If she doesn't start to show some improvement soon, you should consider gathering the family to decide what course you want to take."

"She has no other family. And neither do I..."

"What is that sound? CUT!"

The director launched from his seat pulling his headphones off one ear as he scoured the stage for the source of a low rumbling din.

"Quiet on the set means just *that* people! Where is that coming from?"

"SNORT!"

"You have got to be kidding me! SAM! SHE'S SNORING!"

Burgess leapt from the booth and thundered toward the stage.

"I've got it, Michael!"

Sam rushed by the cast and crew to her bedside once more.

"Shhhh. Faline, honey."

He nudged her gently and her mouth fell open, the tape on her cheeks straining to hold her slacked jaw around the tube.

"That's it, damn it, Sam! Get her outta here!"

Sam abandoned his post at her side and traipsed after the fuming director confessing to the trick he attempted to pull with the valium to this unfortunate end. Faline slumbered on undisturbed and the remaining cast took another "FIVE".

Part Three

1995

Aggie's Second Chance

The sanding didn't stop right away just because the bell rang over the door. After eleven years, everyone in town knew to wait for Aggie to finish what she was doing before they expected her to surface from the back. She knew in an instant it was not one of her regulars when she heard a man's voice.

"Hello, in the shop!"

"I'll be right out!"

She blew the dust from the plank she was perfecting. Clapping the grit from her hands she walked through to the cleaner space and welcomed the stranger to Hupp's Hardwoods.

"Are you Maggie?"

"It's Aggie. Aggie O'Hanley."

She made a last effort to brush off what dirt remained on her hand before shaking his.

"Sorry. I must have heard them wrong. Allen Frank, pleasure to finally meet you."

"Who's them?"

"The guys at the Ace Hardware. They said you were the one to talk to about my projects."

"They did, did they? I'm sorry, did you say *projects*? Plural?"

"Yes!"

"Holy Mary, what have they volunteered me for now?"

"Oh, no. Aggie, I'd pay you."

"Ok, I'm listening."

She walked behind the counter and propped herself up to hear him out.

"I just bought the Morris place up on Canary Knob, just past the cemetery."

"Wow! I didn't know that property was for sale. That house has to be a hundred years old."

"One hundred seven this year. It was built in the summer of 1888."

The man opened a large mailing envelope and spilled photographs in a pile on the counter. They both began to sift through the pictures.

"The realtor said the main house had solid bones, whatever that means but it needs a lot of work."

"Yes. It looks like it."

"I want to restore it, to make it a country retreat for when I want to get out of the city."

She eyed his clean, expensive boots and the creases in his jeans.

"New York City?"

"Yes. I live in Manhattan and work downtown, but I took the summer off to dive into this project and I need someone to help me."

"You want me to *help*?"

She was trying not to castrate this man with her superior knowledge of all things Aggie Rose, a tendency her wife had pointed out to her again, just recently. She gestured to the pictures.

"So, *you* want to do all this work, and you want me to *help*?"

"Alright now."

"I mean, why don't you just hire it done? You just bought a couple hundred acres of farmland in upstate New York for a summer home, surely you can afford to hire this work done."

"I get it. City mouse, country mouse. I don't think you quite understand what I'm after here."

He picked up one of the photos and studied it for a second then tossed it on top of the others and tried again.

"I *could* just have it done, you're right. But I want to learn how to do the work with my own hands. I am forty-eight years old and I've never done more than change a light bulb."

"So, this is your mid-life crisis project?"

"Sure."

He laughed at himself but then taking a minute to think, agreed completely.

"I think you've nailed it, no pun intended."

"None taken."

She looked through the photos again.

"This is a lot. I mean, are you prepared to get into it all? There's plumbing and electrical, plastering, tons of wood restoration, and if you're going to tackle that garden, that's pavers and concrete. You'll be building a house in essence."

"Everything but the bones, right? The realtor said it came with bones."

"I can't say for sure, without looking it over, but I'd guess it comes with some pretty hearty bones."

He challenged her.

"Well…you up for it?"

She thought about what her dad would say, smiled at the man, and extended her hand again.

"Why not?"

Frank vigorously shook her strong but beautiful hand, and she closed the shop and followed him in her truck just out of the city limits to Canary Knob to survey the project.

The first summer with Allen Frank, Aggie worked harder than she ever had. They started with the roof, repairing holes, installing vents and shingles. Then they replaced the windows in the attic. They worked as fast as Ace Hardware could order supplies and by the time Allen went back to the city, the place was weather proofed enough to leave it for the winter.

They kept in contact until spring, planning and ordering more materials and the weekend after Easter he was back on his property eager to begin again.

They started on the second story, knocking tracts out in the plaster walls to uncover the old cloth-wrapped wiring behind it. They replaced fuse boxes with breakers and wired the gas light fixtures for electric. Now they could work after dark…and they did!

The second summer proved more fun and less physically demanding. She taught Allen the art of plaster mixing and repair, they blew in insulation, then they got started on the woodwork, her favorite!

They repaired the hardwood floors they could salvage and replaced what they couldn't with aged wood scouted from other old home places of that era. He really did have the financial resources to do it right, and now Allen could also say he did the work himself, with a little help.

It was the 'help' quizzing him one day while waiting for a coat of stain to dry on a bedroom floor that started a snowball to roll. She poured them some lemonade from her thermos.

"Allen, you said you worked for that financial firm in the city, but you didn't tell me what you do."

"Oh yeah. So, we essentially raise capital for people wanting to create a product or business. There's a transportation line that invests in cruise companies and chartered bus lines, an energy division that is looking to sponsor solar and wind producers, and an entertainment division for TV and movies."

"That's a diversified company."

"Yes. We handle just about everything."

"Which division are you in?"

"I'm in TV. I'm an executive producer."

"So, you raise money for pilots to be made?"

"Yes. That's an aspect of my job that not very many people know about."

"I was just a few credits short of my master's in communication at North Western when my mom got sick and I had to leave school."

She gathered the condensation from her cold drink and wiped it across her forehead and down her neck.

"I wanted to be a talk show host."

"You? A talk show host?"

She shot him a scowl.

"What's wrong with that?"

"I can't see you dressed in a skirt and blazer sitting on a living room set interviewing celebrities about their rehabs and break-ups and fitness tapes."

She thought about the wardrobe and the set and the fact that she'd never considered her 'style' not being the kind that translated to the talk show format.

"Besides, they're overdone. Oprah will never be beat and really who's going to give a talk show to a sweet but mildly butch gay girl from nowhere? This is the reason I keep taking these summer sabbaticals. I can't come up with anything original that's safe enough to produce. Everything's been done."

He paused in thought for a moment.

"Now a home improvement show with a female host, I could definitely see that working."

Just then, as if they were animated by a low, steady current, Aggie and Allen began to contemplate the possibility they'd stumbled on to. He turned to her squinting in the sun.

"It could be a how-to kind of thing where the host tackled minor and even some major home improvements all on her own."

Aggie joined in.

"She'd have to use all the right tools and techniques. She'd have to have a knowledge of wood and electricity, and plumbing, and…"

"And she'd have to be an all-American type; red-headed, green-eyed. Opie-frickin'-Taylor! Holy shit, Aggie, are we on to something here?"

Allen was standing now in the shade of the porch and Aggie spun around on the five-gallon plaster bucket she'd been resting on to face him.

"Where could we film it?"

"Right here!"

He stepped back into the house to survey for camera angles and lighting opportunities. She followed.

"It would be *This Old House* meets *The Woodwright's Shop*!"

His enthusiasm infected her, and she began to visualize the whole thing.

"Could we feature the shop?"

"Hell yes!"

He was on fire for it now.

"You can take pieces back to the shop to recreate newel posts or banisters, or whatever was the finial of the day. You could demonstrate proper painting and staining technique. You could do little plumbing tutorials before updating a sink or a tub. Aggie, this could be the biggest thing since game shows!"

A wide smile spread out across her face and she waited for his formal proposal.

"Aggie Rose O'Hanley, do you want to create a do-it-yourself show with me?"

She was already there.

"I do!"

»«

Aggie returned to her family with the news that her career in television just might not be a pipedream after all and they were elated.

Bill was full of questions about production and royalties; insisting that Aggie let her call a friend from school who had become an entertainment attorney to look over all the contracts before she signed anything. Thatcher was stoked that his Ma was going to be a star! And Eloise, though she didn't have a complete understanding of everything her daughter was explaining to her, was none the less thrilled by the contagious excitement the news created in the house. She was grateful that she was around to see Agatha Rose so happy. After all her sacrifices for everyone else, she was taking her turn.

The phone calls began back and forth to the network of writers and directors in the city. Aggie and Allen inventoried the jobs they had left in his house alone and came up with enough ideas for more than a dozen episodes. They hired Allen's favorite photographer to come and do Aggie's headshots on location at the shop and in the house. They put a pitch together and made an appointment in the city.

Aggie Rose was a knockout in her jeans and flannel, but when she dressed for the trip to Allen's office, she looked stunning. She tamed her wild, red mane into soft waves that hung just below her graceful neck. She wore a sky-blue shirt and a dark brown pinstriped suit that fit her like a glove, accentuating all her curves. After Bill did her make up, she drove herself to the train station, and she was on her way.

Allen met her train and had a car waiting to take them downtown to their meeting. Aggie took in the walls of glass, metal, and concrete that bordered the avenues and felt the tiniest thrill when a flash of memory took her back to preparing for the senior trip she missed a lifetime ago. The tall buildings and mobs of pedestrians made her miss Chicago. They arrived at their destination and walked past security and executive secretaries until they reached the board room. She would wait outside until he made the pitch and then he'd send for her as the big reveal. She was tingling.

It wasn't as long as she anticipated, and an assistant came for her. She walked into the rectangular space and Allen stood, arms out, to present her.

"And this…is the face of the show!"

The room was still. She smiled nervously.

"Hello. I'm Aggie Rose O'Hanley."

Crickets…

Then the gray-haired man at the head of the table spoke.

"Do it again like you'd do it on the show."

She knew in an instant where to go with it. She took her blazer off and laid it over the back of the nearest chair and began rolling up her sleeves. She spied a rubber band on the conference table next to a couple of paperclips in front of one of the board members. She snatched it up with a wink and pulled her gorgeous red hair up on top of her head, then set herself.

"Hi! I'm Aggie Rose and this - is *Just DIY*!"

Allen repeated the gesture of presenting her. No air moved.

Then the gray-haired man responded.

"Yeah…ok…I'm starting to see how it could work. Thanks Allen. We'll call you."

The rest of the room began to hum in collective agreement as Allen gathered her coat and walked out with her. His car took them to a coffee shop near the train station. They went in and sat down to decompress.

"It was so quick! Can they really decide on just that little bit of time with me?"

"That's how it's done, Aggie."

"Brother, I've taken longer to order a meat sandwich!"

"The pitch was sharp and succinct, just the way they like'em. And you, Miss O'Hanley, were superb!"

He had never expected her to run with the prompt she was given. Even with her exposure from college, not everyone can perform on the spot like she had. She was a natural. He was seeing dollar signs.

They parted at the station and the whole way back to West Fort Ann, Aggie dreamed about the near future. She could marry her love of working with her hands with her long-lost love of TV. Her head was swimming with possibilities. She was once again on the cusp of having it all.

The family prepared a fresh leg of lamb with all the trimmings for supper that night and after the dishes were put away, homework checked, and showers taken, Aggie and Bill crawled into bed together tired out, but too excited to sleep.

They pulled in close and took in one another's scent. They whispered I love yous into each other's ears and traded kisses on lobes and necks until their passion closed the space between them. They kissed and tumbled under the cool sheets, touching and tasting tongues, breasts, and inner thighs. They entered and rubbed and teased, their breath heating their skin. Deeper and deeper, tender and safe, they played hard at holding wrists while tongues flickered, and lips dripped with sweet, salty sex. Each woman arching and quivering at the hand of her wife, dropped off the edge of craving and into satisfaction and then they lay sweating and spent, still tangled together.

When their bodies cooled, they settled into their sleeping spots; Aggie on her back with an arm hooked around her sweet wife, Bill resting her head on Aggies chest. Bill was out in an instant and Aggie stared at dancing shadows of the trees outside her window, cast on the ceiling by the barn light.

Her path was coming up to meet her. She ignored her calling long enough and now she would take the road she passed up the year her dad died, and finally be in sync with the universe again.

What a long road back to her truth.

Bill snored quietly in the crook of her arm. Aggie looked down at her peaceful face, kissed her eyes, and then closed her own and let sleep come in and relieve her busy brain and grateful heart.

Faline's Last Chance

"She is only the twenty-seventh makeup professional to be assigned to you, Faline. Can you please just let her do her job?"

"I need better work, Sam!"

Examining herself in the mirror, Faline pointed out dark circles under her eyes and sagging lids and crow's feet.

"This shit can be covered up. I know it can!"

"No matter how much makeup you cake on, you can't hide the damage you've done to yourself with the smoking and drinking and the pills, Faline. You're asking for a miracle!"

Her eyes welled with rage and she steamed.

"Get out!"

"With pleasure!"

He left and slammed the door. She jumped, and swallowed angry tears, and screeched into the empty room.

"Fuck this place! I shouldn't look like this at thirty-five! This place is killing me!"

She reached in her bag for her flask and tipped it back. The familiar burn to the back of her throat soothed her and she took in a deep breath through her nose. One more big swig and she'd let the makeup girl back in. Ok…one more. She replaced the flask and opened the door poking her head out into the hall.

"Makeup! I'm ready!"

Sam sat in Michael's office for the umpteenth time discussing her latest offenses and what measures they might have to take in order to keep her on the show.

They remembered a nearly three-year-long stint in the middle of her patchy sobriety, when the actor who played Nathanial Hart died in real life and the producers thought it would be a good idea to move Faline into the lead role since the story line indicated that her character was the only true heir to his fortune. But shortly thereafter, she began drinking again, which led to the pills again, and they had been struggling to keep her ever since.

"She made us sorry for that decision too. And you're out of favors, Sam."

"I know. I don't even know why I'm still doing this, to be honest. I hate her guts! I know I shouldn't say that out loud, but I do. I hate her God damned guts sometimes."

"I know, man. Remember when she first started?"

Sam smiled nodding.

"I do."

"Sam, she was so sweet and grateful for everything."

"*So* sweet. And humble!"

Michael remembered and shook his head.

"*So* humble! What happens to these people? It's not every one, you know?"

Sam thought of some of his other clients fondly and then shook his head.

"I know. You're right. Some of them stay grounded and authentic their whole career. But not the drunks."

"Is that the only thing, you think?"

"It's pretty consistent, Michael. I've worked with a lot of people in this business and just about everyone can handle the fame except the addicts."

"But it must be the combination of the fame and the addiction because I know lots of alcoholics who aren't famous who make it to work every day and live productive lives. Hell, my old man was a drunk and never missed a day of work!"

Neither of the two men were getting any closer to solving their problem. They were both just looking for some logical place to start. Michael made an attempt.

"Ok…so Delia has had the fall and is in another coma. And she's done throwing a fit about that, right?"

"Who cares at this point, really?"

"I need to know she's not going to pitch a bitch on set today, Sam."

"Your guess is as good as mine, Michael. What if she does? Her contract is good clear through these last thirty-two episodes. I'm sure the producers don't want to buy her out before the end of the season."

"I can't ask the rest of the cast to endure anymore of her tantrums or adlibs. I *will* take action!"

"What is there left to do?"

"I have one more trick up my sleeve that will spare the crew and save us from breaching her contract. But you have to back me up, understand?"

"Michael, regardless of how she reacts, this is my last season representing Faline Farah. So, do your worst. I'm already on my way out."

Sam pushed himself to standing and extended his hand in conspiracy against his client.

"Whatever you plan on doing to her, she probably deserves ten times worse. I'm behind you all the way."

They shook on it.

They began the shoot on the hospital set where Delia lay intubated, waiting to see if and when she would wake up. The actors that played her children gathered outside the I.C.U. observation window lamenting the argument they'd had with their mother the night she fell.

ACTION!

"I wish I could go back to that night, Brett."

"Sonya, you can't beat yourself up like that. This isn't anyone's fault."

"But you didn't see her face when I told her about the baby, Brett. I hurt her. She was genuinely hurt."

"You're giving her entirely too much credit, Sonya."

"What are you saying?"

"She wasn't hurt. She was mortified that her daughter got pregnant at sixteen!"

"No, Brett. You weren't there."

"I didn't have to be. I know our mother! She's never thought about anyone but herself. She doesn't care about us. She sure as hell doesn't care about some illegitimate ba-..."

"CUT! Get in there!"

Michael interrupted the scene and motioned to a figure sitting at the ready in the shadows off stage.

"Faline, stay put. Everybody else take FIVE."

"What Michael? I am just lying here like the corpse you people have made me into. What am I doing wrong now?"

"Seriously? You're going to play dumb? Spit it out!"

He presented his hand under her chin and she pushed a wintergreen Lifesaver from between her pursed lips.

"My stomach was upset. I needed a peppermint."

"You were trying to mask the smell of liquor on your breath. This isn't the first time you've pulled this trick, Faline. Did you think we wouldn't notice you sucking on a mint while you were in a coma?"

He waved the surprise figure onto the stage and positioned him in the far corner of the set to get the whole hospital room in his lens.

"Ok. Back to your one, Faline."

"What's this, promotional stills? Nice touch, Michael! What is this for TV Guide or something?"

She wiggled down into the covers and set herself to the beginning of the scene again and the photographer snapped shot after shot from everywhere in the room. When he finished, the director had them run through the scene again for rehearsal and wrapped for the day. The photos were developed, and enlargements were produced just as Michael had directed. The next day, he would reveal his plan for Faline for the rest of the season.

Sam waited in her dressing room with an uncomfortable amount of joy in his heart. After nearly two decades of worrying how she'd react to the various consequences of her abusive, narcissistic, egotistical rants, he was finally done. He couldn't wait to deliver the news to her. She would flip out and he was all out of give-a-damn about it. He rubbed his hands together in anticipation and chirped at her when she entered, hungover…again.

"Morning Faline!"

She opened one of her squinting eyes wider to take in her agent's strangely cheerful affect.

"Morning. What are you so chipper for this morning? Did you sell another piece of my soul last night or something?"

"No. But I do have good news."

She took off her sunglasses and looked at him, waiting.

"Well? Are you going to share this good news?"

"We're on vacation!"

"Say what now?"

"We can take off until the finale. Michael has it all planned out."

"Michael has what all plan -…they can't kill me off, I have a contract! That fuckin' Michael!"

"No! Faline, they are not going to kill you."

"What then?"

"They're using the stills they took on set last night for all Delia's scenes until the finale."

"Wait, what?"

"Yep. You are only going to be featured through the I.C.U. window so Michael just took the stills and had them enlarged and *they* will be what the camera sees in the background of all Delia's scenes until the finale at the end of the season."

"And then what?"

A smile unfurled across the years of wrinkles and age spots and gray facial hair Sam earned taking this woman's shit for eighteen years and he drew a calming breath.

"*Then,* they are going kill you."

She sat stock still in front of her mirror. He watched her reflection from behind. He saw an immediate change. He assumed it was the aura that usually signaled an oncoming fit, but nothing happened. Something *had* changed though. She instantly looked smaller, less threatening, almost vulnerable, though the word 'pathetic' came to his mind in the moment.

She stared into her own eyes and gave up.

"So, they're finally going to get rid of her. Who couldn't have seen this coming?"

Sam suddenly felt guilty for taking such pleasure in telling her and searched his tired heart for some message of encouragement, some shred of hope. He came up empty. She stood and replaced her sunglasses.

"I'll go home and wait to hear what my final scene will entail. Sam, you know where I'll be."

Compromise and Consolation

She had been trying not to jump for the phone every time it rang but Aggie was getting more and more anxious to hear from Allen. He warned that it could be weeks or even months before they heard definitively from the board, but he was encouraged it would be sooner than later. Her hope diminishing with every day she didn't hear from him, she started letting the answering machine pick up.

She listened to the rings until the recorded message began and then she got quiet to hear what came after the beep.

"Aggie, if you're there pick up!"

It was Allen. She scrambled from the workbench to the phone.

"I've got good news. Call me when -…"

She lunged for the phone, fumbling it to the floor.

"I'm here! Don't hang up, Allen! I'm here!"

"You ok?"

"Just dropped the phone. What good news? I'm dying here!"

"Sorry. Yes, good news! No! Great news!"

"What?"

"And also, some not-so-great but still good news."

"Oh my God! Enough already! Allen, did we get it?"

"You are talking to the executive producer of *Just DIY*, televisions first female hosted do-it-yourself show!"

"We did it! They bought it!"

Aggie danced in place behind the counter, thrilled, and then she stopped short.

"Wait…what's the not-so-great news?"

"But still good! Not great but not awful either."

"Allen!"

"Ok…so, they want the show to be live."

"Live?"

She took it in for a second.

"I love it! The other guys never do that! But I sure can!"

Aggie had no qualms about a live show; she was great in the moment and she was rock solid in her skills.

"Why would you call that bad news?"

"Not bad. Just not great. I thought that might be a negative for you. But hey, if you love it, I love it."

He paused.

"There is just one more thing though."

She giggled.

"Oh. The *really* not great news?"

"Yeah."

"I was kidding. What's the rest of it, Allen?"

He tiptoed in.

"So, they loved you…"

"Yes?"

"But they want someone to co-host with you."

"Like an assistant?"

"No more like a color man."

"A man?"

"Just an expression, don't burn your bra!"

He tempered his delivery and waded in slowly so as not to insult his partner further.

"They want to balance your strength with a more feminine touch."

"Like a pretty gameshow assistant, or someone practical to hand me tools or hold the ladder?"

"No. Not exactly."

"Well what, exactly?"

"So, they want to add an arts and crafts portion to the fix-it-up stuff."

"Ok. What would that look like?"

"Well, you would say, repair some damaged plaster for the main part of the show, and then your co-host would use the same material to create a sculpture of something."

"None of the male-hosted home shows have an arts and crafts portion to them, Allen. They wouldn't ask a man to make a craft project!"

He sat silently and let her work it out in her head.

Was she willing to cow tow to the machismo in the industry to create this new platform for women? The first female Phil Donahue? The first female Norm Abram? Did this detail cancel out everything she'd be bringing to the show? No. The answer was clearly, no.

"Ok."

"Ok? Ok? I was sure I'd have to sell you a little harder on that part, but ok!"

"Well, I mean, as long as I get to do my part, I don't care what else has to happen. The very first female-hosted, live home repair show, ever!"

"Right? Great!"

Allen breathed a sigh of relief and returned to the details he called to convey.

"We couldn't get a buy in from the national market, so we tried the local PBS station, but they already have their line-up in place for next year. So, we're just starting out with a local cable hookup to get a season under our belts."

"That doesn't sound bad. No traveling?"

"No. Everything will be done locally, in the shop or at my place for the first season. You never know who will see this and want to pick it up. The possibilities are endless, Aggie. I'm stoked!"

"Me too! When do we start?"

"I'm waiting for a call back from TV8 out of Glenn Falls for the schedule, but our production crew is assembling as we speak. We need you to make a list of materials and logistics for the projects so we can start mapping out production. We need scripts for the whole season complete by the end of the year. Do you think you can be ready to start broadcasting in the spring?"

"Sure! I'm ready now but what about this cohost person, Allen?"

"I'm not sure which way they want us to go with that. I'll ask the TV8 people if there's a local celebrity or news person who would be suitable. You don't happen to know anyone famous do you?"

Sarcastically, Aggie dropped the only name she knew.

"Well, I don't like to brag but I did go to high school with Faline Farah."

"Whoa! Yeah but isn't she like a nightmare to work with or something?"

"Probably. I was only kidding; we haven't spoken in years."

"Still, I heard that they were penciling her into the script on her soap because she's so impossible. Could you imagine that drama on live TV?!"

The two erupted in laughter and, quickly, the conversation switched to the definites and away from the hypotheticals and ended with Aggie and Allen excited for the coming months to pass. She wished she could have been serious about asking MaryAnne to do it. What fun! But what she knew of her old friend was long gone and what she knew of Faline Farah was that she wouldn't even come back to Lake George for her own mother's funeral. She surely wouldn't be returning to be on a do-it-yourself show on local cable TV. She put the thought to bed and set herself for her debut.

One Last Last-Chance

The buzzer to her apartment rang and she leaned into the button with her shoulder, both hands full of wet delicates, to bark at the doorman.

"What Tony?"

"Miss Farah, Mr. Burgess is here to see you."

"Alright."

She shifted her bundle and freed a hand to unlock the door. It drifted open a crack and she kept on to the balcony where she intended to hang her things. She heard the elevator "ding" just as she stepped outside, and Sam was in her foyer seconds later.

She dumped the lump of clothes on her patio table and motioned to him to join her on the terrace. He obliged.

"Good to see you out, Faline! Beautiful day, huh?"

"Beautiful, Sam."

She plucked the cigarette from her teeth that had dangled there the whole way through the apartment and opened up the conversation.

"What's up?"

"What's up? What's up she wants to know."

"Yes, Sam. I know you didn't come all the way uptown to help me with my intimates."

She shook a bra free from the pile, wiggled it at him, and draped it over the arm of a wrought iron chair then reached for another.

"Ha! You got that right, Faline, honey. I sure didn't come all the way-…"

"Spill it Sam. What do you want?"

"Michael is ready to start on the finale."

"What?"

The cigarette fell out of her mouth and landed in her laundry. He jumped to the rescue and grabbed it up even though it had gone out as soon as it hit the mound of wet silk. He fussed with the ashes and uncovered an ashtray in which to snub the butt while she acquiesced.

"Well, we knew this was coming, eh old friend?"

Sam was leery of her response; so calm, so resigned. He hung in suspense and watched her face. She turned toward the city and stood resting her hands on the railing, quieted and still. He walked toward her and placed a hand on hers.

"You knew what to expect when he laid it out mid-season, Faline."

"No. I know. I guess I just thought I could get one more reprieve, you know. One more last chance to stay."

"Everyone has their limits."

She jerked her hand away.

"Boy! You didn't come to help with the laundry, and you didn't come to mince words."

She walked back inside in search of another cigarette. He followed her in and watched while she lit up.

"I came here to tell you; you are under contract to appear at the studio this coming Monday to tape your final episode of *Hart's Desire.* And then we're done."

She exhaled, the smoke filling the space between them.

"What's this now? What do you mean *we're* done?"

"Faline, I have served you faithfully for years. I have taught you, fought you, and nursed you through your entire career. A career I dare say you may never even have had if it weren't for me!"

Now he was pacing.

"I've struggled with this Faline, I really have. But I can't go on representing you once your contract with the soap is up."

He stopped moving and faced her.

"I'm sorry."

She sat down hard on one of the overstuffed sofa's in her well-appointed living room and looked around, cataloging all the material things she'd amassed in her career. In an instant her mind kicked over to money and she wondered how she'd be able to keep these things she loved or the apartment for that matter without the soap.

"Sam, we'll find something else. I'll do anything. Commercials. Talk shows. Hell hook me up with a game show, that's always a safe bet between gigs."

Her voice sounded soft in her head. She felt more of an urgency than her tone was conveying and turned it up a notch.

"Something, Sam. Please find me something. Don't just drop me after all this time. I won't know what to do with myself."

"I can't keep throwing myself under your buses, Faline."

He felt sorry but promised himself not to cave in this time.

"I've tried. I have tried to think of some way we could stay connected and still protect my sanity, but I just can't. You're not my only client you know."

"I know. I know, Sammy. I've taken a lot of your attention over the years. It's only right that you want to spend more time and effort on some of your other people. It's all good."

She sounded desperate now.

"Just put me on the back burner for now. You can all but forget about me for a little while if you want. I won't ask for anything else, I promise. Just don't let me go. I don't have anyone else, Sam. You're my only friend."

The trouble with actors, good ones at least is that you can never tell when they're sincere. But Sam knew this was the real Faline. He hadn't seen this level of pain and fear in her since she was seventeen. It's what caught his eye; her honestly broken heart. Everything after that had been an act. An act that afforded them both the luxury to which they'd become accustomed. But now she was that broken-hearted teenager again all of a sudden. Only this time he didn't want to cash in on it, he wanted to run. He shook his head and looked down at the tops of his shoes, tracing his eyebrows with his fingertips.

"Faline, I told myself nothing…nothing! I promised myself, this would be the end of things."

She leaned forward on the couch, smudging her butt out in the ashtray on the glass top coffee table in front of her. She folded her hands, bowed her head, and waited while he struggled.

"I told my wife. I told my secretary. I told myself over and over again. No matter what she says, don't do it. Don't give in. Don't let her change your mind. Not for any reason, Sam. Nothing!"

He finished arguing with himself and stood over her like an angry parent. He wouldn't put any effort into it. He wouldn't lose any sleep. He wouldn't even take her calls. But he'd keep her on the books.

"If anything comes across my desk that I think you won't screw up, I'll call you. But that's the extent of my involvement. Do you understand me?"

She stood without looking at him and put her arms around his neck and just held on. She knew exactly where they both were and what this meant to them.

"I'll be at the studio Monday. Thank you, Sammy."

Monday came and just as she promised, Faline Farah arrived on time at the studio where she had worked her entire career as the character Delia Blackwell. She tried hard not to recognize the finality of the day's events but somewhere in her heart she knew this was not just the end of her run on *Hart's Desire;* this could be the end of everything. She fought back the dread and put her best face forward.

She was uncharacteristically kind to the makeup artist assigned to her as well as the costume assistant who drew the short straw. She glanced at the script for effect, even though she knew she'd have no lines or even open her eyes for the duration of Delia's last scenes. And when the bell rang, she took one last look in the mirror and bid a silent goodbye to the woman whose skin she'd been hiding in since leaving St. James Academy.

The set was subdued. Michael stayed out of reach and whispered his direction to his assistant who came on stage and, in turn, whispered direction to the players. She gently handled Faline by the elbow and lead her to bed. The crew set the props in play and the set was cleared.

ACTION!

The actors had begun their lines, gathered around her bedside in I.C.U. but Michael's voice calling the scene into 'ACTION!' was still ringing in her ears. This sound, this tone was what she was born to respond to; like a priest's calling, animating her character into life every season.

That one word, 'ACTION!' and she was no longer a confused, bastard orphan from some obscure country town in the Adirondacks. That word transformed her into who she chose to be. That one word she took for granted every day of her career until today. And today, it rang in her brain as if Quasimodo was pulling the rope himself. “Sanctuary! Sanctuary!” she thought. This place, this set, these people, Sam, and Delia, it had all been her sanctuary. Where would she go now?

“Brett if there’s no hope of saving her, I know she wouldn’t want us to keep her alive for our sakes.”

“And Sonya if we can save one life with her organs, then we have to let her go, so that her life will have some purpose.”

(Another patient wheeled into frame.)

“And she is a perfect match for me, Kenton Blackwell. Because she is my mother too.”

“Aaannd CUT!”

Funny, but ‘CUT’ didn’t ring the same bell. Not this time at least. Faline, eyes open watching the actors reset, stayed put in her hospital bed while the stagehands tweaked the props and readied for the next scene. This time Michael approached the stage and addressed the cast directly.

“Ok, now this is the big event. You’re all agonizing over this decision to let Delia go. Even Brett who never forgave her for having an affair with his best friend from tenth grade, and Sonya who she competed against her whole life. And now here’s Kenton, who she gave up at birth because she was only a homeless teenager, and even though he’ll never know her, she’s giving him a second chance at life by donating her heart to replace his.”

He paused and turned his face toward Faline’s.

"This is it. And no matter how hard this decision is, it must be made."

She kept eye contact with the only director in the business with whom she'd ever worked. This set, *his* set was her home, and they were saying their final goodbyes the only way they could.

"Ok?"

She bowed her head in agreement.

He returned the respect.

The set was cleared, and Delia's death scene commenced.

ACTION!

The scene began with a tight shot on the clipboard to which Sonya and Brett were signing their consent to disconnect Delia's life support. Brett began to cry and fell over his mother's legs and held on. Sonya moved to his side and placed a comforting hand on her brother's back. Kenton wheeled up to the other side of the bed and held Delia's hand in his, weeping.

The doctor entered, read the consent, and walked over to the ventilator. Camera on his face and then the control panel of the vent. He turned one knob, then another, and then looked at Delia one last time, and flipped the final switch. The machine's hum quieted and then went silent and the only thing heard on set was the *'beep…beep…beep'* of her heart monitor.

The actors remained on their marks and the camera zoomed to Delia's face where a single tear escaped the corner of Faline's eye and disappeared into her hair. The truest bit of honest work, in her whole career, literally in her last moments on set.

"Beep…beep…beeeeeeeeeeeeeeeeeppppp."

Flatline.

The doctor reached over Sonya's shoulder and turned off the monitor.

"Aaaaaannnnddd CUT!"

Now 'CUT' rang like 'ACTION' and she lay still for just another moment letting the words fall to the bottom of her empty mind.

Michael was pleased.

"Great job, everybody! Great job!"

She opened her eyes, and the cast and crew were all standing and looking at her. It was Michael who began the applause. Soon the entire sound stage was thundering. Faline arose from her deathbed and took one final bow. Awash with the respect she knew she only partially deserved, she returned the applause to her coworkers and humbly exited the stage to the safety of her dressing room. Once inside, she sat down in front of her mirror for the last time and took a good look at the woman in the reflection.

"End of a run, MaryAnne. What's next?"

She waited for tears or rage or some extreme to erupt, but she couldn't react. She stared blankly into her own eyes and thought about everything and nothing at the same time.

"You look like you could use a drink, sister."

»«

Rumors circulated leading up to the season finale about whether or not Delia would make it out of the coma, but once the final episode aired, the industry reporters were all over it, igniting Faline's life like a brushfire. She naturally contacted her broker and her lawyer to review her assets and make provisions should she remain unemployed for a stretch. They showed her how poorly her stocks had done and how she'd probably need to liquidate some real estate if she wanted to remain in New York. She agreed to sell the vacation home in Maui, the condo in Vale, and two of the three cars she owned but never once drove. She'd keep the champagne Cadillac and the penthouse, but she'd get rid of the original artwork and sell out her half of the restaurant she silently partnered. This would afford her the next two years expenses and surely in that time, she'd be working steadily again.

The hiatus ended and the day-time lineup commenced without her for the first time in her adult life. She tried to watch the show but couldn't. She called into Sam's office twice a month only to get transferred to his voice mail every time. She worked hard at leaving these messages before she began drinking for the day but after she'd gargled and warmed her voice up for a half-hour or so, to give the impression she was keeping her instrument in tune.

That first winter was brutal. She stayed inside for weeks at a time but ordering takeout food and paying extra for the delivery boys to stop at the liquor store proved an expensive proposition. Her real estate sales hadn't yielded what she'd hoped, and her funds were dwindling faster than anticipated. When her HOA check bounced in the spring, the super called Sam, who for better or worse made the trip to her apartment to see what could be done.

"Come in, Sam!"

She beamed throwing herself around his neck.

"It's so good to see you! Hell, it's good to see anyone! It's been a long winter. How are you?"

He patted her insincerely then untangled himself.

"I'm good, Faline. I'm doing just fine."

"You look good. Come in. Sit, sit."

"I have a car waiting downstairs, I can only stay for a minute."

She followed behind him into the living room, breathing into her palm to check her breath.

"I got a call from your building that your check bounced."

"What? I don't know what you're talking about."

"You can cut the act, Faline. You know we have the same broker. He told me you're already running out of money. You need to get serious about this. You need to stop spending."

Flushed with embarrassment, she defended herself.

"I need to work, Sam. I'm not spending that much. I never go out anymore. I haven't bought any new clothes in months; I don't even drive my car!"

"No but I bet you're never out of liquor for more than a minute-and-a-half are you?"

He launched himself from the sofa and trodded into the kitchen throwing cabinet doors open. She remained in her seat bracing for his discovery.

"Empty!" - SLAM. "Empty!" – SLAM.

He found no food, or staples in her whole kitchen, unless he counted the left-over takeout condiment packets. Instinctively, he proceeded into the pantry where he uncovered a mound of empty bottles hidden out of sight, spilling over the garbage cans.

"Aaaand EMPTY!!"

He smoothed his hands over his hairless, heating head and slowed his breathing while she sat motionless in the other room waiting for him to return. He grabbed hold of the louvered doors and kicked the pile of bottles to release the fraction of his anger he was afraid might lead him to actually hurt her. He waited for his pulse to quiet and then shrugged his upper body back into his suit and returned to her.

"Do you feel better now that you've caught me?"

"No. I haven't felt better since 1978. But that's on me."

"I'm sorry, Sam. I drink because I have nothing else to do."

"You have nothing to do because you drink!"

"Find me something and I'll quit!"

"Bullshit!"

He turned to leave, and she jumped up to block his exit.

"Ok! You're right. I'm sorry!"

She held his coat sleeves and set herself to keep him from the door.

"Please, Sam. I need your help."

"I've tried to help you, Faline. I've tried for years to help. I've tried so long, I'm not even sure I know what that means anymore."

"I know. I know how hard you've worked. I know."

He freed his coat sleeves.

"Do you? Do you know, Faline? Do you know the nights I slept on your floor, held your hair while you vomited, missed events with my own family to square your legal claims? Do you really know what I've done for you?"

She slumped in shame.

"No, sir."

"*That* may be the most honest thing you've ever said to me."

He shook his head and fished his hands through the change in his pants pockets to keep from slapping her. She stood fast, humbled, as he turned away arguing internally with himself for ever taking her as a client in the first place. She broke through, sheepishly.

"Sam?"

"I will loan you this money, ONCE!"

He held his finger in front of her face in a stiff threat.

"ONCE! Do you hear me?"

"Yes."

"And I have ONE job - …"

"What? A job? You didn't tell me there was a job. Oh Sam, thank you! Thank you!"

"Don't thank me yet, you don't know what it is."

"I don't care what it is. It's work and I'll do it! So, is it another soap? No. A commercial? A gameshow! I'm sure those are fun at least and I'll get my face out there again. Oh Sam, I'm so excited! What is it?"

The Reunion

The crew had arrived in town just as the trees were beginning to bloom, setting a picturesque backdrop for the show. Aggie and Allen had been hard at work with the writers and sponsors and the details were coming together beautifully.

With the first episode set to air that Saturday afternoon, Allen arrived at the farm early Wednesday evening just before the crew broke for the day. He popped out of his car in the drive.

"Aggie! Aggie! Can you come out here, honey?"

She looked confused at the camera man and boom operator in the dining room with her.

"Honey? Did he just call me 'honey'?"

They shrugged and she and the whole crew exited the house and stood on the wide, wrap around porch shielding their eyes against the late, afternoon sun. Aggie called back to mock him.

"What's up, *honey*?"

A champagne Cadillac lurched its way up the dirt drive.

"I've got a surprise for you, Aggie!"

He beamed and raced to the driver's door of the Caddy, swinging it open.

"Tada!"

And out stepped Faline Farah.

The moment hung in the sweet spring air, stuck to the scent of the lilacs. Faline bowed and a round of applause erupted from all hands on deck.

All hands with the exception of Aggie's.

She couldn't believe what she was seeing. Allen took Faline by the arm and walked her up what length remained of the drive to the walk, then stopped at the foot of the steps to the porch.

"May I present, Miss Faline Farah, your new co-host for *Just DIY*."

He bowed ceremoniously and missed the shock on Aggie's face.

"Faline, this is Ag - …"

"We've met! As a matter of fact, I told you months ago, Allen, MaryAnne –…"

"I go by Faline, hun."

"Miss Farah and I went to high school together."

Faline, who genuinely didn't realize who she was talking to, was trying to impress.

"No, darling you must have me confused with someone else. I was born near here, but I went to a private school way up North. You wouldn't know it."

Aggie widened her stance, and her hands found her hips.

"St. James Academy in Chateaugay. It's me MaryAnne. It's Aggie Rose."

She tore her sunglasses away from her puffy eyes and took another look at the woman in front of her. Slack jawed, she skipped up the steps and grabbed Aggie's arms.

"Aggie Rose?"

She swallowed her in a large, theatrical embrace then scolded their producer.

"Allen, you and Sam didn't tell me I'd be working with Agatha Rose O'Hanley!"

Aggie turned her head to Allen, all smiles on the walk below and mouthed, 'What the hell?'

He took the hint and sprang into action.

"Uh…here, Faline. Let me introduce you to the crew you'll be working with."

He whisked her away from her old friend and gave Aggie the chance to escape. She promptly made the best of the opportunity, hopped in her truck, and disappeared back into town. She went straight for Hupp's Hardwoods where she could be alone to sort out what just unfolded. She dove into the store and locked the door behind her.

"What the actual hell?"

She paced throughout the entire space, figure-eighting between the woodshop and the storefront.

"How in blue blazes did he even *get* her?"

More pacing.

"How am I supposed to work with *that*?"

She stopped in front of the lathe and switched it on. She watched for a moment while a table leg spun without the blade engaged, grabbed her safety glasses off the hook, and went to work on it. She watched as the ribbons of wood curled away from the cubed form and tried hard to get lost in her art. At the lathe she could become so single-mindedly consumed by her process, she thought this would be a safe place for her to compose herself.

She lampooned her former friend to the empty workshop.

"Faline! Please call me Faline…because Faline is a vapid, no-talent, fake bitch with no feelings…and MaryAnne died when she was a senior in high school…and she abandoned her best friend over a stupid lie!"

In her fit, she let her eye off the guide and the blade cut clean into the table leg, gauging it out of shape and knocking the lathe offline.

"Shit!"

She ripped her glasses off and chucked them across the shop. Just then, Allen was on the sidewalk outside the store, banging on the door.

"Aggie! I know you're in there. I can hear that machine! Open up!"

She took a deep breath and retrieved her glasses, then walked to unlock the door.

Allen walked in and watched as she poked her head out to the town beyond, then retreated behind the locked door again.

"She's not out there. I had the P.A. drive her to the hotel."

"What in hell's half-acre, Allen? Why wouldn't you tell me."

"This was your idea, Aggie."

"I was joking. It was a joke."

"I have to admit, I did think it was a long shot when you first mentioned it. But when I was told to find you a sidekick, the board was all over this."

"I thought you said she was too hard to work with."

"Her agent assured me that she'll do anything we want and not cause a smidge of drama."

She cut her eyes at the man.

"Look, Aggie, we need a co-host. She's a major celebrity…from this area…and she neeeeds the work. I mean we got her for a song!"

"Oh my God! This is about money?"

Allen saw her Irish temper begin to surface and tried desperately to back pedal.

"Wait, Aggie. It's not just about the money. But she checks all the boxes, *and* we can afford her. Win-win?"

"I don't need a co-host! It's an extra expense! If we can't afford one, why do we have one?"

"You *do* need a co-host. They won't take a chance on the show without this element. You're just too much on your own, Aggie. You're intimidating."

"I'm what?"

"Agatha Rose O'Hanley, you are a powerful force. The company thinks you'll put people off without this component to soften the show."

Terrified it was all coming apart, Allen chose his next words carefully.

"I want you in front of that camera. I want your expertise, your craftsmanship, your father's shop. All this…on camera."

Her jets began to cool, and her posture relaxed some.

"Aggie, without Faline -…"

"MaryAnne! Her name is MaryAnne!"

"Without her, *Just DIY* doesn't get made."

She looked at his face and saw the sobering truth in his eyes. She wanted the show. She waited so long for something like this. She'd worked around this woman before when she was a lazy teenager, how could she be any worse than that to deal with now? But MaryAnne cost her so much in their youth and Aggie didn't want to have to take care of her again.

"Listen to me, Allen. I won't have any part of her drama. Do you hear me on that?"

"Loud and clear, Aggie. You'll hardly be around her at all. Her segments will be separated from your projects and at most, you'll introduce the show together, make a quick segway into her bits, and then sign off together."

He clapped his hands back and forth.

"One and done!"

"One and done, huh?"

"Ok, technically twelve and done, but literally just minutes together."

He felt safe enough approaching her to take her hands.

"Aggie, I need you to be the bigger star right now."

"Does this horseshit work on people in your real life?"

She glared into his face until he released her hands and backed awkwardly toward the exit.

"I will see you on the farm at dawn, Saturday morning, Allen."

Hand on the doorknob, he held up a finger and closed his eyes to speak.

"Aggie, just one more thing."

She relented before she was officially asked.

"*Faline*. I'll call her, *Faline*."

That evening, Bill found Aggie, beer in hand, chucking stones into the pond below the house: a spot she gravitated to when she was struggling internally. She approached her wife with tender caution.

"Hey babe?"

"Oh, hey Billie. How was your day?"

"The usual; break throughs, set-backs, tears. How about yours? Since you're in your 'pondering' spot, I'm guessing stressful."

Aggie attempted a smile then readily revealed the source of her angst.

"Allen revealed my new co-host today."

"Oh!"

"And you'll never guess in a million years, who he hired."

"Is this one of those times that you say I'll never guess, but you really want me to try and guess anyway?"

"Faline Farah!"

"No. Ok. Oh no, wow!"

"Oh yes, wow!"

The couple had spent hours throughout the years since they got back together, processing their respective stories, and healing their old wounds, so Bill knew all about MaryAnne, or Faline. She was fully aware of all the past pain Aggie had endured because of her, but they never discussed what she'd do if she ever got the chance to reunite with her.

"What kind of shape was she in? I know the gossip columns were full of stuff about her being a hot mess after they killed her off her soap."

"She appeared to be alright. She looks rode hard and put away wet, but she seemed ok, I guess."

"Did she remember you?"

"Get this, she claims that neither Allen nor her agent told her I was the person she'd be working with!"

"Maybe it just didn't register with her, you know. She might have never guessed you'd be the same Aggie Rose they were talking about."

Aggie cut her eyes at her wife.

"Really? That's what you're going with? Come on, Bill. You know damn well if they told her they were setting her up with a how-to show in West Fort Ann, New York with a red-headed, carpenter named Agatha Rose O'Hanley, she'd have recognized the name! Jesus! How many Aggie Roses' do you think there are out there anyway?"

"Ok. You're right. Sorry."

Aggie reached for her to communicate her regret for snapping. Bill took her hand and squeezed.

"So, what are you feeling? Do you think this could affect your commitment to the show?"

"No! I won't let it. This is *my* show! Nothing will keep me from doing this!"

"Ok. That's great. So how will you get through it?"

Aggie squinted toward the sun setting over the hills of their farm, looking for the answer to that question and all the old ones she and MaryAnne left unasked from their old life together. She shook her head.

"I don't know, Billie. I'm not going to take care of her again. I won't be made to do that. I already told Allen. That's not part of my gig."

"Right. That's Allen's job. He's the one who hired her. So, you have to let him manage that."

"Do you know how hard that will be if she messes things up?"

"Aggie, you can't control everything. You only have control over your own actions. You have to come up with a way to release that urge to take over and fix everything!"

They two women chuckled at the irony of it.

"What can I do when it hits me, Bill?"

"Try a mantra."

Aggie rolled her eyes.

"Stop it, Aggie. Really. Try it."

"Ok. What is my mantra?"

Bill ran through her old standards.

"Try, too many cooks spoils the broth."

"No."

"How about too many chiefs, not enough Indians?"

"Racist."

"Oh! I have the perfect one. This is an old Polish idiom; not my circus, not my monkeys!"

Aggie let out a genuine laugh and drew her wife into her arms for a sweet, grateful kiss.

"I love you, Bill."

"I love you too, babe."

Another kiss and Bill would drive her point home.

"You know you can do hard things, Aggie. We all can. Maybe even MaryAnne can."

She smiled her knowing smile and left her wife to finish her beer and her thinking, alone.

»«

With the crew to begin preparation at six that first morning, Aggie arrived at the farm by four. Too anxious to stay in bed any longer and eager to get herself set in her new role, she pulled up to the barn, surprised to see the champagne Cadillac, and cut the lights. She walked through the cavernous structure to the open field beyond it where the trailers had been set up for the cast and crew to prepare and break throughout the day. Hers sat dark but lights shone in the windows of the other.

She stood still thinking to herself.

"Hmm. Ok, she's here early, that's a good sign."

She took a step toward the occupied trailer and stopped to continue her train of thought.

"Or she's been here all night, drinking!"

She shook those two options and all the possibilities falling between them out of her head in the next instant and reminded herself.

"Not my circus!"

She followed the path to her own trailer, entered, put on the coffee, and sat down with the script. As the sun rose over the eastern pasture, the parade of vehicles started up the farm road from town. The sound guys, the camera men, Allen and Sumner, the director, and a host of assistants scattered out around the farm to begin setting up.

They'd stage the project, time a few rehearsals, and then after a break they'd be ready for the real thing. Once the set was ready, someone went to retrieve Faline so they could do their first walk-through. Aggie watched as the girl returned without her charge to whisper in Allen's ear. He looked up to Aggie across the room and smiled nervously, then disappeared with the assistant.

Aggie had spent her whole adult life distancing herself from her raw feelings about MaryAnne and the way their relationship ended, yet here she was again, with that heartsick knot in her guts, waiting to see what this woman would do next. Would she come through like the friend she was for so long? Would she selfishly screw everything up like she did at the end? How on God's green earth did Aggie find herself back in a position where she was depending on MaryAnne O'Hara to call the shots between them? She was right back at St. James reliving her last awful night there all over again! Her director drug her back.

"You ok, Aggie? You're starting to sweat. Is it too warm in here?"

"Am I? It's a little stuffy, Sumner. I'll just go out on the back porch for a sec and get some air."

She turned to leave the room and saw Allen and the P.A. flanking a sunglass wearing Faline as they came in the side door. She kept on out the back exit, letting the screen door slap closed behind her, a sound she always registered as comforting. She straightened her spine and inhaled deeply, filling her lungs with the cool morning air, then exhaled and took the pause she needed to silence the ghost fights in her head. She thought about Bill and Thatch, and every road that lead her there. This was *her* show, and she was going to make it a success. She took one more deep breath and went in to find her mark.

Faline, shades still on, sat in a folding chair off camera while Aggie stood to rehearse the intro.

ACTION!

"Hi! I'm Aggie Rose O'Hanley and this – is Just DIY! Today's project will be plaster patching in our beautiful nineteenth century farm restoration here in lovely Washington County, New York."

Following the cue cards, she paused, and her eyes darted toward her 'co-host' still sitting in the folding chair off camera.

"This is my co-host, star of daytime drama's Hart's Desire, Faline Farah."

Faline remained seated.

"Ok. Is she supposed to join me on camera now or what? Allen, didn't you say we do the intro together?"

Sumner intercepted.

"Yes, Aggie. We're changing the line to 'daytime drama's own Faline Farah'. For legal reasons, we can't mention the show by name."

"Oh. Sorry."

She looked in the direction of her producer and co-star. They both nodded.

"No problem. Just a last-minute change. And yes, when we're all set to broadcast she will join you for the intro. Allen's just letting her observe for a few of these takes, ok? Paula will stand in for Faline."

He shoved the assistant toward Aggie, and she set herself just out of the shot and waited for her cue.

"So, let's try that again for timing. Back to your one, and...ACTION!"

"Hi! I'm Aggie Rose O'Hanley and this - is Just DIY! Today's project will be plaster patching in our beautiful nineteenth century farm restoration here in lovely Washington County, New York. This is my co-host, day-time drama's own Faline Farah."

Paula stepped forward and read from the cards.

"Hi, Aggie. When you're all done patching things up, stay tuned and watch as I use some of your left-over materials to create a beautiful keepsake hand sculpture."

"Great, Faline. Let's get started."

"Time?"

A young man to Sumner's right showed him a stopwatch.

"Ok, great, Aggie. Now Faline will exit camera right and you can make a half turn to the buckets and trowels."

Aggie turned toward her tools to mimic the combining of the water and the plaster mix as she explained the process to the camera.

"This old girl has authentic horse-hair plaster walls over wooden lath, par for the construction of homes in the 1800's. But today's products are more practical and economical, and the horses get to keep their hair."

She knelt to vogue with the plaster mix.

"This dry mix is available at your local hardware or home improvement store and comes in bags of five, ten, and fifty pounds. For a repair job like today's, ten pounds may be all we need. For our project we'll need the plaster, a mixing bucket, a stirrer, a trowel and tray for application, and a drop cloth for both under the mixing bucket and under the work area. Wet plaster can blanch out untreated wood flooring leaving bleached spots that may not absorb stain or vanish properly. So, protect your floors whatever the job. And as always, protect yourself. When working with dry ingredients, always wear a mask and eye protection. This mix is a fine powder, and its particles can cause respiratory issues if inhaled. I also wear gloves when handling plaster. It can dry out your hands, leaving them rough and cracked. We want to fix our cracked walls, but not at the expense of our soft hands. Right girls?"

"Time?"

The rehearsal went on with the director timing each segment of the job and Aggie adjusting to the few tweaks he insisted would make for better TV. Her portion of the hour was shaping up nicely. A couple times through and they were satisfied with the results. Aggie broke and retreated to her trailer and Faline was up.

They set Faline up in the kitchen where they could use the large, wooden farmhouse table as a work area. Her craft was premade, and she was essentially just supposed to explain how someone would create this thing without actually doing it. Measurements for sound and light were taken and the director was ready to begin. She positioned herself behind the table and shook her hands out to prepare for the practice scene. Sumner addressed the star.

"Are we rehearsing with the glasses on, Miss Farah?"

"Honey, please call me Faline. Everybody! Everybody, I'm just Faline. Just call me Faline. We're all friends here, huh?"

She ignored the question.

"I'm ready when you are, sir."

"The glasses, Faline?"

"My eyes are so sensitive to these bright lights, love. If they're exposed to these spots for too long, they'll start to dry out and look just awful. I'll leave the glasses on until we're a go. Ok?"

"Ok. Leaving the glasses for now. And…ACTION!"

"Thank you, Aggie. And thanks for the left-over plaster. This is just what we need to create this lovely, personalized hand sculpture. We also have a few things we picked up at our local craft store. We have the wooden base, which we're leaving unfinished, but should you want yours painted or stained, you'll need do that first and let it dry overnight. Remember how Aggie told us that the plaster could bleach out our wooden surfaces. We also have a carton of silicone mold mix and an empty coffee can. Remember to cover your work surface with a drop cloth and protect your clothes with an apron or work shirt."

"Time?"

Allen sat pleased with himself as Faline went through the spot a few times, each one tighter and smoother than the one before. This was shaping up to be a successful first day.

The local channel was wrapping up their morning programming and everyone was standing by to go live in minutes.

Aggie and Faline stood a few feet apart as the makeup techs blotted the last sweat away and the countdown came in.

"Five, four, three..."

The women caught each other's eye in the final two seconds before air and Faline smiled sincerely and mouthed, 'Break a leg!'

The red light atop camera one clicked on, and so did they.

"Hi! I'm Aggie Rose O'Hanley and this – is Just DIY!

The plaster repair segment went off without a hitch as Aggie was sure it would. She concluded on time and was pleased with her performance.

Faline had been off set, presumably in her trailer for the duration of Aggie's bit but was delivered to the kitchen during the last station break to begin hers. Her sunglasses still donned, came off a split second before her cue.

"Thank you, Aggie."

She looked over her left shoulder as if she were speaking directly to her cohost. When she looked back in the direction of the cue cards she lost her focus and couldn't read what came next, so she improvised.

"And now on to the farts and craps segment of our show..."

Allen whispered into his hands.

"Oh my God!"

"And thanks for the left-over plaster."

She could see the cards now.

"This is just what we need to create this lovely, personalized hand sculpture. We also have a few things we picked up at our local craft store. We have the wooden base, which we're leaving unfinished, but should you want yours painted or stained, you'll need do that first and let it dry overnight. Remember how Aggie told us that the plaster could bleach out our wooden surfaces.

We also have a carton of silicone mold mix…wait…you can buy silicone at the craft store?"

She looked at the container as if to read its ingredients.

"I could have saved a bundle at the plastic surgeon's if I'd have brought my own silicone!"

Returning to the camera she jumped right back in.

"And an empty coffee can. Remember to cover your work surface with a drop cloth and protect your clothes with an apron or work shirt."

The crew grew uneasy and everyone looked to the director for an emergency cut away. Aggie was brought in from her trailer to stand by in case the whole thing went south. Allen kept his hands on his mouth and barely breathed.

"Two-to-one water and mold mix stirred until the consistency of pudding in the coffee can."

She tipped the can toward the camera to show the contents to the audience and the stage manager pointed to the camera mounted over her head that was following the action from above.

"Oh yeah!"

She looked straight up into the overhead lens and waved.

"I forgot about you!"

They cut to camera one and she continued.

"Here now? Ok, so, now you plunge your hands into the coffee can!"

The air escaping around her hands produced a long, bubbly fart sound that instantly struck her funny bone and she giggled.

"Excuse me!"

An audible laugh from someone in the crew got Sumner out of his seat; an act which threatened fines if there wasn't quiet on the set.

"This is definitely the fun part! Now you hold your hand in the position you want your sculpture to display, we're doing hands clasped in prayer, until you feel the mixture begin to soft set. Anywhere from three to five minutes."

The director took his seat; she was moving along.

"Once the mold is gelled, remove your hand and fill the form with Aggie's left-over plaster mix."

She poured the tray of plaster into the coffee can to overflowing and quickly tried to scoop up the raw plaster with her hands.

"Whoopsie!"

She fumbled in the gray mix slopping it everywhere. She looked up into the overhead camera.

"You getting all this up there?"

Camera one tightened up on her face while the stage crew cleared the mess away just out of sight and Aggie was sent in for a diversion until they could get done.

"Looks like we're almost out of time, Faline."

"Hi, Aggie! It's Aggie everyone! I'm almost done."

Aggie stood nervously by as Faline honed back in on the cards.

"Let your piece set up in a cool dry place overnight and in the morning poke some holes in the bottom of the can to release the mold. Then pull the silicone away from the plaster form and voila` - you've created your own keepsake hand sculpture!"

Holding up the premade sculpture she was given by props, Faline's hands were still covered with the gray plaster mix, making it impossible to tell her own fingers from the fabricated ones. Trying not to damage the thing, she carefully held it by her fingertips when presenting to the camera.

The shot was clear and perfect; two hands "clasped together in prayer" with Faline's plaster-covered middle finger protruding from the center knuckles of the fists. Aggie put a hand on Faline's to gently lower the obscene mess out of sight and went into her sign off.

"That's all the time we have for today. Join us next week on Just DIY when I'll show you how to recreate original crown molding. Thanks for tuning in and remember if you want something done right, - ..."

"Just do it yourself!"

Both women signed off in unison and froze staring straight into the camera until the red light went black again and the whole set breathed a collective sigh.

Then a bead of sweat trickled down Sumner's back.

"Ok everybody, the local basketball tournament has begun, and we are off the air. Good first show."

"Are you kidding me?"

Aggie's shock was wearing off and her anger was about to take center stage. Allen saw from across the set and made a beeline for his star grabbing her by her shoulders and walking her out the back door of the house toward the lilacs.

"Allen, she's drunk, isn't she?"

"I think she's not used to the whole demonstration thing; you know what I mean?"

"You mean the 'farts and craps'?"

"Is that what she said, I barely heard her."

He followed her while she paced.

"Your piece was flawless, Aggie!"

"I know! I was fully conscious for my piece; I know it was flawless! Allen, I told you. I told you I wasn't on board for this shit!"

Faline came flying triumphantly out the back door and swept down into the lilacs.

"Great show, Aggie! And what fun!"

Allen shot Aggie a pleading look.

She growled through clenched teeth.

"Are you - …oh my God! Great show. Yes, thanks, Faline."

"I can't wait for next week. Are we all going to lunch together? What's everyone doing?"

Allen reached for Aggie's hand.

"That's a great idea! An afterparty luncheon!"

Aggie ripped her hand away.

"I have plans!"

She stormed past the two to her truck, spitting gravel as far as the chicken coops in her wake. She drove all over West Fort Ann so angry she couldn't even cry. She tried the mantra in her head, but she kept envisioning a farm overrun by monkeys, wrecking everything. She shook her head to clear it over and over again until she found herself on the highway out of town.

She was halfway to Glenn Falls when she realized where she intended to go.

She'd go tell Zeke about it. She'd tell on MaryAnne. She was sure after swallowing everything he'd ever wanted to say about his stepdaughter, that Zeke would be the perfect sounding board. She flew through Glenn Falls and headed for Warrensburg. She passed the signs to Lake George and her energy began to wane. She started to think about the pain this woman had put everyone through. She thought of Dottie and the Halpennys and how disappointed they must have been when she didn't stay for Patsy's wake. How broken-hearted Zeke would have been to know as Aggie alone did, that she *was* there but didn't come down to the church or to the clubhouse after. He didn't deserve that; not then and certainly not now. She couldn't bring all that up again just for the sake of venting to someone. She couldn't break his heart all over again like that. That would make her just as bad as MaryAnne! She pulled over at the next ramp and drove to the nearest Dairy Mart. She went in, bought a bottle of 7-up and a bag of Doritos and sat against her bumper while she fed her angry heart and calmed her head.

She hated the surrender of it but the thought that 'it is what it is', kept running through her mind. She wouldn't tell Zeke. She would spare him. She would soldier on and manage herself. Tipping the bag of chip crumbs into her mouth, she chased the last bite with a swig of her pop, then mumbled her mantra.

"Not my monkeys."

»«

The next Friday night was tense. Aggie had rehearsed the crown molding episode for hours and created some amazing work. She precut all the scrap pieces from which Faline would be making her picture frame project. The twist with this week's show was that it would be filmed at the shop and that was creating a whole new level of anxiety for Agatha Rose. Bill read the signs at the dinner table.

"Not hungry, babe?"

Bill studied her wife who had apparently come to dinner in body only and wasn't aware of the question.

"Ma?"

"What son? Sorry. What did I miss?"

"Mom asked if you were hungry."

"I'm so sorry. No. I mean yes! It's delicious...my favorite!"

Aggie began shoveling ham and mashed potatoes in.

"So good!"

Eloise led and her grandson followed.

"You finished, Thatcher?"

"Yes ma'am. Mom, may I be excused?"

Bill nodded to the two of them.

"Thatcher take your plates to the kitchen; I'll get the rest."

Bill watched as the couple left the room, plotting to challenge each other to a game of chess on the porch, and her wife once again gave up on her dinner plate.

"Thinking about the show, babe?"

"Huh? No. I was just thinking about the show."

Bill giggled.

"I wish I'd have said that."

"What? Did you just ask me that?"

Aggie abandoned her fork and reached for Bill's hand.

"I am so sorry, Billie. I am just world's away right now."

"It's ok. I get it."

Aggie smiled a little condescendingly.

"Do you? No offense, Bill, but I'm not sure you get it every time you say you get it."

Bill squared up in front of her.

"Let me take a stab. You can handle Faline on location at the house. It's Allen's, you have no emotional attachment there. But you're broadcasting from the shop tomorrow…your dad's shop…your shop, and that's a whole other ballgame."

She waited for her argument, but Aggie offered none.

"Hm. I guess you *do* get it a little."

"Aggie, Faline can't change that place for you. You are the only one that can do that. You've had people come in there before that you didn't want to wait on, whose projects you didn't want to finish or take on. But you did it anyway because you were honoring the way your dad did business. What would Hupp do?"

Aggie breathed deep, absently smiling at a memory.

"When we spent the summers here, we'd ride bikes into town and dad would give us money for the pop machine. I'd always get a crème soda and MaryAnne -…"

"See? Why stop yourself from enjoying that memory, Aggie? It's ok to remember that stuff; you two have a history."

"That was a memory of MaryAnne, not Faline!"

Aggie rose from the table too abruptly and flipped her silverware to the floor.

"Shit! Bill, I'm sorry. Jesus! That's all I can do! I'm just sorry all the time for everything!"

Bill watched as the woman she loved struggled with the flatware and hurriedly began clearing the table. She stood reaching for Aggie's wrists and guided them to release the dishes.

"Babe, what are you truly sorry for?"

"I am truly sorry when you do this, Bill."

Aggie didn't always object to being analyzed by the family therapist and, while it hadn't happened often in their relationship, Bill never attempted to camouflage it when it did.

"Just be still a moment and ask yourself if you truly are sorry for something. And then see if you can do anything to make it right."

The two sat still at the table waiting for Aggie's revelation. After a moment, Aggie started to hear the theme from *Jeopardy* in her head. When too much time lapsed for Bill, she rolled her eyes.

"You're doing the *Jeopardy* theme again, aren't you?"

"You're right, doctor, you know me so well!"

Aggie mocked her wife as she returned to her chore, bent on completing it without further interruption.

Bill knew not to push her and deferred to the comedic break.

"Funny! Laugh it up."

She joined in clearing the table and dropped the subject. The seed was planted.

»«

Sumner signaled the cast and crew after the second episode concluded.

"That's a wrap! We'll turn the mic down a little more when the lathe is being run next time but another great show, ladies. Good work!"

Faline begged for more attention.

"Thank you, Sumner. Do you really think I was good?"

"Faline, you were fine."

"I know I flubbed that one line about the mitered corners. I'm sorry, I just read the card wrong."

Aggie took the reins.

"No, Faline, really every picture frame needs 'mighty corners' if it's going to hang properly. And the microphone probably didn't pick up on the glass you broke or the fart that squeaked out when you bent over to pick up the pieces."

Sumner attempted to diffuse the situation.

"Ladies let's calm down."

Faline was less drunk than the previous week, but she'd taken her pills with a couple shots of vodka that morning and she had repeated the same level of sloppy performing.

"Agatha Rose, you're mad!"

Aggie *was* mad.

"I know this is just some po-dunk cable TV nonsense to you, Faline, but I'm serious about doing this show."

"I'm a professional, Miss O'Hanley. I know that every show is important, no matter how tiny and insignificant the performance is. Whether it's a major role on a network TV show or the farm report from West *Fart* Ann!"

The director tried a second time to prompt a truce.

"Ok, girls. Let's take FIVE."

"The farm report was good enough for you when you were a kid! What's the matter? Can't muster the effort to be great for the people you came from?"

"Aw come on, Ags! Let's just get a pop and forget about all this!"

Faline produced a quarter to drop into the slot of the soda machine and Aggie lunged for it.

"NO!"

She grabbed the coin from Faline's hand and hurled it over the ducking heads of the crew into the bowels of shop beyond. It banged around echoing in the uncomfortable silence that followed her tirade. And Sumner halted the action.

"That's enough!"

They cleared the shop, sending Faline hurrying out to be tended to by assistants and the crew to return the equipment to the farm, leaving him alone in the space with Aggie.

"What is up between you two, Aggie?"

She was regretful of her bad behavior but unwilling to be reprimanded by her director for it.

"We have a history! Ok, Sumner? It doesn't matter."

"Oh, but it does matter. It matters to me because I have to work with you two."

"I just mean, the past, our past doesn't matter."

"And I'm saying that it does. Aggie get your head right around her. She's done in this business, but this could be the beginning of something for you."

He put a quarter in the machine and pushed a button. A bottle fell into the chute. He pulled it loose and used the opener under the coin slot to pry off its metal cap, pausing to listen to it jingle to the bottom of some hidden receptacle within. He placed the bottle on the counter for his star.

"Crème soda, right?"

She nodded.

"Faline told me it was your favorite."

The bell over the door, played him out. She put her hand around the cold drink and brought it to her nose to smell it. She took a swig.

"Hmph. Still tastes like summer."

»«

"After Aggie's tongue and groove project, we have all these lovely different tones of sawdust to work with."

Faline drew her hand along a row of open containers with different shades of brown shavings on the kitchen table for the overhead camera, glancing up into the lens just before the cut back to camera one.

"Today we're going to turn all this waste into sawdust art. You'll need a decorative vase, your shavings of course, and your imagination. We begin by layering the colors in the jar like so. Make sure you start with a deep layer because all the other layers will rest on this one."

She took a handful of the first color and sprinkled it in, repeating until she got enough, and held the jar at eye level to examine her work.

"Give it a gentle tap on a hard surface to pack the dust ever so slightly."

Tap, tap, tap on the table.

"Then you add the next color."

She repeated the step, holding the jar up to camera one to show the design taking shape.

She made two more layers when a couple strands of hair broke free from their sprayed assignment and tickled the outer edge of her right eye. Instinctively, she reached for her eye with her saw dusted fingertips, replacing annoying hair with abrasive saw dust.

"Oh!"

She began to tear and blink.

"Be careful with your dusty fingertips around your eyes."

Her mascara started down her cheeks and she attempted to blot her face with her palms, depositing more dust in clumps on the sticky black tracks.

Aggie looked on from just off stage and found herself smiling as she whispered to the crew watching around her.

"What a hot mess!"

Faline grabbed the hem of her apron and tried to stop the endless stream of black tears but only served to flip the dust from *it* into the air in front of her. She could barely make out the movement underneath the table and assumed it was the finished product she was normally handed toward the end of the demonstration and reached for it. Grateful for the rescue, she took a deep breath to deliver the final line in the script but instead released a bellowing sneeze.

"WHAAAAAACHOOOO!"

The sneeze launched the dust, covering the set in an opaque cloud and the fumbled vase went crashing to the floor shattering into a million pieces, releasing a second puff of debris.

Coughs and sneezes from the crew could be heard through the fog. Aggie grabbed the backup vase and walked calmly to Faline's side.

"Sawdust art. Thanks Faline. That was fun."

Faline bobbed her head, coughing into her elbow.

"You bet, Aggie."

"Join us next week on Just DIY when we'll show you how to plane your old, warped wood doors and

Faline will show us how to make wooden rose bouquets. And remember if you want something done right..."

Aggie led her blinded cohost to their joint sign off.

"Just do it yourself!"

They held their marks until the final call…and "CUT!"

Sumner rushed in.

"Mask up everybody and clean this shit up and somebody get Faline to the emergency room!"

Aggie laughed audibly now as her costar was led away coughing and spitting.

She turned her head back and giggled in the direction of Aggie's voice just before they helped her out onto the porch.

"That one is destined to become a classic, right Ags?"

Aggie realized that Faline was committed to the show even though her desperation to remain working was the driving force behind her commitment and not necessarily *Just DIY* itself. She came to accept that any motivation was good enough if it kept her costar showing up. After once again following some advice from Bill, Aggie came to accept Faline, where she was; an alcoholic at the end of her acting career, clinging to this little show as her last vestige of hope. She stopped expecting more and settled for Faline's current best. It was the only way she could get through the weeks without flipping her lid.

Faline's screw ups left everyone involved with the show in stitches, sometimes literally, and she didn't seem to mind that they were obviously laughing *at* her. Agatha Rose was confident that her own efforts would lead her on to the next big thing, without this albatross. So, she tolerated what came next with her sights set somewhere well past Faline's last hoorah. Overall, Aggie moved on less uptight about all the bloopers, and embraced the part of the show that was Faline's disaster.

Even while Faline's performances continued to skirt the edge of the ridiculous second to her drinking and general ineptitude, Aggie's were spot on. She was getting fan mail from women in the tri-county area who were tuning in every weekend, following her projects, and even taping the show to view as a guide when they went to work on their own repairs. The local media lapped them up. The two were invited on radio shows and TV8's human interest and entertainment news spots. They were asked to be the marshals of the July 4th parade and signed headshots in a booth at the fair.

Allen was enjoying the building hype around the show and its personalities. He kept his finger on the pulse of the industry, checking in with his agents back at the office for interest in the concept.

He frequently spent the beginning of every week in the city, sometimes taking Faline along and dropping her off to 'rest' at her apartment. Every time they shared the commute back, she presented with more and more luggage. By mid-July, they were nearing the end of their twelve episodes, and when he picked her up to head back she had bags on bags of her stuff.

Unbeknownst to Allen or Sumner or anyone else for that matter, her creditors had been sending final collection notices one-by-one to Faline's place uptown. Every time she left for the show, she left behind a stack of unpaid bills and shut-off notifications. She took empty suitcases from the farm to the city, filled them with more and more of her things and transferred the mess to her trailer. It was beginning to look like a replica of her penthouse. She poked around the farm when no one was about and secreted the overflow away in the root cellar, smoke house, attic cubbies, and the loft in the barn. None of those spaces were being used for the show and she was sure her private stashes would go undetected.

»«

The final show aired the last Saturday of the summer just ahead of TV8's coverage of the region's semi-pro footballers, the Green Jackets', first home game.

Aggie had replaced copper plumbing in the wall behind the claw-foot tub in the second story bathroom and Faline had used the left-over lengths of pipe to make a windchime. In the first minutes of her segment, as per her usual, Faline had managed to lodge her thumb in a piece of the pipe and worked through to the end with a nine-inch tube of copper affixed to her right hand.

Presenting the counterfeit project at the show's conclusion, she tapped it with her copper thumb and, as the sound gently tinkled through the set, she and Aggie drew near to sign off for the final time.

"Thanks, Faline. That's beautiful."

Faline, sweating and panting as always, hair a tousled mess, nodded.

"And that brings us to the end of our very last episode of Just DIY. I hope you've enjoyed watching as much as we've enjoyed bringing our show to you. For Faline and all our crew, I'd like to thank you all for tuning in and making this show such a success."

The crew that could assembled behind the women to take their collective bow.

"And as always, if you want something done right..."

Aggie lead the group in unison.

"Just do it yourself!"

»«

The wrap party was an all-day affair on Allen's farm complete with pig roast, piles of picnic food, and kegs and kegs of cold beer. The cast and crew brought their families, and that meant Bill, Thatcher, and Eloise would be accompanying Aggie to the celebration.

When they pulled onto the property the party was in full swing. Thatcher helped his grandmother from the truck and walked her around to the back of the farmhouse where she could sit in the shade and watch the festivities. Allen had sprung for a pony for the littles to ride and face-painting. West Fort Ann's favorite local band, Hot Tub Monkeys, played live all day and into the night. Aggie introduced her family to Sumner, the crew, and their respective clans.

She finally got the family settled and was in line at the buffet for her own plate when Faline joined her.

"I saw you and your wife come in, Aggie."

"Oh, hey, Faline. Thatcher is loving this. He's really into this band."

"It's been so long since I've seen your mom. Do you think she'd remember me?"

Faline sounded coy but there was real insecurity in her voice.

"I mean. Would it be ok if I said hello?"

"Faline, she would love that."

Faline's face spread out in a sincere grin and she surrendered her plate and navigated her way back to the table where Eloise sat enjoying the day.

Aggie watched as she leaned in and Eloise's face turned toward the awkward visitor. Then, they reached for one another and embraced. Aggie caught herself choking back a tear and quickly recovered to present her empty dish to the man in charge of the barbeque. She ignored the reunion and watched as the animal in front of her surrendered it's flesh in great slabs. She made the rounds for corn on the cob, potato salad, and homemade rolls with butter, then balanced her bounty in the crook of her arm and pumped herself a cold beer before returning to join her family. Faline was still there.

"Aggie, your wife is lovely, and your son is such a fine young man."

She accepted the compliment then smiled and cut her eyes to Bill, who sat quietly observing.

"Thank you, Faline."

"And your mom hasn't changed a bit!"

Eloise ignored the famous version of the child she knew all those years ago and addressed her in the familiar.

"It's been a long time, MaryAnne. You look a little different from what I remember but you sound the same. It's still her voice, isn't it, Agatha Rose? She still sounds like your friend."

Aggie nodded to her mother.

Such an innocent observation, but the weight of it could be felt by both women. Aggie had put so much effort into distancing herself from Faline's persona that she'd failed to notice that she had connected some to the bit of MaryAnne that remained. And it had been so long since Faline had been around anyone she could truly call her friend, that she too had missed the fact that basic bits of each of them remained intact enough to recognize.

She didn't linger much longer. And Bill was proud of Aggie for tolerating the short-lived intrusion. She watched the two women as Faline parted company with a gentle touch of Aggie's shoulder and a grand wave and invitation for them to enjoy the cookout as if she were hosting.

Bill smiled in Aggie's direction in between bites.

"You did well, babe."

Aggie smiled back around the ear of corn rotating in her buttery hands. Bill was right about a lot of this experience and Aggie felt grateful for her insight.

As the partiers carried on, sweatshirts and sweaters emerged to cover bodies, quilts and blankets were broken out to warm bare legs, and shoulders huddled together around a bon fire. The band played on under lights strung between the porches and outbuildings. People went around again at the buffet and new kegs were tapped to keep the festivities going strong into the night. Eloise was starting to show signs of wear, so Bill offered to take her home, leaving Thatcher and Aggie to stay and enjoy.

Thatcher connected with the band's lead guitar and he let him strum a quiet chorus when they took a break, and Aggie sat nursing her third or fourth beer, she wasn't exactly keeping track. When the group took the stage back, Agatha and her son took a walk around the farm. He asked her about the experience of completing the show and she told him how satisfying it had been, and that she was sure her dad would have enjoyed it.

They found themselves wandering around the trailers behind the barn and Thatch asked if he could peek inside. She granted him entrance to the one she and the bulk of the crew used and then she pointed out Faline's.

"Could we see inside hers too, Ma?"

"I guess it wouldn't hurt. I doubt if she has any of her personal things left in there since the show's over."

He grinned.

"Ok. Let's see what ole Faline Farah's got going on in there."

Aggie opened the door and she and her son stepped into what space remained just inside. The place was jam-packed. Aggie stood slack jawed.

"What the what?"

"Ma, she's living in here!"

"No!"

"Look at this stuff. This is all her stuff."

Aggie took a quick scan of the mess and assured her son.

"No. Now son, *that* is inaccurate. This is only a fraction of what this woman possesses."

"Still, though. These aren't the basics you bring with you when you're staying away from home. This is her *stuff*."

Aggie surveyed the items and realized her son was right. Not just clothes and shoes and toiletries but lamps and furniture and art; all stacked and crammed into every square inch of space in that tiny trailer.

"Even so, we should probably get out before she finds us here."

Thatcher didn't argue. He felt like they were imposing. The two backed down the steps leading to the path back to the party without saying another word.

Faline watched from just out of sight in the barn while they came down the bank. It was only when they were right beside her that either of them knew they'd been made. She ambushed the pair.

"See anything interesting?"

"Oh!"

Aggie and Thatcher jumped.

"Sorry Faline. I…um…we. Thatcher just wanted to see the trailers. You know?"

"Yes…I know."

Aggie shoved the boy to rejoin the party and braced herself for her due.

"We just looked inside, Faline. We didn't touch anything."

"Well, then you've learned my secret."

Aggie shook her head.

"Secret? I saw nothing secret."

"Come here, I want to show you something."

Faline took hold of her co-star's hand and led her up the ladder to the loft above the barn. The two crossed the hay-strewn expanse to a corner behind a stack of bales. There in the striped light sneaking in between the boards and battens was a pile of possessions similar to the ones cluttering her trailer.

"What's all this?"

"More of my things."

Maybe it was the beers mixed with the relief that the show was over, but Aggie felt mildly confused.

"Am I missing something here, Faline?"

"There are three or four more reserves in and around the house and grounds that belong to me too. I can't go back to New York."

"What does that mean?"

"I lost the apartment. I'm broke."

In the dark barn, Aggie could only see bits of the woman's face before her, but she could definitely read the defeat and desperation in her vibe.

"MaryAnne, I'm sorry."

Aggie stiffened against her misspoken sympathy the second she uttered it and Faline waved it away and forgave it just as quickly.

"Psht! Don't even bother with that shit anymore, Aggie."

She shook her head and looked down at the contents of her life stowed in a barn in West Fort Ann.

"I'm no more Faline Farah than the man-in-the-moon. I don't know if I ever was."

Aggie instinctually reached for her friend but checked herself before contact.

"What are you going to do? Have you talked to your agent? Does Allen know?"

"My agent dropped me, finally and completely. And I was waiting to see if we were going to do another season in the house before I asked Allen if I could squat."

"But the house isn't done, MaryAnne. And we can't finish it for you to stay here if we're going to use it for another season."

Faline shrugged.

"I'll think of something. I'll just do it myself, eh?"

Both women feigned a faint laugh and Faline left her old friend behind in the loft. Aggie walked to the hay door and looked down on the party below. She honed in on her son's face as he kept time to the music with his growing feet. She smiled at what the day meant to her; the accomplishment of the show and the beginning of the possibilities it could signal, the closeness of the crew, the family she was so proud of. But none of those things were the same for Faline. This could very possibly be the end of everything for her. She lost her house, her agent, and she was so bad in this production that it could have ended her career. Agatha Rose felt a crushing guilt that overpowered her own celebration. And she felt driven to save her friend once more despite her best judgement.

Bill rose without waking her and Aggie slept on well past her usual morning routine. When she finally stirred, dry mouthed and headachy, Bill appeared with hot coffee for her wife and sat down on the bed next to her.

"Did you have a good time last night, babe?"

"Oh yes. Thatcher and I danced hard after you left. I may have overdone it a bit on the beers."

"Ya think? I'm glad you had the presence of mind to ask for a ride home."

"Yeah, we'll have to go get the truck this morning."

"I have a session in Glenn Falls in an hour. Get up and splash some water on your face and I'll drop you."

She delivered her demands, kissed her wife's smokey hair, and turned to leave.

"Bill."

She stopped in the doorway.

"I love you."

"I know. I love you back."

"I know."

Bill returned to the bed.

"What? What's going on?"

"Faline is living in her trailer."

"What do you mean?"

"I was showing Thatcher around the farm and we looked inside her trailer and she has been bringing her things from the city and storing them on Allen's farm."

"In that little trailer?"

Aggie left the bed and stood at the window with her coffee.

"In the trailer, in the barn. She has stuff stuck in every nook and cranny we didn't use for the show."

"Why? What happened?"

"She lost her place in the city. She's out of money and has nowhere else to go."

"Babe, that's just awful."

Bill shook her head and then began to think aloud.

"Aggie, I don't know about all her things, but we certainly have enough -…"

"Wait."

Aggie held up a cautious hand.

"I know what you're going to say, and it was my first instinct too, but I didn't think that was the healthy thing to do."

Dr. Bill was in the house.

"Ok, fair enough. What's unhealthy about it?"

"It's my old pattern with her, from our old life. She'd get into trouble and I'd get her out. It's our old codependence leading to my passive-aggression. But then when I really needed her, she abandoned me!"

Aggie looked deep into her coffee when she discovered more.

"See! There's another one, abandonment!"

"Ok, babe. I'm glad you're doing this work. I think it *is* healthy to identify all these feelings you're having right now. And you're not wrong. But you are also not fourteen anymore, Aggie."

She smiled and took her place next to her love.

"You are consciously aware of all these emotional snares. I think you can do this."

Aggie put her arm around her wife and kissed her head.

"Are Mom and Thatcher up?"

"You're the last one out of the sack today, you old lush!"

"Very funny."

She kissed her again.

"Let me run it by them first and then we'll see. She may not take the offer."

"No one is going to take anything you offer until you brush those hairy teeth, babe."

She smiled up at her disheveled partner and grimaced at her breath. Aggie held her tighter and breathed heavily into her face.

"These teeth, Willena? Is it these hairy, smelly teeth you think I need to take care of?"

Bill balked and wiggled free, spilling a few drops of Aggie's coffee in the process. Aggie overacted the accident and sent her off giggling. When she was alone again, she returned to the window, leaned her achy forehead against the cool glass and wondered.

"Who knows? Maybe this will be a good thing."

Her breath fogged the pane and wafted back to her and she scolded herself.

"Whew, brush those cobs, Agatha Rose!"

Aggie's talk with Thatcher was a short one. They were raising him right; when a friend is in need, you help. She was more worried about Eloise. She wasn't sure how much her mother knew of Faline's drinking. Eloise had gone a long way toward forgiving her son since Rex got clean and Aggie wouldn't jeopardize that progress for anything. Not to take anything away from Rex's sobriety, but Eloise's acceptance and forgiveness was also a result of her waning memory. Aggie was convinced that her mom just lost a good bit of the bad stuff that happened when Rex was drinking, as she had other memories. She felt a little like she was tricking her but at the same time, she counted on her blurry cognition to make this work.

"Weren't you girls awful close in school, Agatha Rose? Why wouldn't we help her until she figures something else out?"

"I just didn't want to offer unless you and Bill and Thatcher were on board."

"Baby, this is your farm now. You decide who you share it with. You've earned that."

Aggie looked into the fading eyes of a woman who never stopped surprising her.

"I love you, Mom."

"Me too you, girl. Me too you."

Allen was back in the city politicking hard for a network deal for the show. Faline played hard to get for about ten minutes then orchestrated the packing and transfer of her belongings to Aggie's farm. They had plenty of room for storing her things, and Bill offered to move her home office out of the fourth bedroom at the house and into the apartment above the shop in town. She could play without disturbing anyone and she could catch up on notes and make calls without being interrupted. They laughed about how smart that would have been all along.

Faline moved the last of her things on a balmy day toward the end of the summer and breathed a quiet sigh of relief for the sense of safety she felt. She was hanging the last of her wardrobe up until supper her first night 'home'.

Thatcher tapped on the open door to her room.

"Mom told me to come get you for supper…uh…um…I'm not sure what you want to be called."

"Faline is fine, doll. Or MaryAnne. Whatever you want. I have no preference."

"It's funny, Gram has been telling me so much about you and Ma that I feel like I should call you *Aunt* MaryAnne."

His sweet, open heart caught her by surprise, and she beamed.

"Thatcher, my sweet boy, it would be my honor to be considered your aunt. Do you think that will fly with your moms?"

He shrugged.

"Let's see."

She went all in.

"I'm game if you are."

He grinned and waved her on to supper.

Over Bill's amazing cooking, they talked and laughed as if no time had passed since their last life. Thatcher was his usual charming self, Eloise told stories that couldn't possibly be all true, and Aggie watched as MaryAnne let her guard down a little more.

"So, Billie, tell me more about music therapy."

"Well, I am working with a grant from the New York State Mental Health Association to travel between a couple of different facilities to work with a range of clients."

"What kind of facilities?"

Aggie watched beaming with pride while her wife fielded MaryAnne's sincerely asked questions. MaryAnne watched Aggie, watching.

"I have a youth home with at-risk kids, two addiction treatment facilities, a pediatric occupational therapy office, and I work with the recreational therapists at the skilled nursing facility where your mom -…"

Everyone stiffened but Thatcher. He had forgotten MaryAnne's connection to the Nursing Center at Glen Falls.

"Where her mom what?"

Bill felt awful and attempted a save.

"Thatch, it's where -…"

"She died there."

MaryAnne blurted it out. She said the words and thought for a moment that it may have been the first time she heard them, in her own voice, outside her own head. She took in the shocked faces at the table. Thatcher was reddening and she reached for him.

"Don't you dare! Thatcher, it's fine. Really."

"I'm sorry, Aunt MaryAnne, I forgot."

Another shockwave hit Aggie. Did he just call her 'aunt'? What was happening? She opened her mouth to speak and Eloise beat her to it.

"That's the same place I was when I recovered from my stroke, Thatcher. You were awful little then; it was just about then that you and your mom came to the farm. Remember Agatha Rose?"

"Yes. Gram was in there for over a year after her stroke."

Aggie was caught between lives for an instant. Her reflex was to make it ok for MaryAnne and Thatcher and everyone but really…'*Aunt MaryAnne*'?

It was Bill who'd reel the whole thing in.

"I would love to show you what we do there sometime, MaryAnne. It really is a nice place."

"I'd love that."

MaryAnne was warm from the flare of shame the exchange produced but remained brave in the face of it. The bravado may have been from Faline's acting reflexes, but the shame was all her own and she was strangely comforted by the fact that she felt that and recognized it for what it was. As uncomfortable as the moment was, she was glad it happened. She helped the family clear the table and excused herself to her room.

Alone in her privacy, she took an airplane bottle of bourbon from a new stash in her underwear drawer. She tipped the tiny bottle upside down and breathed in the scent as the golden-brown liquid trickled down her throat. She kept her eyes closed well after she swallowed as if she was waiting for a signal that never came. She opened a second one and chased the first with a loud gulp. She held the back of her hand against her closed lips to mute her gullet.

Two shots.

If she could just stick to two shots a night, she could manage. If those were the first two shots of the day, her plan might have made more sense. As it was though, those were just that last two shots of the day.

This new road would be mostly uphill.

»«

For the most part the O'Hanley farm was just as it had been before Faline came to stay. School took Thatcher away early and with football practice right after, brought him home late. Bill visited her clients and returned to her office at day's end for notes and prep for her next day's schedule. Eloise puttered around the house, wrote to the boys, and watched her shows. Aggie sandwiched her hours at the shop with farm chores at dawn and dusk.

They let Faline find her way into whatever she desired. The idea was the less they expected of her the less disappointed they'd be. She enjoyed the freedom but after just a few days of it began to search for ways to combat her boredom and hold herself to her half-hearted pledge to sober life.

She began to lean into the others' spaces.

In late October, she was delighted to help with the annual apple butter party they threw. Thatcher and his defensive linemen spent one whole Saturday the first weekend after the tournaments picking the heavy trees bare and washing, peeling, and coring the fruit. Faline helped Eloise measure out the plentiful portions of brown and white sugar, cinnamon, nutmeg, and vanilla to be mixed in with the softening McIntosh beauties. A copper kettle hung on the spit over an open fire, and Bill and Aggie took turns churning the mixture with an old hockey stick the family had used specifically for this chore for forty years. The young men summoned their girlfriends, and, before dusk, the farm was alive with pre-teens donned in warm flannel and down vests swarming around the cooking pot like bees. Eloise could tell what it needed by the smell of it and the girls added ingredients as directed.

Faline took a turn at the stirring and listened to the kids recounting their middle school football season with a sincere love for the game. She attended the last post-season game with Bill and Aggie but still wasn't sure she understood the sport. In charge of the pot, she felt secure enough to interject a technical question or two here and there so she could learn more about it. The players were kind and respectful in their explanations and their dates were star struck by Thatcher's Aunt Faline. There were just as many questions about *Hart's Desire* and *Just DIY* as football.

As the cool night air chased the sun below the horizon, Faline turned the churn over to Aggie and excused herself to dart into the house for another layer. She noticed that Bill was already inside preparing homemade pizzas for the troops. Faline stole away to her room for her sheepskin-lined denim jacket and swallowed one of her tiny shot bottles, tucking the empty deep in her pocket before she joined Bill in the kitchen to see if she could help.

Bill was happy for the offer and employed her to slice mushrooms and peppers for the pies.

“I love it when Thatcher brings his people over. These boys are the best, most respectful kids. Of course, their mothers would snatch them bald-headed if they were ever anything but.”

“I have to admit, I felt sorry for you and Aggie for getting stuck back here with the farm and her mother and everything, but it does look like it’s been the best place to raise a family.”

Faline’s compliments were sometimes vague, even backhanded. Bill considered the source and took nothing personally.

“You couldn’t be more right, sister.”

Faline smiled at the family tie.

“Thatch was born in the city and I thought I’d raise him in the city. But there hasn’t been a single day since we came back here that I’ve regretted rearing him right here, on this farm.”

“You’re lucky, Billie.”

Faline studied the pieces she was cutting free from the vegetables they had grown a few yards away from the kitchen table where they worked.

“You and Aggie are so very lucky to have found each other and made such a fine family life for your boy.”

She continued to cut and talk.

“I never thought about kids with anyone. I had a couple of serious – humph- what’s serious in the world I came from?”

"We read about a couple of your more public affairs. Is that a fair term, *affairs*?"

"I suppose. I mean I told myself every time that I was in love, but I don't know how anyone really knows that anyway."

A silent pause hung uncomfortably between them as Faline finished with the last pepper and plowed the bits with the blade of her knife toward the chef.

"Is this what you wanted?"

"Since I was sixteen."

"Huh?"

"Oh! I thought you meant my life!"

An awkward laugh escaped Faline.

"Peppers and mushrooms are pretty easy to come by, I hope you haven't been waiting all your life for these."

"Right?"

Bill laughed a little too and spying a few black flecks from the mushrooms on the woman's face, offered her dishtowel.

"You have a little garden dirt on your cheek, Faline."

"Thanks, I think I have a tissue in my pocket."

She rummaged in her jacket to retrieve it when the empty shot bottle fell onto the countertop. Both women froze in a dead stare. Faline blinked first.

"I know what this looks like."

Bill shook her head.

“No. I don’t think it looks like anything.”

“Bill, I’m off the pills altogether and I have cut down to six of these a day.”

Bill repeated the number to clarify.

“Six? Six shots a day? Every day?”

“You need context, I get it. I was drinking whole handles-a-day at my worst. Believe me, this is such – I’ve come so – please don’t tell Aggie.”

“Faline, I appreciate what you’re trying to tell me. And I have no intention of ratting on you to Aggie or the family.”

Faline braced herself for the ‘but’.

“But you realize I can help you with this, right?”

“But! I knew it. There’s always a -wait, what?”

“I am a therapist, Faline. I help people in recovery all the time.”

“With your music?”

“Yes. I utilize music as a tool to facilitate treatment for addiction, depression, anxiety. You can treat all kinds of health problems with music therapy.”

She watched as the dots connected in Faline’s wet brain, hoping for the lightbulb to click on.

“I meant what I said about coming along to my clinics.”

“I don’t know.”

"You could just come and observe. You wouldn't have to participate."

"I really am doing much better."

"I would agree if you're down to just six of these a day, that *is* progress. But you might find a way to figure out the reason you still need those six a day."

"The reason I need them is - …"

Faline could not fill in the blank. She was so sure she knew but when faced with the actual question, she came up empty.

"The invitation is open. I visit one of my recovery groups day after tomorrow."

She returned her attention to assembling the pizzas and put them into the oven.

"Will you let the kids know it's fifteen minutes to pizza."

Faline smiled and nodded her response to the directive. Lost in the query in her own head Bill so deftly placed there, she walked out into the chill of the night toward the fire, weighing her thoughts.

»«

The day after tomorrow came swiftly but Faline was determined to be open to what came next. She set her alarm and was dressed and on her second cup of coffee when Bill and Aggie came down for breakfast. Aggie seemed mildly stunned but said nothing to shame her co-star and whispered a wish of good luck into her wife's ear as she donned her gloves and headed out into the barn.

It was a short ride to the treatment center where Bill facilitated her group. She had seven people in this recovery group so Faline would round it out nicely if she chose to jump in. The suite she used was in the transition wing of an inpatient treatment center so some of the clients were still patients in house and some were returning from outside the facility. She and Faline got to the room ahead of the rest save one, Shelby.

Shelby was always the first one there. She had been in recovery for sixteen months this time and was determined to make it to two years. She took great pride in arranging the chairs and starting the coffee. She greeted the two women with a smile and her customary offer to help Bill with her cello.

“I’ve got it, thanks.”

Bill always insisted on wrangling the mammoth instrument alone to demonstrate that doing difficult things was part of life and manageable.

“Shelby, this is -….”

They hadn’t discussed Faline’s anonymity, so she deferred to the former.

“This is Shelby.”

Faline decided in the moment to try and just be MaryAnne.

“Hi, I’m MaryAnne.”.

“Nice to meet you. Has anyone ever told you that you look like Faline Farah?”

“I get that a lot.”

“Do you want some coffee?”

The ease with which this young girl skipped right over Faline's public presence immediately relieved her. This could be exactly what she needed to reset. Maybe she could really relax and see what it was like to be herself again.

The room filled in with the rest of the members and Bill began the session with a quick nod to their guest and an invitation for everyone to check in where they were in the moment.

She wasn't prepared for MaryAnne to take a turn but when everyone else had reported in, she did too.

"My problem is mostly with alcohol…and sometimes pills. I am staying with friends, waiting to see if a career opportunity comes through so, I'm kind of in limbo at the moment. Anyway, I am trying hard not to drink or use anything to get through this time of uncertainty."

Bill was impressed.

"Ok. Thanks everyone. Now let's get started."

She moved to engage with her instrument and instructed the group.

"I'm going to play a piece and I want you to try to listen and relate the music to your inner self. Just try and connect, no shame in the game if you don't. But practice being open."

The people around her instinctively closed their eyes to block out any visual stimulation that might detract from the song of the cello, and MaryAnne watched their faces for a second before following.

The sounds were deep and low, slow, and heavy. Faline first felt self-conscious and was unable to relax. After peeking once or twice and realizing that no one was watching her, she inhaled slowly and calmed her closed lids. She breathed in the deep tones of the vibrating strings and sunk into the center of herself.

Bill concluded the piece and waited a beat.

"Is there a feeling that the music evoked that you could associate with using? Remember, no war stories. A feeling."

A hand raised.

"Malcolm."

"I felt alone. Like when I used to wake up in the middle of the night in jail."

"Aloneness is a powerful thing. And remember the difference between alone and lonely. Being alone is a state of affairs, feeling lonely is the sadness we feel associated with being alone."

Nodding heads agreed. Malcolm's neighbor reached over to touch his hand. Another volunteer.

"Rosie."

"I felt the regret in those minutes between snorting a pill and falling out."

"Regret is a powerful emotion. One that every human feels at one time or another. Good. And we also need to be aware that regret is always a past tense emotion. It's always in the rearview mirror. We have to *invite* regret into the now."

The responses continued with sadness, anger, craving, and hopelessness rounding out the group. Then MaryAnne raised her hand.

"I felt confused. I feel like I've been down for so long, it's almost comforting to hear that in the music even though I know it's not where I want to be."

A familiar hum circulated among the participants and again, Bill was pleased she was taking part.

"Ok. Another arrangement with a completely different range of tones. See what this one brings to you. Remain open to whatever comes."

Bill played the cello beautifully. She composed her own music and borrowed from others but always with such reverence to the instrument itself, asking it for help in leading these broken and bruised souls to new lives. The second set was up tempo, lilty, and light.

MaryAnne didn't peek this time, but she felt the smiles on every face as well as her own. This was a stark contrast to the moody dirge that conjured negative feelings around dark memories. This tune was like life renewing itself. It felt good.

When she had concluded, Bill waited again then queried her patients.

"And this one? What are your feelings and are they associated with using or no?"

Heads began shaking even before eyes opened fully, and every hand raised at once.

"Wow! Great!"

Bill left her cello and rejoined the group.

"Let's just start around the circle. Shelby start us off."

"It made me feel summery. I had the feeling that I used to get playing with the hose in my side yard when I was little."

"Good. Summer is carefree."

Bill explained and the girl repeated.

"Yes. Carefree and summery!"

"Jamie?"

"It made me feel like I did when I floated on tubes in the river when me and my family camped."

"Weightless?"

"Floating above but still connected to the current."

"Good. Floating but still connected. What an amazing feeling that must be."

"Deacon?"

"I felt comforted like I do when I sleep on clean sheets. Clean, cool sheets and heavy blankets. I felt the cool clean sheets my wife used to put on the bed."

The huge man dropped his head and folks on either side reached out to comfort him.

"I miss her so much!"

Bill made room for his tears and gave him a moment to find his composure before going on.

"But what a beautiful memory of her."

The entire circle checked in, recounting more goodness and joy. MaryAnne was the last to share.

"I grew up on a lake and it made me think of that."

"What was the emotion attached to the memory of growing up on that lake, MaryAnne?"

Bill was as skilled at leading the group as she was at playing the cello.

"I felt…loved."

It was really MaryAnne and *not* Faline who sat still in that room with those people, staring off into the blinding summer sun reflecting off the water of Lake George. *MaryAnne* heard the gulls and the vacationers chirping and calling, laughing, and splashing in the wake of the boats and skiers. *MaryAnne* saw Aggie's sunburned freckles and her easy smile…and *MaryAnne* felt loved.

"I chose these two very different pieces to show you the extremes to which we can evoke feelings about our pasts. It's unrealistic to think that you can ever be completely free of some of the memories associated with your addiction. But when you experience a moment from the past, you have a real-time, in-the-here-and-now choice about how to react to it."

Heads bobbed in agreement.

"Even if the emotional response is a negative one, you possess the power to 'change your mind' from the negative to the joyful. You did it today in just the last thirty minutes and just by listening to some upbeat music. Many of you will be returning to the places you last used, the people you lied to, stole from, or used with."

Worried faces stared back at her.

"But you have a choice with every trigger to counter it with something that triggers your joy. You each have to find your 'joy song'. It won't keep the bad things from happening, but it will be a tool to use to keep you grateful and hopeful and on the path of your recovery."

The messages about environment were always hard for the group to digest and their newest member was no exception. MaryAnne was sheltered on the farm. No one used there, there was no stress or pressure to perform, even *Just DIY* hadn't been a strain; of course, she was scronched the whole time. Bill was hopeful that this lead would make MaryAnne wake up to the fact that if she went back to a life in the limelight, her old demons could come to call again. She had a lot to work through before she was strong enough for that test.

With no more than a few well-placed prompts, Bill was able to get MaryAnne to return to the clinic twice weekly, through the fall. The group members invited her to AA and NA meetings that she attended with a true commitment to working the steps. When she thanked her therapist for all she had done for her, Bill offered her yet another opportunity for growth when she suggested MaryAnne come with her to volunteer at the Nursing Facility at Glenn Falls. Giving back was good work and Bill thought she was ready.

»«

The girls entered the day room at the nursing home and set up in the stage area, a one-step raised platform at the sunny end of the hall. Bill fixed her music stand and handed MaryAnne the song sheets to distribute to the residents as they began wheeling and shuffling in.

MaryAnne smiled and greeted every guest as if they were entering her home. She met the lost eyes of dementia and the gnarled bodies of arthritis with a compassion that surprised her. She hadn't returned after that Christmas visit when Patsy was a resident because these people made her sick and sad. It was only now, in her sober mind, that she realized they personified her mother's terminal condition and perhaps even her own mortality. She looked at Bill preparing to serenade them with her calming strings and beamed with gratitude for what being part of Aggie's family was doing to heal her own heart. She was happy to help Bill in her effort to bring these souls that same joy.

The cello played sweet and low while the crowd settled in and the recreational therapists took center stage to lead the sing-along and musical games that followed. MaryAnne stayed on the fringe of the group to watch and jumped in when signaled to help. When their quiet applause died out at the end of the activities and the residents slowly began clearing the room, a senior nurse approached her.

"You're Faline Farah, aren't you? I remember when you came to see your sweet mom."

"You have me confused with someone else. I'm MaryAnne, see."

She pointed to the paper name tag stuck to her sweater.

“Yes, MaryAnne O’Hara, stage name, Faline Farah.”

MaryAnne grinned.

“Your mom talked about you all the time. And the pictures! Every magazine cover and celebrity interview. I’d know you anywhere.”

“Ok. You got me.”

“I knew it was you.”

MaryAnne leaned in toward the old girl and winked.

“Don’t rat me out to the others, ok?”

The nurse winked back and leaned in still more.

“Your secret’s safe with me. It’s funny, we were just talking about Patsy and Zeke the other day at lunch. Your dad came back on the regular after your mom passed, to volunteer.”

MaryAnne listened intently.

“He helped us with the water feature in the Hospice Garden, he rebuilt the old Koi pond. He used to come back to inspect the pipe wraps every year before winter.”

“Used to?”

MaryAnne was suddenly stricken with fear that something had happened to Zeke and she hadn’t heard. She was flush with shame for abandoning her parents and doubly so if Zeke was still around and she hadn’t given him a single thought until now.

"What do you mean, 'he used to come'?"

An unintended judgmental frown appeared in the woman's wrinkles.

"He retired from plumbing a couple of years ago. Don't you two keep in touch?"

MaryAnne was red-faced and warm with guilt.

"I've not been the best daughter."

The nurse instinctively reached around the woman and gave her a loving squeeze.

"It's not too late, darlin'. He's still in Warrensburg. He went back to the beginning."

Bill lumbered toward the two with her cello in tow just in time to read the mild shock on MaryAnne's face as the nurse hobbled away.

"You alright?"

"Yeah…I'm good."

"You look like you've seen a ghost."

MaryAnne shook off the jolt.

"I'm fine. That nurse just told me that Zeke is still around, in Warrensburg."

Knowingly, Bill smiled.

"He'd love to see you."

Aggie had made Bill promise that no one would tell Zeke that MaryAnne was back in town. She had appointed herself his unofficial guardian and was intent that no more emotional harm would come to that kind man as long as she had a say in the matter. The fact that MaryAnne hadn't even bridged the subject of her parents in the entire time they'd been working together, angered Aggie. Bill took the leap knowing full well she stood a pretty good chance of catching hell over it; but she thought MaryAnne was ready to confront some of those shadows she'd been trying to outrun with the booze and the pills. Bill felt it was time.

That night after dinner, Eloise retired to her room to read, Thatcher disappeared to talk on the phone to his girlfriend until curfew, and MaryAnne shooed Bill and Aggie outside to start a fire while she cleaned up the remnants of the meal. She could see from the kitchen window the couple's faces glowing in the firelight and she smiled. Aggie saw her spying and waved her out to join them. She grinned, grabbed her coat, and joined the girls. She tucked a quilt into her lawn chair and presented her hands to be warmed.

"This is such a perfect night for a fire."

Aggie and Bill were wrapped together on the glider. Bill snuggled deeper into her wife's side.

"We love a good fire night, don't we, babe?"

Aggie agreed.

"We do. We *do* love our fire nights."

"It's a shame they don't do this for your residents at Glenn Falls, Billie. I'm sure they have good memories of apple butter season and fire nights."

"They'd love it! And you know what's sad about that MaryAnne, is the families and the residents would be all for it, but the regulations built into the licensure of the place forbid the residents from being outside the facility after dark."

"That's right. I asked to take mom out once to see the harvest moon and was told it was against regulation."

"That sucks! *My* mom probably would have loved that too."

Bill saw MaryAnne's speculation as her lead-in to the subject of Zeke.

"I'm sure Zeke tried to do that kind of thing all the time with your mom, MaryAnne. He was always sweet talking those nurses into letting him take her to do this or that. Wasn't he Aggie?"

Bill felt her wife's body tense against hers. Aggie stared blankly into the flames without responding.

"Aggie, I was talking to a nurse there today who said Zeke kept coming around fixing things even after Mom passed away; all the way up until he retired a couple of years ago."

Aggie just nodded, waiting to see where MaryAnne was headed.

"She said he's still in Warrensburg. She said he went back to the beginning. Kind of cryptic, huh?"

"There's nothing cryptic about it, MaryAnne. He sold the one-story place they moved to when we started at school and now he lives in the apartment where you all started out."

"He's back at the Libby?"

"Yes. Been there since just after Patsy died."

"Not in the same apartment? What are the odds he could get that same third-story apartment?"

"Pretty good when he never gave it up."

"Say what now?"

Bill decided to take over.

"MaryAnne, the house they moved into after you left for school was handicap accessible and easier for them both. But they never gave up the apartment, so when he didn't need the ramps and shower bars anymore, Zeke sold the house and moved back into the Libby."

"That *would* be the beginning. Well anyway, I've decided that I'm going into Warrensburg in the morning and surprise him."

"Wait! Have you even so much as called him or sent a card since you've been back here? Couldn't you surprise him by calling ahead first?"

Aggie was heating up. Bill felt it and tried to defer to her friend.

"I think MaryAnne needs to be the one to decide how she reconnects with her dad, babe."

"Really?"

Aggie was on her feet now, asking Bill but staring straight into MaryAnne's face.

"Do you also think MaryAnne should have never gone this long without contacting him in the first place? Do you think that she would have known where he was if she even bothered to call or write EVER over the past eighteen years, when that man did everything imaginable for her mother, watching her waste away in front of his very eyes…ALONE IN THE WORLD!"

"I WAS A ROTTEN DAUGHTER!"

Now MaryAnne was up.

"I know, Aggie! I didn't give up my life like you and sacrifice my dreams to take care of my crippled mother!"

"She loved you more than anything else in her life, and you just abandoned her! All of us!"

"Us? You left ME the night of the senior trip, Aggie Rose! You just disappeared! POOF! And I was alone!"

Bill stood as the ground between the angry women narrowed. She could see her wife reaching her limit. Aggie turned away from the fire to find her way back to the house.

"I'm not putting myself through this again!"

MaryAnne called after her.

"Yes, run away! Just like you did in school!"

Aggie stopped in her tracks and turned back to the posturing woman.

"You think I ran away?"

"I didn't know what to think, Aggie. You were my best friend. And I felt like I didn't even *know* you. Thomasina said - …"

"NO! Thomasina does not get a say in this now! Do you hear me?"

Thrusting a finger in her face, Aggie squared off with her old friend. Her teeth were clamped tight and her words were seething out between them.

"This is MY house, MaryAnne. No lies in this house. We were more than friends, but you believed someone else's lies over the truth. And then YOU abandoned US!"

Bill watched Aggie's eyes begin to glisten with tears of rage and pain.

"I wrote to you every day for a year! Zeke and your poor mother wrote and called and wrote and called! And all our attempts to get through to you just fell flat."

"Don't you think I know all this? Don't you think I torture myself every day with regret over losing my family? Why do you think I drink and take pills?"

The confession might as well have made an audible clang in all three of their heads. The charge of it made MaryAnne flinch and tears she'd always swallowed with bourbon filled her lids to the brim and held there illuminated by the flames of fire night. She could taste the salt in the back of her throat.

"I was hurt. I was confused. And I was alone."

"That's funny. I was all those things too, MaryAnne."

"But you were home. I was all the way up in Chateaugay, with only Thomasina to rely on."

Aggie shook her head at the disconnect that persisted between them.

"And as long as you keep relying on what Thomasina told you about me, we will never get past this."

"Aggie, you were the love of my life…and you lied to me."

"I never lied!"

"You never told me that you were gay."

"I didn't lie about it, MaryAnne. I was just afraid to tell you."

"Why? Because you were afraid I wasn't attracted to you?"

"For God's sake! You still have no idea, do you?"

Aggie's tears streaked down her cheeks and she couldn't remain in the space. She left the fire, and Bill and MaryAnne listened as the truck started and disappeared down the farm road.

"What don't I get, Bill?"

Bill responded as Aggie's wife and not MaryAnne's therapist, as what she said next was not the most therapeutic.

"You know something? You were the love of her life too, you stupid twat-waffle! She was afraid to come out to you because she thought you'd judge her or reject her. You were her sister. She wasn't in love with you. But she loves you…more than you'll ever know."

Angered by the line she crossed, Bill kicked at the dirt under her feet and stomped away chastising herself.

"Aww, fuck me running!"

MaryAnne stood wide-eyed, watching her retreat to the house and then fell back into her lawn chair. She stared into the fire searching scenes from her days at St. James for any glimpse of a feeling that would support Thomasina's rhetoric and found nothing.

Nothing.

Why hadn't she done this on the bus to New York City? Why was she so quick to discount her dearest friend when the stakes were so high? The mistake was hers alone. It clicked. Knowing meant she had to make it right. A simple peace washed over her that she hadn't felt since she was a kid; it made her laugh.

"Twat-waffle? Fuckin' Bill."

»«

The champagne Cadillac sloshed through a band of freezing rain that often showed up ahead of winter's official beginning around the west side of Lake George. MaryAnne had resisted the urge to turn off and drive to the lake on her way to Warrensburg, and Aggie resisted the urge to call Zeke and warn him of his stepdaughter's visit.

MaryAnne pulled up in front of the aging brick building and counted the windows to her old bedroom with a smile. She gathered the groceries she bought and braced against the wet cold between her car and the main entrance. She slumped in front of the 'out of order' sign on the lobby elevator and headed for the stairwell.

Out of breath, she panted on the second-floor landing.

"Damn girl, you got to get in better shape!"

She lighted just outside the entrance to the third floor to allow her pulse and heaving breath to slow before proceeding down the hall to 314. The brass numbers were blackened with age and the tiny strip of braided detail around the doorknob was nearly worn smooth. She took one more breath for courage then knocked and waited smiling while the muted footsteps grew closer on the other side. The door opened wide.

"Hi Zeke! It's me, MaryAnne!"

He flinched with a start and stood stunned in place.

"Aggie told me to call but I wanted to surprise you."

She stared at his blank face.

"Are you surprised?"

His sweet smile appeared.

"You might say that, yes."

She relaxed a little.

"Well, don't just stand there in the hallway, come in! Let me help you. What is all this?"

He stepped aside and reached for one of the grocery bags. She surrendered it and shimmied free from her coat to hang it on the hooks she remembered just inside the door. She followed the old plumber into the kitchen and they both deposited their parcels on the table.

"I just picked up the stuff to make us some dinner. If you don't have plans."

He began unloading the groceries.

"Let's see, tomatoes, hamburger meat, lasagna noodles!"

"I remembered how much you used to like Mom's lasagna."

"I sure did! I haven't had good, homemade lasagna in so long."

"Well don't get your hopes too high. I haven't cooked it in as long as you haven't eaten it."

"This *is* a treat! It's good to have you home, MaryAnne."

He reached for her hand. Her heart stalled in her chest for a split second as she let the word sink in…*home*.

She pulled a kitchen chair out for him and began busying herself with preparing dinner. They talked and talked about the cost of tomatoes this late in the season and how the chain grocery stores didn't have the same quality of meat you used to get at Whitey Thompson's butcher shop. The small talk got them through until the casserole went in the oven, then she excused herself to pee and agreed to meet him back in the living room to pass the time until the buzzer went off.

Nothing so far was different in the whole place. Every rug, every towel, every dish, and pot, and pan was just as she remembered it. Before she popped up from the toilet to wash and caught a glimpse of her weathered face, she might have expected to hear her mom's voice calling from the hall to 'Hurry up in there!'. But those were the differences; her mom was gone, and she was not a kid anymore.

She dried her hands and snuck out of the bathroom and into her old bedroom. It was like a time capsule. She tiptoed to her desk and picked up a resin Ziggy figurine, a mood ring sitting in a bottle cap, and the frame displaying her school class picture from eighth grade. She challenged herself to name every one of her classmates and won! It was as if her life was frozen in place. She replaced the items and wandered around thinking about the upheaval of leaving for school and Patsy and Zeke moving into the little house all in the same summer. Now she realized why her mom's MS symptoms worsened so quickly that year; the sheer stress of it all.

She walked to the dresser and picked up her old hairbrush. It still had her long dark hair tangled in the bristles. She pulled it clean and put it through her hair again. She thought about her mother's fingers combing through her hair to calm her at night.

What she wouldn't give to have just one more moment to share with her.

A wave of shame and guilt washed over her. She fought the negative emotions with the joyful thought that Zeke, the only father she had ever known was just sixteen feet away and alive and well and she could enjoy his sweet face and hear his thunderous laugh again if she could get herself in there and have the hard talk. Before she could get turned around, she heard music coming from the living room. It was Dino!

"Zeke! You still have my old records?"

"*Your* old records?"

"My Dean Martin collection. Sam shipped all my things back home when I left school for the city. I'm sure of it."

"Yes, he did. But those weren't your records to begin with."

"What are you trying to pull, old man?".

"MaryAnne O'Hara, I'm surprised at you! Your mom bought every single one of these albums for me. I love Dean Martin!"

"No!"

"What do you mean 'no'! I'm telling you for the truth. I can tell you when I got every single record."

He reached into the stereo cabinet and pulled them out one by one.

"*Relaxin'* my thirtieth birthday, 1966; *Christmas Album*, that same year for Christmas; *Dino – Like Never Before*, from you and your mom on father's day '67; *Gentle On My Mind*, to celebrate dating for one year; *Swingin'* Christmas '68; *My Woman, My Woman, My Wife* on our wedding day!"

"That's what you danced to at the reception, in the clubhouse at the lake, I remember that!"

MaryAnne stared off lost in the memory playing in her heart of her mother in that pale-yellow suit and Zeke holding his face pressed against hers, whispering things that changed her expression to sheer blushing bliss.

"How do I remember that Zeke? I can't even remember where I put my keys when I came in?"

"We remember what's most important."

He tilted the cover and the disc slid out into his rough hands. He lifted the needle from the current selection and gently switched the two, seeking out the track he had memorized from decades of playing it for Patsy and to the empty apartment after she passed.

When the intro began to play, Zeke extended his hand to his daughter, she took it, and they danced. The crooner sang on with the orchestra's support for verse after sweet, heartwarming verse. The story of a man unworthy of his beautiful, strong wife.

At the top of the last verse, Zeke began to sing.

"When she reaches that river Lord, you know what she's worth.

Give her that mansion up yonder, 'cause she's been through hell here on Earth.

Lord, give her my share of heaven, if I've earned any here in this life.

Because God I believe she deserves it, my woman, my woman, my wife."

As Dino and his backup singers repeated the title for the finale, Zeke's forehead dropped to MaryAnne's shoulder and she held her father's trembling frame as they wept together for their lost love, regrets, and joyful memories all at once. They kept dancing and crying and laughing to the next song and the next until the timer on the oven signaled the lasagna was done.

She kissed his cheek, then darted off to silence the noise interrupting their moment. She tossed the salad and plated dinner, and he chose another record to play low in the background and poured some red wine. They fed their bodies with the meal and their souls with the company.

MaryAnne was so relieved at the reception she got from Zeke. He could have shut her out, refused to forgive her for any or all of it.

But he didn't.

His belly full, Zeke started the hard talk with a smile and the best compliment.

"Patsy would have been proud, that was delicious."

His eyes narrowed ever-so slightly.

"Your mom and I really did appreciate everything you did for us at the center, MaryAnne."

He wiped a hand over his mouth.

"But why did you just leave us there? She didn't deserve that, honey."

"I know. I couldn't take it, Zeke. I was so weak."

MaryAnne hung her head, and even though she had no valid explanation, she just spoke from the heart…and he listened.

"I couldn't take seeing her waste away. I couldn't take seeing her taken care of like that. Some stranger bathing her, dressing her, feeding her."

"Only when I couldn't! I was there every day to do for her so she wouldn't suffer the embarrassment of a stranger tending to her like that."

"And I couldn't handle that either. I'm so sorry. She was everything to me. She was all I had…until you."

Her shame swelled in the base of her throat and she swallowed hard to get it down. He reached across the table for her hands and the very touch of his brought her to tears.

"I thought I'd come here and have the door slammed in my face. No one would blame you for disowning me, Zeke. But you didn't. You let me come home. Here! We're back home at the Libby, eating lasagna like nothing's changed."

Her tears fell freely but she didn't look away from his steady eyes.

"She always knew you'd come home, honey. That's why she insisted on keeping this place. She said, 'Zeke, when she's had enough of the fast lane, she'll need a quiet place to lay her head and think about what's important. She'll be back.' And here you are."

She gave his hands a squeeze then let go to wipe her face. He straightened against the back of his chair and dug into the pocket of his dungarees to offer his handkerchief. She accepted it and composed herself.

"I've been back since the first of Spring! I did a TV show with Aggie Rose in West Fort Ann. I had no idea you were even still around here until I heard it from one of Mom's old nurses in Glenn Falls yesterday."

"I know all about your TV show, honey."

He got up from the table and crossed to the window seat raising the hinged shelf under the cushion to reveal a collection of VHS tapes; every episode of *Hart's Desire*, and twelve new ones marked *Just DIY*.

She stood at his side and looked at him, confused.

"You never told Aggie you knew about the show?"

"Nope."

"And she never told you I was back to do it either?"

"Nope."

"What the devil does that mean, Zeke?"

"MaryAnne, Aggie's been here all along. She visited your mom every chance she could. One year when I was out with the flu for a couple weeks, she came every day and sat with her; reading to her, doing her nails. She brought me groceries and buckets full of soup and cornbread. She never stopped being family. She never spoke an ill word about you; not that Patsy would have allowed that anyway. I'm sure she was just trying to protect me from any more grief."

He choked up a little and she reached for his hand. He held hers tight in his and they understood each other; she was sorry she'd caused him *any* grief; he forgave her; and they were both grateful for Aggie. Parents never stop loving their children no matter what the condition of the relationship though, and that meant their love for each other was right where they left it.

Reconciliation

It would be two days before Aggie would be caught around the farm for MaryAnne to run into. She could go two days without tending the sheep this close to winter and Thatcher did the heavier chores anyway. She stayed at the shop all day, got sandwiches from the Palace Restaurant for dinner and slipped into bed well after the rest of the house was down to keep from getting into it with the lot of them.

Bill came and went from her office over the shop without letting her know. She wasn't upset with Aggie, more herself for losing it with MaryAnne on fire night and not being able to effectively comfort her wife. She had been optimistic that the women would reconcile their past and build something new, but their pain ran so deep, she was starting to question the wisdom of taking MaryAnne on at all. But hope dies hard in a wise heart and she thought if she backed off a little, they had a chance at finding common ground on their own.

MaryAnne was determined to make that happen.

She rose early to try and catch Aggie before she left for the shop. She came down to an empty kitchen and a full coffee pot. Someone was up. She looked out the window and saw Thatcher running for the school bus and Bill loading Eloise into her car. She thought she remembered seeing something about a checkup in Glenn Falls on the calendar that hung on the cork board above the kitchen phone. She double checked and it was as she recalled; meaning that the full pot of coffee might be a sign that Agatha Rose was still about. She poured two black cups and donned her boots and flannel jacket over her pajamas and headed to the barn.

She squinted in the cool wind, the steam from the coffee swirling in her face. She saw the light in the crack of the barn door and heard Aggie calling for Culpepper to come in from the back pasture. She squeezed through the nearly closed door without a sound and walked to the other end of the barn. She needed to call loudly to be heard over the barking.

"You're at it pretty early this morning!"

Aggie tapped the sheep gently on the rump with her staff without looking up.

"Thatcher was up most of the night studying for his big tests, so I let him sleep in. I told him I'd clean the pens out this morning. What are you doing out here?"

"I thought I'd buy you a cup a coffee."

Aggie turned away from her flock and saw her friend shivering in her night clothes and smiled at her generous gesture.

"Give me a second to get these girls back in."

"I can wait. Take your time."

Aggie and Culpepper worked quickly and when the last ewe was deposited safely, Aggie pulled the rear barn door shut and praised her good dog.

"He's so smart. Was he bred for this, Aggie?"

"Naw, he's just a good ole' mutt. Culpepper is a good boy."

The dog wagged and licked and went from stall to stall sniffing at the latches, checking on his charges. Aggie straightened as she approached MaryAnne, taking her dirty gloves off and sticking them under one arm. She reached her bare hands out to receive the hot cup.

"This is nice. Thanks."

The two women sat down on bales of hay on the other side of the stalls from the sheep, warming their hands and faces with the coffee, their hair and coats being nibbled at through the planks of the enclosure.

Their noses wet from the warmth of the drink in the cold barn air, they sniffled in unison then called out together.

"Coke!"

It made them laugh.

"That was so dumb! Who started that silly shit anyway?"

"I honestly don't know. I think I heard it in grade school."

"Yea, my brothers did it all the time, but they said, 'buy me a Coke or join the punch club' and then they drill you in the arm."

"Oh my God! I remember that, Aggie. Man, they were rotten ornery."

"They were that."

A pause and more coffee and MaryAnne made the first move.

"I seem to be remembering a lot of things I think I was trying to forget."

"Is that right?"

"I went to see Zeke the other day."

Agatha stretched her back as if she were preparing for a fist fight.

"You don't say?"

"You know, he knew I was in town."

"He knew?"

"Yep. I took the stuff to make lasagna and we cooked, and talked, and listened to records, and we even had a father-daughter dance."

Utter surprise and relief overtook Aggie's expression and she smiled.

"I bet he was in hog heaven, MaryAnne."

"I think he was happy to see me. It was a very good visit."

She smiled too and then hesitated just a beat.

"We talked about you."

"Me?"

"Mm-hm."

"What on Earth for?"

"He told me what a help you'd been to him. How you took care of mom at the nursing home when he was sick and how you brought him soup."

"That's nothin'. Nothin' anyone else wouldn't have done."

"No, not nothin', Aggie. You were there for them when they needed you. When I should have been there."

Aggie shook her head.

"MaryAnne. I was really there...*for* you."

"I know that now, Aggie Rose. You know your wife called me a twat-waffle the other night after you got mad and drove off?"

Aggie erupted in laughter at the slur.

"She doesn't have a lot of experience insulting people. A twat – what was it a waffle?"

"Waffle, yes. A twat-waffle. I've never even heard of such a thing! Have you?"

"No. But that's my wife. She kills me sometimes."

"She was right you know?"

"I knew it! You *are* a twat-waffle!"

They laughed out loud again at the name-calling.

"No, seriously. Bill was right about me. I had it all wrong from the very start. All I needed to do was think about it even a little and none of what they were saying about you, about us, was even remotely the way I remember it."

Aggie sat nodding as her friend continued her confession.

"I think it was everything all at once. Remember Mom was getting worse, we were just months away from graduation, I had just lost my virginity to Jason, and then you were expelled!"

"Oh my God! I forgot about you and Jason."

Aggie looked to the rafters to conjure the image of the boy.

"I can still see his stupid face that night when you drug him out of The Library…he was terrified!"

"Yeah he was."

The girlfriends laughed easily at Jason's expense and continued reminiscing.

"I never got to hear how it was."

"Oh! It was pathetic. It lasted seconds and then he cried all over me!"

"Poor Jason!"

"Poor Jason? Poor me! I was the one that had to spoon his sobbing ass to sleep. What a night!"

"It was a hell of a night!"

"Was any of it the way she said?"

Aggie took a deep breath and turned her body toward her friend.

"I thought she loved me, MaryAnne. We had been together, secretly, for a year. I let my guard down and she set me up."

"She moved into our room. Did you know that?"

"No. I didn't hear anything, from anybody after that night."

Aggie could feel the loneliness she succumbed to on the bus ride home all those years ago.

"That's why you're not a twat-waffle, MaryAnne. Because you can't know. You can't possibly know what it was like to lose everything like that. I was rejected. Just spit out. And I dreaded going home."

"You hadn't come out to your family either?"

"They knew but they didn't understand it. They made up some lie about me graduating early and got me shipped off to Chicago as quick as they could."

"It's so weird that we both went through the hardest things without each other, when we had been through so much together up to that point."

They thought about it a little longer while they enjoyed their coffee.

"I missed you, Aggie."

"Me? In all that fortune and fame, you missed little old Aggie of Green Gables?"

"I missed my sister."

MaryAnne's words broke the spell of the cold and the coffee and all the memories.

"I know what you mean, MaryAnne. I missed you too."

The two confessed in unison.

"I'm so sorry -…"

They looked stung for a split second.

"Coke!"

They giggled and Aggie raised her mug.

"To all the places we'll run to and from."

Raising hers to clink, MaryAnne finished the toast.

"And to all our safe returns to those we simply cannot leave behind."

“Get On With Your Livin”

The holidays would give the girls the occasion they needed to come together even closer than in the months before. They shopped for gifts together and got Zeke out to the farm for Christmas Eve. They cooked and entertained and rekindled their kindred hearts. The busyness of the season effectively distracted them from worrying about the fate of their show. They hadn’t even spoken about it in passing. Early on New Year’s Eve they were gathered at The Libby to watch the ball drop with Zeke when the call came in from Allen. Thatcher was first to the phone.

“Ma! Aunt MaryAnne! It’s New York!”

The women ran in different directions to pick up the extensions and listen in together.

“Girls, are you both on?”

“Yes!” “We’re here! What’s the word, Allen?”

“Well, are you sitting down?”

“Come on!” “Get to it, man!”

“I just sold your show to HBO!”

They both screamed and stretched the phone cords around to see each other in the doorways. The family clustered in around them.

“HBO! He got us on HBO!”

“A couple of their guys saw an episode live and reached out to me to see the tapes. I sent them, and months went by without a word. I thought it was a dead end."

MaryAnne pumped him for more.

"But then they called back?"

"And they just called me back to-day!

Aggie relayed to the spectators.

"They called him today!"

"That's right. They called today and said, 'We want to make *Just DIY* for HBO."

Aggie slowed the roll.

"What does it mean make it *for* HBO?"

"It wouldn't be live. They want to tape it. They love you both and want you both just as you were in the original, but they want to make it *about* you two. Aggie will still be doing her fix-it bits and MaryAnne will still do her craft segments, but they want to build the show around your relationship."

MaryAnne began dissecting.

"So, a little more interaction between us on set?"

"Yes. They liked the way you kind of messed things up at the ends of the program, MaryAnne. They think you're really funny. They want to write some new gags for your character."

The two women fell silent and looked at each other, frowning.

"Don't worry about the drinking. They don't mind if you drink. As a matter of fact, they said they'd prefer it if you were a little tipsy to make it more authentic. They're writing some great stuff, you two. Funny stuff for you both."

Their quiet confused him and he tried to decipher their response.

"What's the problem, girls? This is the big time. National exposure. Artistic freedom. You won't be bleeped if you slip up and cuss, MaryAnne. And if you drop something and break it, all the better. We just can't lose with this formula, ladies. It's a sitcom about two friends; one a washed-up soap opera actress clinging to stardom on a home improvement show hosted by the other one who's fixing up this producer's summer home in a tiny town in upstate New York! It's your true story!"

They stood in silence, the family deflating around them.

"It's not funny, Allen. She has a problem with pills and whiskey. It all but ended her career. She's clean and sober now, man. You can't ask her to go back to that life for the sake of a TV show."

"It's not TV, it's - "

Aggie stopped him.

"We know the tag line, Allen."

He waited again and no one spoke.

"What are you saying, ladies?"

They waited too, staring into each other's eyes for the answer.

Then it hit her and MaryAnne broke into song.

"Everybody loves somebody sometime."

Aggie covered the receiver with her hand.

"What are you thinking? I won't let you do this!"

MaryAnne covered hers too.

"This is your big break, Aggie. I won't let you NOT do this!"

"What's going on? All I hear is muffled talking. Is somebody singing? Is anybody going to tell me what's going on here?"

Allen was getting uncomfortable.

"Aggie, MaryAnne, this is the chance of a lifetime. We can't get better than HBO. What am I supposed to tell them?"

MaryAnne took over.

"We'll call you back, Allen."

She hung up her receiver and grabbed Aggie's to do the same. She snatched their coats from the hooks by the door, and took her friend by the hand, and assured the family.

"We'll be back before the ball drops!"

Aggie followed the wild-eyed woman to the elevator pulling her coat on.

"I don't know what you've got up your sleeve, but we can't possibly do…"

"Shhhhh! Shush it! I know you don't owe me one thing, Agatha Rose O'Hanley, but please just shut your pie hole for once and trust me."

When they landed in the lobby, MaryAnne bolted out the doors toward her Cadillac and Aggie sighed, shook her head, and followed. They rode through the dark, cold through the familiar twists of the road between their childhood homes.

"Can I ask where we're going?"

"No."

MaryAnne's eyes glistened in the lights of the occasional headlamp or lighted Christmas decoration they passed. She looked different tonight. What ever it was, it comforted Aggie somehow. She'd never felt at ease with MaryAnne in charge…ever. But tonight, she was ok with it. She watched as the signs for the turn off to Lake George came and went; so, that destination was out. They rode silently on. As they neared the exits to West Fort Ann, she thought maybe the farm, but MaryAnne took the left at the 'y' and headed downtown.

The main street off 149 was all but abandoned. The ancient decorations put up on the few light posts along the storefronts blinked off and on feebly. This poor old town had had it! It didn't even clean up that well all decked out. But still Aggie felt at home, and so did her friend. MaryAnne pulled to a stop in front of Hupp's Hardwoods and parked the car.

"Let me buy you a drink."

Aggie smiled and trailed her friend to the door to unlock the shop. The two stepped in without reaching for the lights and inhaled the scents that had fueled their childhood memories. The moment hung in the air with the fumes of the wood glue and sawdust. Aggie walked around behind the counter by the dim glow of the streetlights coming in through the front window. MaryAnne crossed in front of the illuminated soda machine and deposited her change. After the muted mechanical racket, two 'thunks' produced their drinks. She popped the tops and crossed back to her friend.

"What was it we used to toast?"

Aggie grinned.

"Drink up to the Lord in May!"

MaryAnne smiled too and they tapped the necks of their pop bottles together.

"Drink up to the Lord in May!"

They each chugged a gulp of the soda and Aggie started the dialog.

"Why in the world would we have to come all the way back here to talk about this, MaryAnne?"

MaryAnne took another drink of her soda and nodded.

"I needed you to be home to hear what I'm about to say. Home, here, in this place where you feel the most like yourself."

Aggie looked around and nodded.

"Ok. I'm home. Now what? I just can't imagine any argument you could make that can change the way I fell about this thing, MaryAnne."

"Just listen. This is your home. This town, this shop; you have it all. You have the farm, Bill, Thatcher. But you have it all because you came when they called. You've never once let anyone down. You never chose yourself over someone else's needs. Yes, you went away to college, but you dropped everything when sweet Hupp died, and Eloise needed you. I think it's because you were so selfless that the universe turned around and brought Bill back to you, and that sweet boy."

"What are you getting at?"

"I asked you to be still!"

Aggie's eyes widened and she locked her lips and bowed in submission.

"I have never done anything like what you did…for anyone. I paid some bills and sent money. Money! My mother needed me too and all I did was write checks."

Her head dropped under the weight of her shame and she swallowed hard to keep the tears from discrediting her message. She raised her head again to look her friend in the eye.

"I know that's why I started using, and I promise you I'm going to keep working on that. But this is a chance for me to do something good…for you! *You* get the gift of support and recognition. *You* get the attention. This is *your* show, Agatha Rose."

"But…"

"And I can do hard things! You taught me that, Aggie. You taught me that in Algebra in ninth grade, a hundred years ago and you've been teaching me that every day since I came back home. Look, we 'fall' into depression', we 'backslide into old habits'. It takes no effort to go backward; it's all downhill, it's easy! But it takes strength, and presence, and conscious intention to stand your ground without losing any. It takes discipline and endurance to keep trodding up the hill, rolling that stone up that hill. And there is no other side. It's all up hill until the end! There might be some temporary relief when one rough spot is overcome, but then it's plant your feet and keep rolling up hill again to the next one. And absolutely no one on Earth can 'just do it themselves'. If this past year, these past thirty years, have taught me anything it's that no one does it alone. I finally get that Aggie. I won't be alone. I have you and Bill and Zeke and your sweet mom and son. And me! I finally have me on my own side."

Aggie chuckled then continued to be quiet and listen.

"And you all have me too. You especially, Ags. *You* have me. So, yes…home. That's what I don't think you're getting. I'm home too. I know who I am again. I am Patsy O'Hara-Goodwin's daughter, God damn it! I was raised in The Grand Chancellor Hotel by a mishmash of hardworking people who loved me. I had the best friend in the world. And even though I was not selfless in my life, the universe has turned around and put me right back where I feel the most like *myself.* I can do this, Aggie. I can do this and stay safe. I can do this thing. I truly can. Please, be gracious this one time and let me do this *one* thing…for *you*."

Aggie remained silent as she was commanded, and MaryAnne searched her face for concession. A single tear dropped onto Aggie's freckled cheek just as one also fell from her friend's honest eye.

"I can't believe we actually get to do this."

MaryAnne smiled, raised her soda bottle, and the two friends toasted again.

"Happy New Year!"

...Six Years Later

The stage manager came to the greenroom to retrieve them as they checked each other's teeth and noses for the final time. Wading through the narrow halls backstage they whispered like schoolgirls again.

"I can't believe how nervous I am. I can't believe we're really here!"

"Me too. I mean six seasons of Just DIY, five Emmys, two People's Choice Awards, and a citation from The Woodworkers Guild of America and nothing until now!"

"Maybe it's because we have all the prizes now that we rate an interview."

The stage manager put a finger to her lips to signal the women to be still and held her headset tighter to her head to listen for direction. The girls winced behind the set partitions and MaryAnne carried on even quieter.

"Maybe she was tired of hearing in every other interview that you wanted to *be* her when you grew up and finally decided to size you up and see what kind of a threat you are to her kingdom, Aggie Rose."

The stage manager leaned into her in a panic.

"She doesn't threaten, she conquers! Now shut up or she'll have us all for lunch!"

MaryAnne huddled against her friend, bracing against the menacing girl. The three women froze in place until she finally mouthed a silent apology.

As they listened for the cue just before the introduction, Aggie's excitement grew with the smile taking over her face, and she looked at her friend, her sister, who had risked so much to get them there and she was overcome with love for her. She whispered her simplest, most sincere gratitude.

"Thank you."

MaryAnne smiled back and matched Aggie's sentiment with grace.

"You're welcome."

And then the thrilling call from the queen.

"Please welcome from the hit HBO series Just DIY, Aggie O'Hanley and Feline Faraaaahhhhhh!"

About the Author

Diana Johnson grew up in Fairmont, WV not far from where she lives now with her husband and daughter. She began her first attempts at storytelling over 30 years ago, outlining novels and screen plays on a used word processor between her sons' T-ball games and loads of laundry; but these works lay incomplete at the bottom of her dresser drawer for decades.

After two divorces and a number of jobs, she met her current husband and had her daughter and shortly after that decided to fully answer her calling to write.

Compiling a bank of stories and characters from all her other lives, she began to weave them into her own signature tales of life and love.

Since then, she has published her debut novel, the near future, sci-fi, feminist novel *Cold Daughters*, and her second, the friendship fiction you've just enjoyed, *Just DIY.* All Diana's titles are available on Amazon and directly from the author. Visit her website at dianajohnsonwriter.com for full details and upcoming projects.

Made in the USA
Monee, IL
22 February 2021

60807533R40187